DEADMAN'S REVENGE

(THE DEADMAN BOOK 3)

LINELL JEPPSEN

WOLFPACK
PUBLISHING
— EST 2013 —

Deadman's Revenge
Linell Jeppsen

Wolfpack Publishing
6032 Wheat Penny Avenue
Las Vegas, NV 89122

wolfpackpublishing.com

Paperback Edition

Paperback ISBN 978-1-64119-517-1
eBook ISBN 978-1-64119-139-5

DEADMAN'S REVENGE

Two children ran into the dugout yelling, "Mama, Mama! The man is sick, maybe dead!"

Unbeknownst to them, their father was home from tilling the fields early and they came to a skidding stop on the dirt floor, sending up small plumes of dust. Both of them stared at their feet, knowing they were caught barehanded doing something they had been forbidden to do.

Eight-year-old Toby Ferguson gulped and placed his hands on his buttocks, which were already warming up in anticipation of his pa's belt. His little sister, Susan, sniffed back tears as, indeed, her father had stood up from the edge of his bed and was pulling his belt out from the loops of his dungarees.

"Pull your britches down, son" Joseph Ferguson sighed. His back was paining him something fierce after his draft horse had spooked sideways from the rattled warning of a dozing snake. He had called his plowing quits for the day in hopes that his muscles wouldn't tighten up from the strain of keeping the horse from bolting and the last thing he felt like doing now was disciplining his wayward children. Rules were rules though, and his kids had just broken one of them.

Toby sighed and tried to keep from crying... he didn't want to look like a sissy in front of Susan. Still, his pa's belt, on those occasions it fell across his tender bottom, stung like fire and usually raised welts that would throb for days.

His ma, Ann Ferguson, watched from across the room. Her husband brooked no nonsense from their children, but she knew Joseph loved them dearly and would do no lasting harm. Still, she felt sorry for the kids as their neighbor, Mr. Wilcox, was a fascinating character who had won their hearts with his grave courtesy and occasional treats like hard rock candy, wooden figurines and once, a handmade sling-shot which was now Toby's most prized possession.

That was before he had become so angry, aloof and frankly, frightening. They had known the man for the better part of a year now and had only recently put a stop to their children's visits. Joseph had begun to suspect that the man might be some sort of outlaw, although Ann thought there was more to it than that. Nevertheless, she didn't doubt that he was a dangerous man and one her children had no business dealing with.

The boy bent over and grasped his ankles even as his sister gulped back tears of shame. Joseph drew his belt up high in order to give his son's butt a smart lick but Susan cried out, "Pa... wait!"

Of his two children, Susan was the most obedient and it was almost unheard of for her to try to interfere with her papa's discipline. Joseph raised his eyebrows and let the belt drop. Studying his six-year-old daughter's worried face he said, "I'll hear you out, Sis, but don't think I'm going to change my mind."

The little tow-headed girl shook her head. "No sir, we know, but before you give us our spankin's, we just wanted to tell you we never went down to Mr. Wilcox's house. We were playing close by, though, hoping Trickster might come and play with us but all he did was howl and howl! That's when we went up on the rise behind Mr. Wilcox's house and saw him a laying by the well. We think he might be dead!"

With those words, Susan's cornflower blue eyes filled and she burst into tears. Joseph and Ann looked into each other's faces and then, without a word, she stood up and started gathering what little medicinal supplies remained in her meager stores.

Joseph looked down at his son, who still stood hunched over with his bare bottom in the air. "Stand up, Toby. I guess your whipping will have to wait."

"Yes sir...thank you sir!" Toby gasped and pulled his pants back up.

A few minutes later, the little family rode their wagon through their own fields and up an overgrown and rocky trail toward their reclusive neighbor's log cabin.

Matthew woke up with his face in the mud. His dog, a mixed-breed descendent of his beloved wolf Bandit, whined and nuzzled his owner's ear in anxiety.

Groaning, he sat up and gazed about with swollen, dazzled eyes. *What am I doing here?* he wondered uneasily and then he commenced to coughing. He coughed so hard his stomach almost turned inside out but he couldn't get any air. Willing himself to stillness and trying not to wheeze, Matthew made himself breath slowly through his nose.

Feeling somewhat relieved with the thin but blessed oxygen, he realized that he had pneumonia and had been stricken for days on end. He had been in the grip of fever, as well, and alternately sweated and shook with chill or lie thrashing on his rumpled blankets, delirious with fever.

Sometime in the last few hours, he had run out of drinking water and tried to bring a bucket up from his well, but he figured he must have passed out in the attempt. Trickster reached out his long muzzle and licked his human's cheek.

Matthew tried to pet his dog but he was weak and as shaky as a newborn colt. His arm dropped and he sighed. Staring down at his britches, Matthew frowned. They were filthy and stained and somehow, he had lost his socks.

Looking away in disgust as another wave of chills racked his bones; he leaned over sideways and tried using his hands and elbows to rise to his feet. It took two tries but finally, Matthew got his feet under him and staggered upright. Hearing an anxious whine, he looked down and saw his dog standing close by his side.

The animal was quite tall at the shoulders and Matthew was able to use Trickster's head as a makeshift crutch. Moaning softly, he and the dog moved slowly onto the front stoop and into the cabin.

Once inside, Matthew pitched, face first, on to his rumpled cot. He managed to pull his feet up onto the bed and then he fell, shuddering, into the swirling red mist of dream... and nightmare.

Trickster whined and placed his long white teeth on Matthew's left hand. He clamped down gently, trying to pull his master into wakefulness. Failing, he sat on his haunches, staring at his master's face and panting with worry. He stayed like that for a while and then stood up and paced back and forth by the side of the bed. Then, he whirled around, facing the cabin's open door.

Growling deep in his throat, the fur on his neck and back rose in alarm. Lowering his large, square head, he stalked to the front door and stared out at the approaching wagon. His soft growl rose in volume and he moved out onto the dirt, snarling.

"Whoa... whoa," Joseph Ferguson pulled back on

the reins and his draft horse settled to a stop about twenty-five feet from the snarling dog. Then, as if just realizing the threat, the horse jinked sideways in its traces, spooky and white-eyed. "Knock it off, damn you!" Joseph yelled, the muscles in his back throbbing from its earlier assault by this same nervous nag.

Trickster's ears rose up as he recognized the people who approached—especially the little ones. Playing with these children was one of the dog's principal joys and suddenly, he knew what to do. Moving swiftly out into the front yard, he ran up to little Susan and seized her wrist in his teeth, carefully tugging her toward the cabin.

Ann let out a soft scream of fright, but she saw that her daughter was not hurt or even scared. The huge, wolf-like dog was simply leading Susan and her brother toward the house. "Don't go all the way inside!" she instructed the children.

Grabbing her basket of medicinals, she heard Joseph say, "Be careful, wife. That dog could turn on you..."

She nodded. "I don't think it will, Joseph. It's just worried for its master. The children and I will take care, though." Then she climbed down off the wagon and walked slowly up the stairs. Peering inside the darkened interior, she wrinkled her nose against the sour odor of sickness and despair.

Ann was half Crow Indian—a fact that caused her both great pride and searing agony. She had attended the white-man school in north Idaho, and suffered under her fellow student's taunts and ridicule. She had learned, firsthand, the pain of prejudice. So, when Joseph came along and asked her to be his wife, Ann had fled her tormentors and never looked back.

She did not, however, leave her family's legacy behind. She was the niece of one of the tribe's greatest medicine men, Turkey Feather. Although taking a young girl as an apprentice was considered scandalous, her uncle had flouted tradition and taught Ann much of what he knew. From herbal remedies to the recognition of and communication with all manner of spirits, Turkey Feather poured his life's work into the young girl's heart and soul.

That was why she used caution now. Stepping up to the front door, Ann turned both of her kids around and instructed them to stay outside with their father until she called for them. Not only because their neighbor might have succumbed to a communicable disease but also for the fact that, she sensed an evil presence inside the small, darkened interior. A foul spirit had taken up residence in Mr. Wilcox' home—she could feel it in her very bones.

Stopping just outside the front door she called for a flint and watched as her husband lit a small bundle of grass. Walking slowly toward her, Joseph bent over, shielding the flames with his body while she lit her sage stick on fire. Then, she put a damp, comfrey-laden rag over her mouth and holding the burning sage high in the air, entered the cabin.

Matthew dreamed about the time his wolf, Bandit, had come to him one morning and took his wrist in his mouth. The wolf was old and grey now, content, usually, to sleep his days away in the shade of a tree. That particular morning, however, Bandit's golden eyes were alight with joy and his whole body seemed to vibrate with excitement.

Allowing the animal to lead him about a mile and a half away from the house, Matthew followed the wolf to a rocky outcropping. "What is it, Bandit?" he asked as the wolf stopped and wagged his tail, turning to look at what lie hidden in the rocks and then spinning in circles and yelping in excited impatience as he waited for his master to come and look.

He heard them before he saw what had piqued Bandit's interest. Matthew crept up slowly and saw three puppies tucked into a stony ledge. They were very young—perhaps only a couple of weeks old but their eyes were open, shining blue and gold in the sun.

They tried to flee when they saw the huge, human looming over them but there was no place to go. They tumbled over one another and let out yelps of fright as Matthew hunkered down next to them. Bandit nosed them, snuffling noisily and began to lick them all over as they cried. Then, as if they remembered, all three animals ran toward the big wolf, squealing hungrily.

They looked like Bandit—the same gray and tawny fur, the same black mask. But their noses were more blunt and their ears comically long and floppy. Rubbing his pet's head, Matthew murmured, "Why you old rascal, Bandit. You went and got yourself some pups."

Bandit sat down, whining anxiously. Picking one of the pups up, Matthew saw that it was starving and there was a white scrim of dried saliva on its muzzle. Understanding the wolf's anxiety suddenly, he realized that the puppies had been abandoned. Perhaps the bitch had been killed or just wandered off but these tiny pups would perish if he didn't do something and quick.

"Okay buddy, don't worry... I've got 'em." Matthew tucked all three pups into his jacket and headed home, while the old wolf walked beside him—its tail going around and around in joyous circles.

Suddenly, the happy dream turned to nightmare—as dreams sometimes do. Matthew's smile turned into a grimace of fear as he heard a wolf snarl. The fever raging in his blood kept him from knowing that the sound was real—issued from the one pup he had chosen to keep out of the litter he had found so long ago. What Matthew thought he heard was Bandit's snarl as he tried, in vain, to save his mistress.

Matthew's head rocked back and forth on his sweaty pillow and he moaned in denial. Having spent the last four months trying to forget what he had found on his living room floor that fateful day, and for the most part succeeding, his mind recoiled at the visions his fever visited upon him now.

For months, revenge had been his cure to memory —the sights, sounds and smell of it filling his senses and washing clean the sight of his beloved wife lying in a pool of her own blood, while his twelve- year-old son, Chance, clung to his arm weeping in horror.

Matthew now looked to his sweet dog, Trickster, to replace the sight of his old wolf whose dead body lie at Iris' feet, riddled with bullet holes. Bandit's long, yellow teeth were crusted with dried blood, though—a fact that caused his owner a fierce sense of pride. The criminals who had destroyed his world did not get away without losing some of their own blood, as well.

Since then, Matthew had meted out his own brand of justice, submerging those horrid memories under a dark, red veil of fury. With wild abandon he allowed himself to become the thing he abhorred most in the world—an outlaw... a criminal, in order to forget his anguish but now those memories came roaring back, and he was as helpless to fight them now as he was able to protect his wife from harm, then.

As Ann Ferguson approached cautiously, sage-stick held high, her blood ran cold as Mr. Wilcox sat up in his bed, stared blindly ahead and screamed one word... a word so fraught with love, desperation and sorrow, her heart ached as if she had been kicked by a mule.

She stood stock-still and listened as Matthew screamed, "Iris!"

REVENGE~~ 1899

IN SEPTEMBER OF 1899, EARL DICKSON WALKED OUT OF Walla Walla State penitentiary after serving seven years for grand larceny, drug trafficking and attempted murder. He walked, alone, down the gravel path leading into and out of the prison gates, enduring catcalls and hissed imprecations from the guards stationed by the entrance.

He gritted his teeth against the insults. He had made few friends inside those tall, brick walls. The guards feared him and the other inmates kept their distance as well. His narrow blue eyes and long, ropy arms spoke volumes to the men incarcerated with him. They sensed, instinctively, that although he came with no convenient handle like murderer, molester, sodomite or road agent, he was a dangerous man, just the same, who would kill, unprovoked, for the thrill of it.

The only friend Earl did make while serving time for his crimes was a simpleton by the name of Josh

Manning. Josh's biggest crime was being born an imbecile and having an outlaw for a brother. Martin Manning depended on his idiot brother for everything from cooking dinner and caring for the gang's livestock... to taking the fall for their nefarious schemes gone wrong.

Martin and most of his gang were all dead now... brought down in a Pinkerton-staged ambush in 1895. The agents had foiled the gangs attempted train robbery and while they milled about the scene afterward, counting the dead and retrieving anything of value left on the outlaw's bodies for their bosses from the Union Pacific, they were amazed to see a fat man wander up with a number of horses in tow.

Josh, who had been left behind, as usual, and not knowing what else to do, decided to go looking for his wayward brother and his friends. Knowing better than to leave the gang's horseflesh unattended, he wandered right into the long arms of the law. Many of the Pinks were all for putting Joshua out of his misery (and taking whatever he possessed upon his person) but the agent-in-charge, an angry but deeply religious man named Murray Pike, called a halt to that notion and placed the bewildered young man under arrest.

Josh suffered greatly in prison. He was abused, both physically and emotionally, until Earl Dickson took him under his wing. It took some time but, eventually, Joshua was like putty in Earl's hands. If Earl said, *"Say, Josh... that man over there... yes, that one with the splay eye.*

I want you to put an end to him—tonight, after lights out..."
that was just what would happen.

And, rightly so. Josh was a big man-overweight and out of shape but with the heavy, elastic muscles of youth under all the flab. Although his hazel eyes seemed dull, a sort of slow, cunning intelligence seethed behind his flaccid gaze, like a hidden but deadly undertow in a still pond.

The two men came to be regarded with fear and respect. No tasty tidbit came onto the prison grounds that Earl and Joshua didn't have a taste of and any aggression toward them was met with swift and irrevocable retaliation.

For two years, Earl and Joshua were as thick as thieves until the summer of '98, when Josh was let go for lack of evidence. The warden and his guards knew that Josh was a simpleton who only did what he was told to do and they figured (rightly) that more exposure to the criminals within the walls of the prison would only set into stone what his brother, Martin, had molded out of soft clay.

Earl studied the road ahead and frowned. *Where is that kid?* he wondered. He had told Josh on the day he left, to stay close and to be ready for a fast get-away upon Earl's release. Had he forgotten? That old, familiar serpent of anger began to coil in his stomach and his flesh grew hot. He had plans—BIG plans—and his success depended upon swift transportation.

He stood on the side of the road watching as farm carts and fast-moving buggies made their way into town and wondered what he was going to do now. He had given everything he had stashed over the last seven years in prison to Josh for the necessary items. Now he had a grand total of ten dollars in his pocket (plus about twenty in his sock), which wasn't even near enough to purchase a horse—much less two horses and a wagon to go with them.

Trembling with frustrated wrath, Earl turned to his right and started walking toward town. His clothes were stiff and sour with mildew and, the rank odor of his own nervous sweat rose up to his nostrils as he made his way down the road. He was thinking fast—he *could* stash his lousy thirty bucks and, perhaps, work as a stoker for the railroad. They hired by the day—no credentials required—if memory served.

"Hey boss, is that you?" a deep voice said behind him.

Earl spun around and saw Josh sitting on the bench of a wagon with two large draft horses in the traces. Still boiling with anger, he snapped, "Where the hell have you been, Josh? I've been waiting over a half-hour!"

The big man flushed and stammered, "Sorry, Earl. Had to ketch the horses an' it took longer than I figured!"

Earl took two deep breaths, willing himself to calm down. He knew—going in—that his partner was a moron, and there was no sense in scaring the boy off… at least until Earl was through with his services.

He climbed up into the wagon and sat next to Josh

on the bench. "That's okay. For a minute, I thought you might have skedaddled with my cash, that's all."

Joshua's eyes got big. "I would NEVER, boss!" he said in his slow, garbled tongue.

Earl nodded. "That's right, son. Now, how much is left of what I gave you?"

Joshua pulled a grimy leather pouch from his pocket and handed it over. "Never was good with counting," he said. "But I got a good deal from the farmer for the rig and horses. I even put what was mine inter this bag for ya."

Earl emptied the bag and counted the bills and coin within, finally nodding with satisfaction. *Ninety-four dollars and change*, he thought. That would be plenty, if he was careful, to make it to the cemetery in Wenatchee.

He had spent years thinking about a conversation he had once had with Fred Marston... an employee of the long dead and buried Patrick Donnelly. Fred was, as usual, in his cups when he let slip the fact that Donnelly stashed a large part of his fortune in a secret vault of the mausoleum in his cemetery in Wenatchee.

It was supposed to be a closely guarded secret but Fred was pissed at his boss at that moment in time and had let slip a lot of valuable intelligence. Now that Marston, Donnelly and his slut of a sister were all dead, Earl wanted to make a play for that hidden treasure.

He only hoped that it was still there, now that the Wenatchee city council had taken over custodianship of the graveyard. If not... oh well. But if so, he would be a rich man. Rich enough, in fact, to mete some revenge on the man who had so drastically changed his life for the worse.

"Let's head on into town, Joshua," he said. "I'm sorely in need of a bath and a new set of clothes. Then, in the morning, we'll head on into Wenatchee. If things go the way I hope, we'll be rich men and then…"

As Joshua watched his boss' face change into something dark and devilish, he wondered, for the twentieth time, if following Earl Dickson was a smart thing to do or just another stupid choice in the long list of misdeeds his life had become.

"Then," Earl continued, "We'll go pay an old friend of mine, Matthew Wilcox, a long overdue visit."

THE FIRST THING Earl Dickson did when he and Josh hit town was head to a bathhouse. He was only forty-two years old, by God, but he looked as old and used up as a dead miner's gold pan. While he washed the stink off his body and allowed a Chinese man to shave his chin whiskers and cut and clean his nails, he directed Josh to run to the mercantile and purchase a new set of clothes—dungarees, a warm wool shirt, socks, boots and a sturdy coat.

As Josh nodded obediently and stepped out the door, Earl wondered, briefly, if the moron would bring back clothes only fit for a scarecrow. He was distracted though, by the pleasant sensation of getting truly clean for the first time in years and the thought of possibly becoming a rich man in the next day or so.

Therefore, he was happily surprised when Josh stepped back inside the warm, steam-filled room a little while later with a paper-wrapped bundle containing a pair of perfectly fitting black wool pants, a snowy, white cotton shirt, brown leather boots with wool socks stuffed inside and a fine tweed jacket. Each piece of clothing fit like a glove and he looked up at Josh with surprise.

The fat man stared at his broke-down boots and said, "I already bought 'em, Earl. Right after you sent me that letter sayin' you was getting' out." I did use some of your cash to get you this though—hope it fits good." He brought a hatbox around from behind his back and handed it to Dickson with a shy smile.

Staring at Josh's face, Earl realized that the dope was halfway in love with him. In his opinion, doing the dirty behind bars was one thing, but engaging in that kind of nonsense on the outside was... well, a perversion of nature. Deciding to have a heart-to-heart with the kid before things got awkward; Earl opened the hatbox and drew in a breath.

Nestled inside the tissues was one of the nicest hats he had ever seen. A dark grey Derby with a black, leather band around the crown; it even sported a tiny black and red feather. Facing the mirror, Earl put the hat on, adjusted the angle and gave himself a jaunty wink. He had half a mind to admonish the idiot for spending so much cash on a hat but he was so impressed by how it made him look—and feel—he didn't have the heart for it.

He had to admit, going to jail might have been good for his health. He looked better than he had in years. He had quit smoking and taking drugs… and dreamed of his new life after jail with no trace of guilt or remorse over what had gone before in his rough and violent life.

Staring at himself in the mirror, he saw a gentleman. No, he acknowledged… not some high-falutin' dandy with a lacy collar and pointy, white shoes but a man of substance. Studying his own clear blue eyes, he saw no trace of his bad, old days as a murderer, a thief, a hopped-up drug-runner or a roust-about for Patrick Donnelly.

Josh was staring at his reflection as well; his hazel eyes open wide in awe. "You look nice, Earl," he mumbled.

Earl spun on his heel and said, "Come on. Let's get something to eat.

Mindful of his money and reluctant to smudge the reflected image he had seen of himself in the mirror, Earl bought dinner for the two of them at a café and refrained from availing himself of the abundant tail offered at the closest saloon. Although his loins itched for relief, Earl didn't want to take any chances… not with the possibility of such a big pay-off only two-day ride from here.

He and Josh were asleep like upright citizens, soon after the sun set that night.

THE NEXT MORNING Earl shook his partner awake. "Come on, let's move out."

Josh groaned, sleepily, and rolled over but Earl took the young man's limp and dirty slouch hat and whipped it across his head. "I said, get up asshole... NOW!"

Josh yelped and sat bolt upright. He stared up at Earl with scared eyes and touched the two perfect welts rising up on his left cheek.

Earl glared. "Now, listen up, Josh..." he hissed. "You and me, we're partners and that's all, got it? I won't put up with any of that nonsense from before and I don't want you mooning around about it, neither.... You hear me?" He watched as Josh's cheeks flushed red.

Then he added, "And don't you go forgetting that I'm the boss of this outfit. You can hang around with me if you like and maybe I'll make you a rich man in the process, but when I say jump, the only thing I want to hear coming from your mouth is, how high? Can you live with that, because if not, you get up and get outta here, right now!"

Tears flowed down both of Josh's cheeks now, but he jumped out of his bed and pulled his old boots on with alacrity.

Earl watched with stony eyes and then he said, "Go in and brush your teeth, Josh. Your breath stinks like the grave. Soon as you're done, we're heading to Wenatchee."

Head hanging low in bewilderment, the big man pulled his seldom-used toothbrush out of his back pocket and commenced to cleaning his mouth. Two hours later, the men pulled out of town heading north to Donnelly's cemetery in Wenatchee.

EARL AND JOSH watched the cemetery for a couple of days before making their move. It looked like a groundskeeper came out every day from 9 am to 4 pm. He would yank a few weeds and scythe away some of the taller grasses around gravestones and monuments. Mostly, though, the old man grabbed frequent pulls off a small jug and took long naps behind the mausoleum.

Earl had wondered if the house that sat behind the graveyard was occupied but it didn't seem to be and there were no guard dogs to worry about either. *Perfect!* He thought, grinning.

Now, as they hunkered down in the weeds behind some leafless shrubbery, Josh muttered, "He's leaving, Earl." They watched as the caretaker staggered up to his small wagon and drove away. It was a little past 4:00 in the afternoon, and the sun was setting behind the low hills.

Earl nodded. "Let's wait for a few more minutes, Josh. By 4:30, it should be almost dark. Anyone who chances by won't be able to spot us if they tried."

A half hour or so later, Earl and Josh ran out from behind a stand of lilac bushes and scaled the fence, landing on the grass behind the mausoleum. A wrought iron gate in front of the building was bolted for the night but it was quick enough work to smash the padlock. Earl's heart pounded with excitement as the tall gate swung open with a rusty screech.

According to Marston, the vault that held Donnelly's fortune was the biggest one on the end. There was supposed to be a rendering of St. Patrick and the word, *DONNELLY* on the front panel.

Turning to his companion, Earl hissed, "Light that lantern, Josh. It's black as pitch in here."

Josh complied and as the feeble light filled the room, Earl saw that the young man's face was slack and wide-eyed with fear. "Don't worry, Josh," he murmured. "There ain't nuthin' in here but dust... and maybe a buried treasure."

Taking the lantern, Earl moved down the room and stopped in front of the last vault. Sure enough, a saint stared back at him from the vaults front cover and *DONNELLY* was etched into metal's fancy scrollwork. The panel had been soldered shut though, and Earl said, "Time for some muscle, Josh."

They each took a side, and using whatever means they had at their disposal, the men hammered and pried away at the seal. It was hot and sweaty work but twenty minutes later, most of the seal was lying in pieces on the floor at their feet. Then, they removed the metal cover and, holding the lantern high, Earl peered inside the vault.

There were no dusty bones or any half-rotted

corpses inside but there was a metal lockbox pushed toward the rear of the enclosure. Grinning in anticipation, Earl reached in and pulled the box out. It was heavy, though, and Earl grunted, "Josh, come here and give me a hand!"

"I'm a scairt to, Earl! Can't you manage it yourself?"

Josh's sudden recalcitrant moods were really starting to get on Earl's nerves. The man didn't seem to grasp that fact he was under orders! He stopped pulling and turned around.

"You do what I say, Josh, or I swear I'll kill you and stick you in one of these vaults!" he snarled.

Gulping, Josh stepped forward and grasped the end of the heavy metal box in both arms. A moment later, it hit the floor with a resounding bang. Coughing against a plume of dust rising into the air, Earl knelt over the lockbox and proceeded to pound at yet another padlock pinning the lid tight.

Apparently, Josh had no qualms about a box that was not hiding inside a crypt and he said, "Move over, Earl. I can get it." He had found a shovel, somewhere along the way and with a mighty heave; he drove the metal blade down onto the lock, which gave away with a dull thud.

Holding his breath, Earl lifted the lid. It stuck for a moment and then lifted into the air to reveal Earl's every hope and dream. There were banknotes—thousands of them, and small boxes of jewelry. There was coin, gleaming gold and silver in the lamp light and files of miscellaneous paperwork—bills of deed, licenses and assorted legal papers representing, Earl guessed, a separate fortune all on its own.

Shaking with greed, Earl straightened and said, "Can you carry this on your own or do you need help?"

Josh shrugged. "I reckon I can manage, for a while anyway. It's about a mile to the wagon... maybe you can spell me if'n I get tired?"

Earl nodded and watched as Josh bent down to pick his new fortune up off the dusty floor. Then he followed, closing the big iron gate behind him and fastening the padlock back into place. It was slightly bent but, with some effort, fit the lock well enough. Besides, Earl had not seen the old caretaker look inside the mausoleum once in the last two days.

He figured that by the time the man bothered to look, and report the break-in (if ever) he and Josh would be long gone. Earl blew the lantern out and watched Josh's wide back as the young man picked his way through the dusk to the back fence.

Earl still needed Josh's muscles for what he had planned next but... he had *no intention,* of sharing his newfound wealth. One more job and Earl would put an end to the sassy moron once, and for all.

2

"GETTING TIRED, IS ALL"

STATE MARSHAL, MATTHEW WILCOX PICKED UP THE latest batch of WANTED posters from the polished wood counter-top of the marshal's office in Spokane, Washington. Thumbing through the paperwork, he saw the usual suspects; bank robbers, train robbers, a few rapists/murderers and two Yakima Indians, accused of torching houses and barns all along the Columbia River gorge.

Sighing, he stuffed the papers in his carryall and stared out the window across the street at his son, Chance, who was talking to a couple of boys his own age. Matthew smiled. His twelve-year-old son was an almost perfect mixture of Iris and himself. The boy's hair was strawberry blonde and his eyes as green as grass. He was growing up tall and lean and his smile was already melting a number of girlish hearts back home in Granville.

Stepping up to the windowpane, Matthew gestured

and saw Chance nod. He said something to the other boys and then led his horse over to the hitch rail in front of the marshal's office, tying it fast. Placing a bag of oats over the horse's muzzle, he patted the animal's rump and then stepped up on the boardwalk.

"You ready to head out, Pa?" he asked, after entering the office.

"Just about... Marshal Adams is fetching the payroll from the safe, and then we'll go home." Matthew replied.

At that precise moment, Matthew's boss stepped into the room with a small canvas bag clutched in his hand. "Here you go, Matthew... and, here are your orders for October. Looks like there's not too much going on— just prisoner transport from the Spokane County jail to Walla Walla penitentiary... um... twice, in the first two weeks and then you need to stand as state witness in four separate trials, from October 15th through the 22nd".

He looked up from the orders with a grin. "Looks like a gravy train for you, at least for now. Of course, that could all change," he added with a sigh.

Knowing how true that statement was, Matthew nodded in agreement. Looking the orders over, he said, "Well, I guess I'll be seeing you in about three weeks, right?"

"That's right. Get on home now and give that wife of yours a big hug for me, won't you?" The portly, little marshal (and confirmed bachelor) was half in love with Iris, Matthew knew.

But, he mused, *what's new about that? Wherever she goes, Iris makes friends, both with her uncommon good sense and her deep compassion for others. She is as pretty as a picture and for many of the folks back home, an angel on Earth.*

Matthew smiled. He had been gone for almost three weeks this time and couldn't wait to get home to her loving arms. The only reason he wasn't home already was that Chance was attending school in Spokane and Matthew had seized the opportunity to ride the thirty miles back home with his son.

He looked forward to hearing about Chance's studies, the latest local gossip... and, just spending time with his boy. He longed for Iris' touch, though. Although she was almost forty-four years old now and gray was beginning to etch its way through her long, red hair, she was just as desirable as ever. Her long, lean body was still straight and strong and Matthew couldn't wait to run his hands over her curves.

"Hey, Pa, did you see this?"

Looking over at Chance, Matthew saw that the boy was staring at a poster on the wall. Walking up to stand beside him, Matthew saw an all too familiar face. It was none other than that little weasel, Martin LeVesque. Matthew grimaced as he read the words, MARTIN LEVESQUE FOR ATTORNY GENERAL!

The crooked, police commissioner was one fish that got away seven years ago, after a sex-slave prostitution ring in Seattle was discovered, and dismantled for good. Matthew was able to prove many people's guilt in that affair but, although he had eyewitnesses and *proof* of Lévesque's involvement in the scheme, Matthew was not able to see the man convicted of his crimes.

The corruption within the King County Sheriff's office had apparently sunk its roots too deep for Matthew to penetrate, and after months of presenting one argument after another and making countless train trips into the rainy city of Seattle, he had grown weary, finally, of trying to grab a hold of that slippery, little snake and shrugged it off as a loss.

"I remember you talking about this guy, Pa," Chance spoke quietly.

Matthew put his hand on the boy's shoulder. "Yes, he's as bent as an old stick, son." Matthew shook his head, adding, "That's why you should never put blind faith in anyone, Chance. Just because there's a nice picture of a man on a wall somewhere, doesn't mean he's good or trustworthy. This particular man made his fortune by selling woman as slaves. He almost got rich selling your cousin Amelia!"

Chance nodded. "I remember, Pa. Gosh, I wish you could have proven him guilty!" The boy's eyes blazed like green embers and his dark, slanting eyebrows lowered in anger.

Over the last few years, Amelia and her husband had made numerous trips to Granville for visits. Since then, Chance had fallen in love with the beautiful young woman, her baby boy and Adam Lowry, the fine young doctor she had married, who also helped

Amelia's father, Lewis Winters, in his medical practice in Marysville, Washington.

Chance was only five years old when Amelia was abducted and, even now, he could hardly believe that something so evil had almost taken his beloved cousin away from hearth and home forever.

Sighing, Matthew nodded. "Me too, son, but that one got away."

Turning back to Marshal Adams, Matthew smiled and said, "See you in a couple of weeks, sir. If you need me before then, though, just wire Sheriff Smithers, okay? He'll ride out to the ranch and let me know."

"Will do, Matthew. Have a good rest." Adams said and headed back to his office.

Matthew and Chance walked outside and mounted their horses. They rode slowly down the busy streets and Matthew marveled anew at all the grand brick buildings replacing the canvas tents and wooden structures that had been swept away in the great fire of '89. They stopped at the mercantile and picked up a bolt of pretty, flower-sprigged cotton for Iris, some special herbs she had ordered and a few sticks of licorice. Then they headed out of town toward home.

Once they hit the road, traffic fell off significantly. Walking their horses, father and son gnawed on the black licorice sticks and chatted amiably about school, outlaws, the winter wheat crop and the fall market. Iris thought the thirty-two calves she was bringing to market would sell at a fair price and she had also talked a number of ranchers in the area into bringing their mares home to the Imes ranch for stud service, rather than having to haul their Quarter Horse stallion out, as in year's past.

Matthew thought of home and smiled. He understood, suddenly, that his vague longing to stay in Granville and work the farm was real—and undeniable. He had been thinking of retiring from the Marshal's service for quite a while, but until now, he had thought it was a passing fancy—nothing a little rest wouldn't cure.

He realized, though, that he was sick of being a lawman. The idea of bringing justice to outlaws, and protecting the solid citizens in his territory from harm was noble in and of itself but it was a dirty business. When he wasn't immersed in the world of bandits and their schemes, he had to think like one in order to bring them down.

More and more, of late, he found himself dreaming of the golden wheat fields and verdant green hollows of home. He wanted to spread grain for Iris' girls... the prize flock of Rhode Island Red chickens that pecked and quarreled in the front yard and he wanted to roll up his sleeves and wrestle calves to the mud during branding season. He wanted to be there when their mares foaled and help build the giant grass—hay mounds that spotted the back pasture.

He thought he could work part-time from home as a lawyer, and help Iris as well, if he finished his study of the law with Judge Abernathy—an ornery but sharp old friend of his uncle Jon, who still practiced law in

Spokane. It would take about a year, he figured, and then he could hang a shingle on the front porch of his own house. Matthew knew that what he didn't know about farming, Iris and her farm hands could teach.

Feeling happy for the first time in a while, he turned to his son and said, "How would you feel about your old man becoming a lawyer and staying home for once?"

Chance stiffened and his eyes got big. Turning to Matthew, he said, "Are you serious, Pa?" A huge smile spread over the boy's face and he added, "That would be fine, sir... and boy, would Ma ever be glad!" Then he frowned. "Don't you like being a US Marshal anymore?"

Matthew grinned back and said, "Well, I'm getting tired is all and I would like to spend more time at home with your ma." He shrugged, adding, "It'll take some time, though, you know. First, I have to give my boss a chance to replace me and then, I will need to study up. I lack about a year of school to actually practice law." Looking his son in the eye, Matthew said, "Maybe you'll find your studies a little easier if you knew your old pa was suffering right along with you, eh?"

Chance blushed. He was as smart as a whip but hated being cooped-up in a classroom all day, which was why Matthew and Iris had arranged for him to study at the military academy in Spokane, rather than back home with his friends. A bored Chance was naughty and prone to playing hooky. At least the academy focused on military techniques, firearms and swordplay—all the things that kept Chance's interest engaged.

A flurry of growls interrupted their musing and Chance said, "There's that mean old dog of the Parkers' again. One of these days somebody's going to shoot him!"

Matthew did not doubt it. He had been so lost in his visions of the future he didn't realize they were so close to home but hearing that elderly, Blue Tick hound snarling in the weeds brought him back to the present with a start. Realizing it was only a quarter of a mile or so from home, he grinned and said, "Hey, about we stretch these horses out a bit?"

Chance didn't need to be asked twice. His eyes glinted and he swept his hat off his head. Using it as a whip, he gave his horse a whack and hollered, "I'll beat you home, Pa!" Then he was off and running.

Matthew gave his own horse, Lincoln, a slight kick. The horse was ugly by most standards with a dappled red and white "medicine hat", and a rat-tail but he was fast as greased lightning and one of the smartest animals the sheriff had ever owned. The big gelding snorted and did a little crow-hop, back legs digging into the dirt road. Then it flew after the other horse.

It was no contest. Feeling the wind rushing past his ears and a keen sense of joy, Matthew yelled, "EEEE-Haw!" and flew past his son in a cloud of dust. Entering the high arch that signified the entrance to the Imes ranch, he flew up the dirt road, Chance hot on his tail.

Staring right and left, he felt a sudden chill. Pulling

back on his horse's reins, he held an arm out so Chance would come to a stop as well. To his left he saw a number of cows milling around an empty feed bin and bawling for relief from the milk straining their udders. To his right, he saw the same scene, only this time it was their herd of horses scattered around the paddock nibbling stray shoots of grass instead of hay and kicking in frustration at the empty water trough.

"What's going on, Pa? The critturs ain't been fed!" Chance breathed.

"Haven't been fed," Matthew answered automatically through fear-frozen lips. His heart was pounding in his ears, because he had just spied the tips of some one's boots in the grass by the side of the road. Turning to Chance, he said, "Stay right here, son. I need to check something out."

Chance had already seen for himself, though, and spurred his horse ahead.

"Chance! Goddammit..." Matthew muttered under his breath and trotted Lincoln to where his son sat his horse, looking down at the body on the ground with tears in his eyes.

He glanced at Matthew and whispered, "Somebody killed old Lenny, Pa!"

Matthew dismounted and checked the old man's throat for a pulse but he knew that Lenny was shot dead and had been gone for quite some time. The body was stone cold and flies lifted in a black, lazy cloud from the man's mouth, eyes and nostrils. Feeling a cold chill, Matthew straightened up and looked over at the house.

"How many folks did your ma have helping around here, Chance?"

"Just Lenny, sir, as far as I know." Chance said.

Matthew took off walking, staring straight ahead at the house. He could hear Bandit's pups yipping and howling from their pen in the backyard, and couldn't help but wonder, *where's Bandit?*

Iris' chickens came running across the yard and crowded around Matthew's legs in querulous complaint, but he ignored them and stepped up on the porch. Standing just outside the front door and seeing dried smears of blood around the doorknob, Matthew's heart froze.

Telling himself that there must be a logical explanation and that the fear he felt was just an over-active imagination run amok, did not quell the tremors that shook his body. Hearing his son step up behind him, he held his arm out and murmured, "I need you to stay out here, Chance."

Then, taking a deep breath, Matthew Wilcox opened the door and stepped straight into hell.

3

JOSH AND EARL~

EARL ROLLED OVER ON HIS SWEATY PILLOW AND groaned. His whole face throbbed with pain and his lips were swollen and cracked. His nose... what was left of it, anyway, was numb and he reached a hand up to feel around and see if the fragile stiches holding his proboscis in place had given way or if the ruined flesh was buried somewhere in the tangled sheets and blankets on his bed.

"Josh! Bring me more of that junk!" he croaked.

Joshua stuck his head around the doorjamb and said, "We're out, boss. You want me to go and buy some more?"

"Yes, goddammit, I'm dying here!"

Josh didn't think Earl was fixing to die, but acknowledged the man might feel that way. That big dog, the one Earl said was actually a timber wolf had come flying out of nowhere and latched on to Earl's face when he was trying to have his way with that red-haired woman.

This had forced Josh to pull his gun and shoot the woman dead but it took some time to get a shot off at that horrible beast eating away at Earl's face. Man and beast had rolled back and forth on the floor of that kitchen, Earl screaming like a banshee and the wolf snarling like a demon from hell.

Finally, Earl was able to sink a knife in the wolf's side, which caused the animal to slink away for a second, whining. Then, it gathered itself to spring on its quarry once more, which finally gave Josh enough time to empty his revolver into its sorry hide.

These events had taken place four days ago, in a little town about thirty miles from Spokane. Shivering, Josh still felt like what had happened was some sort of dark dream from which he could not awaken. Josh had never hurt a woman before and Earl had not said that anything like that would be taking place when they rode up to that pretty farm.

Apparently, the red-haired woman was the wife of an old enemy of Earls named Matthew Wilcox. Earl claimed that she deserved to die, but Josh wasn't so sure. He had been sent to the front door of her house, while Earl lurked outside. He was instructed to ask for work in exchange for food, which he did, but the woman had insisted on inviting him inside and sitting him down at the kitchen table for a nice meal of cold, fried chicken and spud salad.

She was so pretty and sweet as she bustled around

her sunny kitchen that Josh hated to see her get hurt. He was sitting at her wide plank table, undecided, when he heard a volley of shots fired from outside. He watched as she paused, staring out the window, and then moved swiftly to the back of the room, reaching up to grab the rifle sitting on a shelf above the door.

He knew then, that the decision had just been made for him. He flew up out of his chair, wrestled the rifle out of her hands and cold-cocked her on the chin. He had no sooner placed the woman's limp body on the floor than Earl stepped into the room. He stared at the woman and grinned.

"Looks like it's just her and that old man on the premises," Earl jeered. "And *he* ain't any threat now."

"Does that mean we can go on, then, since your sheriff ain't here?" Josh crossed his fingers behind his back. He really didn't want to see the nice lady come to any harm, and he didn't like the look that had come over Earl's face.

"Well… we'll take off soon enough, I reckon. First though…" He unbuckled his belt and popped the buttons on his britches. "I don't know how long it's been since I had a taste of something this fine…"

Josh felt a stirring in his own loins as Earl hoisted the woman's skirt's up and pulled her long johns down to her ankles. Her legs were as white as snow and the hair at her crutch was as red as a handful of new copper pennies.

Earl was about to set to, when that God- awful wolf came a'running in the back door. The rest of that day's events seemed to dissolve into a hazy cloud of red-tinged images that Josh could hardly countenance as happening to him.

Just as the animal jumped on Earl, the woman awoke. Sitting up with a gasp, she grabbed the rifle that lay a couple of feet from where she sat on the floor. She heaved it up to her shoulder, and Josh had no choice… biting his lip in regret, he shot her in the stomach, and then, again, in the chest.

The wolf had paused for a moment then, turning around with blazing yellow eyes to stare first at the woman lying dead on the floor and then at Josh, where he stood with his pistol still belching smoke. Even now, Josh understood that the animal was grief-stricken, and he knew he would carry the look in those wise, golden eyes until the end of his days.

Then, it turned around and renewed its attack on Earl's face, before Josh was finally able to put it out of its misery. He emptied his pistol into the wolf's body but still, as Josh searched for the knobby piece of Earl's nose the wolf had torn off, it managed to crawl over to where the woman lay in a pool of her own blood. The last thing Josh heard as he hauled Earl's bloody carcass out the back door was the sound of the animal's pitiful whimpers as it lay dying at its mistress' feet.

Josh started as Earl snapped, "Well, are you just going to stand there, staring into space like the village idiot, or are going to get me some dope for the pain?" The man's words were garbled and red-tinged spit drooled out the corner of his mouth.

Rushing over to the small leather bag that held most of their cash, Josh pulled out another fiver and said, "Sorry, Earl. I'll go get your stuff and more of that herbal remedy too."

Earl snarled, "Be quick about it!"

Looking at Earl's face, Josh tried to keep his revulsion from showing. The wolf had done horrible damage. Although Josh had managed to sew the man's nose back on, the stiff protuberance that gave it form had been gnawed away and the flesh hung loosely around Earl's nasal cavities.

There were deep gouges on both cheeks, and Earls left eyelid hung over the eye like a loose blind. His lips were swollen to three times their natural size and the tip of Earl's tongue was gone as well. A last dinner for the beast, Josh thought, before it ate no more, ever again.

Josh really did not want to hang around this horrible spectacle of a man anymore, but he did not know how to proceed on his own through life. Especially now, that he was a murderer of women. He knew, though, that Earl might die if he did not find a doctor very soon. Earl had said no to that notion but Josh felt he had no other choice or he would be alone in the world.

Looking away, Josh said, "I'll be back real soon, Earl."

A COUPLE OF HOURS LATER, Earl lay staring up at the peeling, fly-shot wallpaper in the hotel room on the outskirts of Ellensburg. He was rubbing at a spot on his chest where a St. Patrick medal had once resided—a gift to him from his old boss, Patrick Donnelly. He was angry with himself for losing it, and trying to remember the last time he had seen it but he had swallowed a large dose of laudanum… too large, actually, and he was soon lost in a dream.

He was a child again, living in the slums of Hell's Kitchen. He and his friends had just been bested in a skirmish against a rival street gang and the bigger, stronger boys were subsequently, teaching them a lesson.

One by one, Earl and his friends were dragged up to a burn-barrel that glowed like the fires of Hades in a back alley. The young tough who claimed to be king of that gang pulled a red-hot poker out of the barrel and laid the point of the brand against each of the smaller boy's cheeks. He said, "This will show our bosses you been here before—and now if they see this brand on your faces, they will know to kill you for trespassin'."

Earl moaned, the inflamed skin on his face and neck chafing hotly on the pillowcase. The childhood dream fled and then Earl was staring at the long, wrinkled muzzle of a devil-dog from hell. Its large, amber eyes glared into his, and then its teeth dug down and down until Earl screamed in agony, watching as his whole head came loose in the wolf's jaws.

He stared as the wolf walked away a few feet and

then turned around to glare at Earl's body in scorn. Then, a hand reached down and shook his shoulder. Startled awake, Earl reached for the knife at his side, and came up off the bed with a savage snarl.

"Whoa, whoa!" a voice said. "I'm here to help with your wounds!"

Earl fought against the drugs heavy embrace and finally managed to open his eyes. A man stood by the side of the bed, staring down at him. "What do you want?" he muttered.

"Well, your young man here tells me you have cash to pay for surgery and some stitch work. He told me how you two come up on a she-bear a couple of days ago and it almost took your head off. The name's, Talbot...Dr. Lawrence Talbot."

Earl stared over at Josh who stood fidgeting by the door. He was impressed, in spite of himself, for the valid-sounding lie the moron had thought up. Then he studied the character looming over his bed and he wasn't sure he liked what he saw. Middle-aged, the man looked like he'd seen better days and his coat and shirtsleeves were dirty and frayed at the seams. He had long, greasy hair and a face like an old coonhound.

Still, Earl was afraid of dying and equally afraid of living with what remained of his face. "Can you fix my dose?" he asked.

"Do you mind?" Talbot leaned over and gently moved Earl's head back and forth, studying the blob on the front of his face. Then he grunted, "Most of the stitches on the left side are holding and there looks to be an adequate flow of blood to the affected area. The right side, though... if I'm going to save your nose, Mr. ..." he paused, waiting for Earl to supply a name. Seeing that wasn't going to happen, he added, "I need to move quickly. Right now, in fact."

"How 'bout the reth of my face?" Earl still couldn't believe that God-forsaken wolf had burrowed its way into his mouth and tore out a chunk of his tongue during the attack.

Talbot said, "Open wide," and stared down Earl's gullet for a few moments. Shaking his head, he turned to Josh and asked, "Don't suppose you found what's left of your friend's tongue lying around after that bear attack?"

Josh shook his head and the doctor turned back to Earl. "What's done is done, as far as your tongue's concerned. It's not too bad though... a little practice and you will make yourself understood well enough. It's that nose that's going to kill you if you don't let me work on it right now."

"How much?" Earl glared.

The doctor smiled down at him. "One thousand dollars... and a good horse."

Earl sat up with an outraged roar and then fell back down in a swoon. "That's robbery!" he gasped.

Talbot shrugged. "That's business, sir. I'm a good doctor, but I have fallen on hard times since they caught me preforming one too many abortions. Now, I'm one step ahead of the law and I need a new start. You're my ticket."

"I could have my man shoot you dead." Earl replied, wincing as his ruined tongue tried to pronounce the simple words.

"Talbot raised his furry eyebrows. "Really? Don't you want to live with your pretty face intact?"

Earl studied the old coot's long face for a moment. "Okay... half dow, the rest after."

"Excellent!" the doctor exclaimed. Turning to Josh he said, "First bring me my cash and then fetch me a pan of hot water—as hot as you can get it! I'll also need clean towels... lots of them. HURRY!"

Earl gestured to Josh and the young man nodded. Rooting through the leather bag and shrugging in bewilderment, Earl said, "Bring it to me!"

Josh handed the bag over and watched as Earl thumbed through the bills, finally handing five hundred dollars to the doctor. Then he glared up at Josh and said, "Go get the water and towels, Josh!" The young man nodded and ran out the door.

Then, Talbot reached inside his bag and came up with a wicked looking hypodermic needle. Gazing down into Earl's eyes, he murmured, "Take a little snooze now. When you wake up, you will feel like a new man."

4

MATTHEW—DESOLATE

MATTHEW STARED DOWN AT THE RED AND BLOODY RUIN his life had just become and felt his heart crack in two. He wanted to throw his head back and howl in anguish. He wanted to fall to his knees and sob in grief. He wanted to dig a hole in the ground and crawl inside of it and die—but he had work to do. A little voice in back of his mind spoke clearly through the roaring maelstrom of his jumbled emotions saying, "You must think clearly now—Chance needs you!"

His son was clinging to his arm, eyes wide with shock and mouth opening and closing against the suppressed screams in his throat. "Pa...oh, Pa" he whispered.

Turning around, Matthew swept the boy up in his arms and walked out the front door. He didn't realize it but he was pressing his son's face into his chest and whispering, "Take it easy, Chance. It will be all right... Ssh, Ssh."

As if Matthew's words had pushed over a dam, Chance suddenly convulsed in Matthew's arms, keening in sorrow and then he burst into tears, sobbing against his father's chest. Matthew made for their horses, still saddled and nibbling on tall grass by the side of the entrance road.

Putting his heart-broken child down on the ground, Matthew swiftly unsaddled Chance's horse and then led it by the bridle to the paddock. His heartbeat was steady and, for the moment, he operated on instinct alone. He did not know that his face was as gray as a ghost, or that white showed all around his brilliant green irises, like a spooked mule.

Once inside the fence, he pulled the bridle off the animal's muzzle and slapped its rump. Watching, for a moment, as the horse did a little rodeo in front of its herd mates, he closed the gate, walked back and picked Chance up in his arms again. Placing the boy just behind the saddle's cantle, he climbed on and kicked Lincoln up to a trot.

They rode toward town, Chance clinging to his pa's back with trembling arms. Matthew could tell the boy was trying to be brave… to stop the sobs that kept rising up in his chest like a rushing river, but he wanted the boy to let those poisonous waters out. He didn't want Chance to turn out like him—bottled up, cold and remote.

Iris had been the one person in his life who was able to uncork his overwhelming fear… the fear of loss, love, family and friendship. With a large dose of determination and humor, she had reached past his defenses and taught him to love again and to bury the ghosts of his past. Now she was gone and it was up to him to protect his son's heart.

His eyes were burning with unshed tears. He wanted to weep and wail, he longed for the release of his sorrow, but his eyes remained barren. Seeing the church steeple in the near distance and the second story balcony of the town's newest hotel, Matthew placed his right hand over his son's clenched fists.

"I'm taking you to Roy, Chance. I'll have you stay with him while I clean things up a bit at home, okay?" He felt his boy shake his head.

"No!" Chance mumbled. "I'm staying with you!"

Matthew sighed. He knew this would happen but knowing didn't make dealing with it any easier. They were about a hundred yards from the large livery that marked the entrance to his hometown... a new barn but the same place that had brought an end to the "Granville Stand-off," so long ago.

He stopped his horse and slid off the saddle, gazing up at the boy who looked so much like Iris it made his heart ache. Chance stared down at Matthew in defiance.

"I'm staying with you, Pa. Don't send me away... not now."

Matthew stared down at the toes of his boots. Then he looked up at Chance again. "Please, help me out, son. I have to use my badge now, which means I need my deputy's help in figuring out who did this to your ma and to old Lenny. You are smart, Chance, and a great help to me but this time you're too close to the victims to be of any use.

Chance glared. "What about you, Pa? You're close too!"

Matthew nodded. "Yes, I am too close and, eventually, the marshals will kick me off the case. That's the way it works, Chance. Meanwhile, I'm going to do what I can to help find the bast... the men who did this to us, okay?" Green eyes searched green eyes and, finally, Chance shrugged in defeat.

Matthew continued. "I need to know you're safe, son, while I search for evidence, but I'll come and get you later on tonight. While I'm gone, I need you to send for Abby and Sam, all right? Either Abner or Dicky will help you with that. Tell them to make haste, as I would like to lay your ma to rest as soon as possible.

Chance's large, slightly slanted green eyes filled with tears again and his face turned red. Matthew held his arms up and Chance slid off the back of the horse and into his father's embrace.

A few moments passed as the boy wept and then Sheriff Roy Smithers said, "What's happened, Matthew?"

THREE DAYS LATER, Matthew and his children stood close to three newly, dug graves. They were surrounded by the town's citizens, including members of the sheriff's department, the US Marshal's office and a number of dignitaries from the city of Spokane. There was even a representative from the State governor's office.

Chance was standing close to Matthew on one side and Iris' daughter, Abby, on the other. Abby's young husband held their twin sons as their mother was inconsolable and clung to Matthew's left arm as though it was the only thing holding her upright. Iris' son, Samuel, stood at attention in his Calvary uniform, staring at his mother's casket with angry eyes. When he wasn't staring at Iris' coffin he was gazing at Matthew in accusation.

Sam was a good boy but he was no fool. He knew that Matthew was somehow responsible for his mother's death. Not intentionally, he acknowledged, but right at this moment, that was cold comfort. Matthew had made too many enemies during his years as a lawman and now, in Sam's mind, the chickens had come home to roost.

Matthew was well- aware of the young man's scrutiny and felt no desire to defend himself. He *was* responsible for the death of his wife and he knew there was nothing he could say in his own defense. He was careful, though, to avoid Samuel's eyes. Right now, he needed Sam and Abby, both, to be strong and to step up to the task of moving forward in life.

Sam would be going back to active duty in two days, which was right and proper, as time alone would heal the boy's heart. Abby, though, would need to take her little brother, Chance, into her home in Spokane. Maybe for a short time only or… maybe forever.

———

AS THE PREACHER droned on and on and the cool autumn wind nipped at people's coats and parasols, Roy stared across the short distance to where his best friend stared into the dark hole that would house his beloved Iris forever. Then he shivered, thinking about the last couple of days and wondering what would happen next.

In those first few, mind numbing hours after finding Iris lying dead in her own kitchen and her farmhand, Lenny, filled with holes in the front paddock of the Imes' ranch, Roy had decided to ensconce Chance in one of the jail cells of the sheriff's office. He thought, and Matthew agreed, that this was a revenge killing and worried the perpetrators were still at large in the area and possibly intent on wiping out the US Marshal's whole family.

Chance was offended, of course, and wanted to stay as close as possible to his father but there was work to be done and neither Matthew nor the Granville sheriff's department had the time or the ability to keep the boy occupied, while they made final preparations and searched, in vain, for Iris' killers.

While Bean Tolson kept Chance company, Matthew, Roy and the Granville deputies spent the rest of that afternoon and most of the next day searching the town and neighboring farms but found nothing out of the ordinary. Knowing that the doctor (who was also the town's coroner) was tending to Iris and Lenny did not ease Matthew's mind. He had turned to Roy, finally, saying, "I have got to get back to the house, Roy. Will you keep Chance safe and... as comfortable as possible?"

"Of course, Matthew," Roy responded. Turning to Dicky McNulty and Abner Smalley he said, "You two go on ahead... I'll catch up in a bit." The two grief-stricken deputies nodded, and spurred their horses up the road to search the last two farmsteads within a thirty-mile radius of town.

Facing Matthew again, Roy said, "If you will just wait a little while, me and the boys will help you search the house."

Roy's bright blue eyes were red and sunk into tired, gray pouches... it seemed he had aged into an old man almost overnight. Of course, being ten years older than Matthew; he technically *was* an old man now, at fifty. Still, the news of Iris' murder had hit him hard, and he hadn't slept a wink since he ran into Matthew and Chance yesterday on the outskirts of town, and heard the devastating news.

Roy studied Matthew and his heart sank. He had seen that desolation on his friend's face a couple of times during their fifteen- year friendship, and mourned that the expression on those handsome features was just as bleak now—and twice as deadly. Roy knew that Matthew would not let this stand. Come Hell or high water, his friend would move heaven and Earth, leaving no stone unturned, until he tracked down the dirty dog who murdered his wife.

"Did you hear me, Matthew?" Roy asked.

Matthew was staring at the far horizon, where a flock of crows seethed and hissed over something on the ground below them. He started at Roy's words, then turned around in his saddle. He shook his head and said, "Yes Roy, I heard you but, no. I really need to be alone, okay? I'll be able to concentrate better if there aren't other bodies around me."

Roy nodded. He had been at Matthew's side two days ago, when they entered his home. He had watched as the marshal fell to his knees by Iris and Bandit, and winced as Matthew gathered them both up in his arms, weeping silently, his big shoulders hunched and quaking with grief. Abner and Bean Tolson were entertaining Chance at the jailhouse, but Dicky had come with Roy and Matthew and stood in the kitchen doorway, weeping like a baby.

Now, Roy sighed. Iris was lying in a coffin next to where Matthew had already buried his beloved pet wolf, Bandit. He saw the look in his old friend's eyes and, despite the fact that he held his step-daughter tightly and clutched Chance close to his body; Roy noted the chilly distance in Matthew's eyes.

Matthew had taken him aside a few minutes before the funeral service and murmured, "Promise you'll see after Chance, please?"

Roy turned around and stared up into Matthew's face. "Of course I will, but that job should fall to you, am I right?"

Matthew looked down at his boots. "I will make sure he and the other children are taken care of, financially." Expression hidden by the brim of his dress hat, Matthew's tone was neutral.

"What are you going to do, Mattie?" Roy whispered as black clad men, women and children filed past them on the way to the gravesite.

Matthew looked up and his green eyes locked on Roy's face. "You know, exactly, what I'm going to do. As God is my witness, I will find who did this to Iris, to…" For the first time, Roy heard grief trembling in Matthew's voice.

"To me…" he sighed, plucking a handkerchief out of his suit coat pocket and wiping his eyes.

Roy wanted to help. He wanted nothing more than to leave everyone and everything behind and help his friend track down the perpetrators but… he just couldn't. The town of Granville had grown by leaps, and bounds, since he first took office five years earlier. There were 290 citizens within the town limits now, and another three-hundred souls in the surrounding area that he had sworn to protect. He simply couldn't abandon them.

Knowing... no, depending on this, Matthew had looked Roy square in the eyes. Standing straight, he said. "I found a piece of evidence at the crime scene." Patting his pocket, he added, "I'm not sure what it means yet, but I have to track down some sources. I have a feeling that... well, it might take some time." He cleared his throat and watched as Abby led Chance toward the newly dug hole in the graveyard.

Chance was looking his way, his small face pinched with grief and horror. Sam was also staring at his step-father but his expression was a mite more hostile.

"We had better go." Matthew muttered and started walking toward the small cemetery as well. He slowed down, though, and said, "Chance is going to be mad at me, you know. Try to ease his heart, okay? In the meantime, promise you'll keep him and all my children safe."

A while later, as he stood across the burial plot of his oldest friend's wife, Roy understood that Matthew was already gone. Sure, his body was there, doing its best to be a pillar of strength on which his children could lean, but his heart had left three days earlier when he found what remained of his one true love and his loyal pet.

Sighing again, as his wife wept by his side, Roy vowed to keep Matthew's children safe, while their father risked everything to bring justice to the men who had devastated his life.

Unfortunately, Roy Smithers also understood that Matthew strove for more than simple justice. The look he saw in his friend' eyes was as deep and cold as the bottom of an artic lake, and the Spokane County sheriff knew that justice was the least of Matthew's concerns.

What Marshal Wilcox really sought was revenge.

5

EARL

EARL AWOKE WITH A STARTLED YELP FROM A SWIRLING, haze of pain. He stared at the doctor who sat snoring, in a chair by the wall with his flop hat pulled down over his eyes and then at Josh who stood, like a faithful hound, by the door to the hotel room.

"How are you feeling, Earl?" Josh asked.

Earl took inventory. Although he was still addle-pated, the bite marks didn't hurt quite as much and he could tell that the swelling around his eyes and mouth had subsided. He lifted a hand to touch his nose, but Josh stopped him.

"Don't touch it, Earl! The doc did a good job, as far as I can tell, but he said the stitches are... frag..."

It was obvious to Earl that Josh couldn't quite recall the word the doctor had used but ascertained that the elusive term was "fragile". He let his hand drop and demanded, "How long have I been out?"

"Couple of days is all."

Earl glared up at the younger man. "Well, how does it look?"

Josh studied Earl's face for a moment and replied, "It's a lot better, I think. It covers your air holes, anyway. It's still pretty bruised up and swoll, though. You should leave it be, while it heals."

Doctor Talbot was awake by now and added, "I was able to re-attach the flesh and, so far, the stiches are holding. Remember though, the animal that attacked you managed to tear away a good portion of the underlying cartilage. Your nose will heal, but it will not look the same as it did."

Earl smiled. *Maybe that goddamn wolf did me a favor,* he thought. *I have a fortune hidden away, but I also have a record with the law, thanks to Wilcox. Now that I have gotten my revenge, I can go all the way— change my appearance, my clothes, and my whole life. That way, if Wilcox is gunning for me... he'll never know who I am, even if he trips right over the top of me!*

Satisfied, Earl asked, "When can I travel, Doc?"

The physician stared down at Earl's face for a minute. "I think you can get up and go anytime you're ready. I scraped away the inflammation, and I no longer see any sign of fever. You do need the keep the bandages clean, though, and apply this ointment once in the morning and once at night until it's gone." Talbot held a blue jar in the air, and then slid it into his coat pocket.

Earl nodded and started to sit up. Then he heard the doc say, "About my payment..."

Earl grinned and said, "Yes, about that." He winked at Josh, who suddenly darted away from the door and grabbed Talbot up by his grimy lapels. He hit the doctor hard, two times in the face and then let him fall to the floor in a faint.

"Check his pockets for the cash... and grab that goddam ointment," Earl muttered as he got slowly to his feet. Josh rooted around in the doctor's coat and trousers until he finally pulled a wad of bills and the blue jar from Talbot's person.

Handing the goods over, Josh asked, "What do you want me to do with him, Earl?"

Studying his reflection in the dirty mirror above a chest of drawers, Earl knew that the old man had done a good job on his ruined face. His once, rather sharp and pointy nose was smaller now and flatter, but the stitch work was good and he could feel fresh blood bonding the torn flesh.

The smart thing to do, he knew, was kill the old man, leaving no witnesses behind. But... Earl owed the doctor a debt. Leaving Talbot no cash, much less a horse when they left, would serve as a guarantee. Talbot was a wanted man, after all. He wouldn't be getting a hold of a lawman over an unpaid doctor's bill anytime soon.

Peeling a ten-spot off the wad of bills in his hand, he stooped over and put the bill in the doctor's vest pocket. Then he said, "Truss this man up good and proper. Gag him and put him in the closet. Then I want you to go get the wagon and the rest of the cash.

Meet me back here in an hour. We're leaving town now."

After tying the old doctor up and stuffing his mouth with a wad of bandages, Josh put him in the coat closet and left. Then Earl bent down and pulled a large, leather satchel out from under the bed.

Holding his breath, he opened the flaps and saw that everything was still there. It could have gone worse, he knew. The old man could have gotten the drop on Josh and stolen everything while Earl slept but, luckily, good fortune had prevailed. (It never occurred to Dickson that Josh had spent the last forty-nine hours holding Talbot at gunpoint and that luck had nothing to do with the stolen fortune being intact.)

Sighing with relief, he poured water from a pitcher into a stained porcelain bowl, and commenced to washing sweat and dried blood from his face and body. He had worn his old clothes to the Imes ranch in antic-ipation of red-work and he was happy enough to discard them now. Pulling on his new duds, he studied his reflection in the mirror.

He had been clean-shaven in prison (Warden's orders) and continued to scrape his whiskers off since his release, more out of habit than anything. Now, he thought, a beard was in order. For one thing, he saw that his thick, dark beard helped cover the teeth mark and puncture holes on his face, which was good.

Also, if he was going to change how he looked, he might as well start now. Fancy new clothes, a heavy beard, maybe a... monocle! Earl grinned. *Yes*, he thought. A fancy walking stick (like many a fine gent he had seen over the years), a monocle, a beard, fancy suits... all of these things would serve to disguise who he really was—both from the law and from the rarified society he hoped to enter soon.

Three and a half hours later, a gentleman and his all-around man stepped on to a coach heading east-bound toward Montana.

MATTHEW SLIPPED AWAY in the early hours of morning, the day after the funeral. Chance had gone to Spokane to stay with his sister and her family, and although Sam had leave to stay longer, he had chosen to return to base, rather than stay with his stepfather.

Good, Matthew thought, as he loaded the last of his supplies into the back of his wagon. He had no desire to explain his position to the young man and knew that no matter what he said, Sam would disagree on general principal. He was heading up into the hills, to an abandoned cabin he owned, and planned to base his hunt from there.

He had befriended an old miner, once, many years ago. The prospector, named Smiley Hawkins, has run afoul of an unscrupulous banker and had been taken by said banker for over a thousand dollars in gold nugget and dust.

Smiley, not knowing what else to do, had packed up everything he could carry on his back and hiked fourteen miles into the town of Colville to file charges. Matthew happened to be in the sheriff's office the day the old man walked in complaining of devils dressed up like preachers, who were preying on honest folks, like him.

It only took a couple of days for Matthew to find the fake banker. He saw a fancy black carriage with the words NORTHWEST BANK, spelled out on the doors in gold paint, by the side of a rushing stream. Two matching geldings were taking water and their owner was washing his face and arms on the rocky shoreline.

When the marshal walked up and said howdy, the fat little crook had jumped six inches into the air. His shirt was beside him on the rocks, and damned if there wasn't a white paper collar lying in amongst the folds.

"My name is Matthew Wilcox, US Marshal Service," he called out.

Guilt was written all over the man's face and he hollered, "Don't shoot! You caught me red-handed!"

Matthew's guns still rested, peacefully, in his holsters, but he obliged the crook by saying, "Okay then, put 'em up."

He found out that William Moran *was* a retired preacher who had gotten the bright idea of offering false promissory notes from the fictional Northwest Bank, in exchange for the much more cumbersome minerals in many prospectors' possession. It might have worked too, but for the man's fear of his own horses, his tendency toward getting lost in the woods and his own guilty conscience.

After handcuffing Moran and placing him on the front bench of his own wagon, Matthew had found almost five thousand dollars' worth of gold in back, all of which he returned to the jailhouse in Colville, along with the thief who stole it.

A couple of years later, he talked to the Colville sheriff and found out that Smiley had died after leaving the cabin and all his worldly possessions to Matthew Wilcox in his will, along with about three hundred and fifty dollars in gold bullion.

Matthew was mystified... why did the toothless, old miner leave him his property, he asked the sheriff. The middle-aged man scratched his head, and said, "Well, Matthew, for some reason, Smiley said you reminded him of his own son, dead over twenty-years ago. Don't complain now... it's a nice piece of land with some decent ore along the creek beds."

Now Matthew smiled, although no one looking in his direction would call the expression on his face— happy. That was where he headed to now... to that old cabin high up in the Saddleback Mountains. He would reconnoiter there, in relative obscurity and fan his search out in a wide radius.

Reaching into his pants pocket, Matthew pulled out a battered silver-chained necklace. He wasn't sure, but he thought that the medal depicted St. Patrick... the patron saint of Ireland and its people.

There had been so many thieves, outlaws, rapists and murderers in his life since he first picked up his deputies star, they all blended—together in a mad hodge-podge in his mind, and plenty of those outlaws were, originally, from the Emerald Isle. But, one name still stood out clearly. Patrick Donnelly.

Knowing that the man was long dead did not stop the thrill of anticipation in Matthew's heart. There had been many men and women involved in the prostitution/slavery ring in King County that almost stole Iris' niece, Amelia Winters, away from her family for good. And although Matthew had done his best to see the perpetrators jailed for their crimes, some of them had gotten away clean.

Rubbing dried blood away from the chain that Matthew had pulled from the teeth of his dead wolf, he grinned again. At least now, he had a trail to follow.

He tied Lincoln to the back of the wagon and whistled to the puppy that he had decided to keep out of Bandits found litter. He waited as Trickster jumped up on the wagon and then, snapping the reins over the packhorse's rumps, Matthew left Granville to hunt down his wife's murderer.

6

EARL AND JOSH

EARL AND JOSH STEPPED DOWN FROM THE COACH IN THE small town of Orofino, Idaho. According to the driver, Orofino (meaning "fine gold" in Spanish) was experiencing a boom. Not from gold so much (that ship had sailed in the late 1860's), but from the tracks being laid for the Great Northern Railroad.

The driver, a smelly old coot by the name of Dave Spiles, bemoaned the rail lines, ascertaining that train travel would bring an end to independent coach lines in the high northern states. Earl had hired the man and his coach for the long trip from Ellensburg, Washington to Billings, Montana.

It had been an arduous journey, so far, and there was still another three hundred miles to go. Earl would have preferred to take a train but the anonymous old coach suited his needs much better. Train travel required tickets, which required names... something Earl was unwilling to divulge at this stage of the game.

Tiring, in turns too hot or too cold, dusty and bone jarring as the coach ride had been so far, it had also been profitable.

Each time they pulled into a town, Josh (after careful coaching) had gone into one of the local banks and turned Donnelly's gold coin into paper money. Just small amounts, here and there, was turning into a fortune.

Earl spent most of his time inside the coach recuperating from his injuries. He used the ointment had had taken from Dr. Talbot and was careful to keep his wounds clean and the bandages fresh. Whenever he did step out of the coach, he used a bandana over his face, telling Spiles that he had the flux and was trying to keep infection at a minimum.

His torn eyelid had healed by now, and it looked like nothing more than a simple rash, or a case of Pinkeye. Earl was pleased to see that the stiches around his nose (which had loosened and come out of their own accord) were sealing properly and his face, although different, looked almost normal but for some residual bruising and a few remaining puncture holes.

He thought that by the time they reached their final destination, he would emerge from the coach a new man... perhaps not an attractive man but a man of wealth and means with a few scars to mark his progress in life. Earl had spent the better part of his life in the company of wealthy men. Not as a peer but in their employ, and he knew that a handsome countenance could be bought.

He had a good start. His eyes were still as blue as robin's eggs, and his thick, black hair only lightly streaked with gray. Earl frowned, he would need to find a dentist and see if his missing incisor could be replaced. If not... he shrugged. Not too many people he knew had a full set of teeth and one missing fang would not set him apart from the society he sought.

Staring about, he smiled. The small town was nestled amongst high piney woods, and bustled with people, mainly Irish and Chinese workers who were laying tracks for the new railroad. Besides a smattering of crude houses there were a number of bars, a livery, a dry goods store, a couple of restaurants, a bathhouse, a solicitor's office, a funeral home, a post/telegraph office and a hotel.

Eying the solicitor's office, he turned to Spiles and said, "Take this money and see to any repairs the coach may need. Change the horses out, if necessary, and get yourself a bath and a good meal. Don't get drunk though... we may need to leave at a moment's notice."

Spiles stuck a dirty finger in the bag and stirred the heavy gold coins around. Looking up, he stared at Earl and mumbled, "I never seed so much dough. You sure you want to hand over this much?"

Earl's blue eyes glittered, and something in their depths made the old man step back in alarm. "I will pay you, handsomely, for a trip to Billings. I intend to get there and I am simply guaranteeing we make it there in one piece. So far, I am satisfied with your services, but don't think that if you try to rob me, my friend and I won't hunt you down."

Staring back and forth at the two men, Spiles suddenly understood that he must have a couple of crooks onboard his coach. He didn't care, overmuch, as long as they paid for his services but he didn't like the look in the older gent's eyes. Now that he was getting a good look at his mysterious passenger, he realized that this was one tough customer, and the old man knew that his life would be forfeit if he didn't do as ordered.

Tipping his dirty felt hat, Spiles said, "No problem, boys. I'll take the coach to the livery, buy a couple of extra horses to change out, and get some victuals. I'll be…" he stared across the street. "Right there, at that café when you need me."

Earl nodded and said, "Remember, take a few hours for yourself, but be ready to leave at a moment's notice."

"Got it," Dave said and climbed back on the wagon. Earl and Josh watched as the driver pulled up in front of the livery and spoke to one of the hands.

Then Earl turned to Josh. "You do the same, Josh. You stink and need a change of clothes. Go and get a bath and take this money for some new duds. Nothing fancy, but buy a warm coat, some new boots and a couple of warm, wool hats. Dave said it'll be getting colder, the further we get to the Rockies, so we need to be prepared."

Turning around, Earl spotted another restaurant up the street. "Meet me over there in a couple of hours for dinner. I might have some work for you to do, later on this afternoon."

Josh pulled his hat from his head and shuffled his feet. "Aw, Earl," he whined. "Do I have to take a bath?"

Earl glared. "You will do as I say or be on your way. Is that what you want?"

Josh blushed. "Nah... I'll do it. No need to be so touchy!"

"Meet me over there in two hours." Earl growled.

After Josh scampered off, Earl sauntered down a boardwalk and saw a middle-aged woman step out the front door of a building with a large pan of water in her hands. Watching for a moment as she heaved the water onto a muddy side street, he called out, "Ma'am —is this a bathhouse?"

She turned around and answered, "A dime for a bath, two-bits for a load of laundry. Clothes will be ready to wear by tomorrow morning."

Earl had a change of clean clothes in his carpetbag, and although the garments he currently wore would wash up fine, he didn't want to be forced into waiting for them to dry. He smiled at the woman and said, "Just a bath, thanks."

The woman eyed the kerchief Earl wore over his nose and mouth. "What's wrong witcha?"

Earl shrugged. "I have had the flux, but I think I am past giving it to anyone else..." He tugged the bandana down, watching the woman's reaction as his face was revealed.

She studied him for a moment and shrugged,

"Guess you weren't too sick to get in a fight, though, eh?"

Earl sighed with relief. He had thought his face was much improved and this woman's opinion reinforced his belief. Nodding with humility, he murmured, "Yes, an unfortunate disagreement a few days ago."

She smirked, "Oh well... a good bath will fix you up. Come on in and I'll get a tub ready for you."

A couple of hours later, Earl sat down in the restaurant. After scrubbing his body and hair clean, he had donned a fresh set of clothes and set out for the solicitor's office. He stepped up to the front window and peered inside. There were two gentlemen working side by side on matching desks and one old woman who seemed to be sorting through paperwork at a long table in back of the room.

Earl frowned and stepped away. *This place will not do,* he thought and walked across the street toward a grimy tent he had spied earlier. NOTARY! TITLES and DEEDS was painted on a board hanging in front above the tent's flap.

Taking a deep breath, Earl stepped inside. Smiling, he reached out his right hand to shake and said, "Howdy, I wonder if you could help me?"

A scrawny, middle-aged man stood up from where he sat at a long table. Smiling, he answered, "Howdy to you too, sir. The name's Howard Stapleton. How might I be of service?"

Earl spent the better part of an hour inside Stapleton's tent. When he emerged, he no longer sported the handle, Earl Dickson, but the loftier title, Allen O'Donnell. (Earl had wanted to get rid of the O'Donnell name, entirely, but Stapleton assured him that brand new papers would raise more suspicions than a simple rearrangement on the original documents.) It took some convincing and a lot of money, but the name change was accompanied by a transfer of signatures, entitling the wealthy O'Donnell to all of (the long deceased) Patrick Donnelly's properties in Ellensburg, Wenatchee and King County.

Earl put his newly signed papers in his bag and handed the nervous notary five thousand dollars for his part in the fraud. "If I were you," he told Stapleton, "I would head out of town as soon as possible. I doubt if we will ever meet again, but just in case someone does get on to me, it would be better for you if you were long gone, right?"

Stapleton wiped sweat from his balding pate and nodded in agreement. Opening his lockbox and staring at the crisp new banknotes, he said, "Right you are. The lawyers down the street beat me here by two weeks and my business never got off the ground. Now I have enough money to start up new... maybe back home in California! My wife and kids are still there and have been waiting to follow me north but I have, until now, been unable to send for them."

The man's eyes sparkled with excitement, and Earl smiled. *Perfect!* He thought, and shook the crooked notary's hand. Wishing him farewell, he walked to the restaurant and sat down by a window where he had a good view of the notary's tent.

A few minutes later, Josh walked in the front doors and stared over at where Earl sat. He had taken a bath and, apparently, gotten a shave and a haircut as well. His light brown hair was slicked down and oily with pomade, and his new leather boots creaked as he walked up.

Josh gazed down at Earl and said, "Hi Earl, what do you think?" The big man's cheeks were flushed with bashful excitement. (He had never owned a new set of clothes before, much less gotten a shave from a real barber.)

Earl studied the young man and replied, "Well, it looks like someone's trying to make a silk purse out of a sow's ear."

Josh's face turned red with embarrassment and Earl decided to relent a bit. "I'm just kidding you, Josh. You look swell."

Josh sat down and his lips turned up in a pleased smile. "Thanks! I was hoping to do you proud, Earl!"

Earl glanced around and was relieved to see that all the tables within hearing distance were unoccupied. Then he snapped, "Sit down, Josh."

Josh sat and Earl leaned forward. "Now, there are two things I need you to do. First—from now on you call me Mr. O'Donnell or Allen... when we are alone. That's my name now and you need to remember it!"

Josh stared at Earl with such puzzlement, his eyes almost crossed. "Okay, Earl... OW!"

Dickson had just kicked Josh's ankle under the table. "Oh, yeah, sorry... um, Evan!"

Leaning forward again, Earl whispered, "You get my name right from now on, or I'll cut you lose, I swear it!"

Josh's eyes grew damp and he said, "I will, sir... Evan, I promise!"

Sitting back in his chair, Earl stared out the window, down the street. He saw the notary walk out of his tent with a straight-backed chair in one hand. Placing the chair directly under the off-kilter sign, Stapleton climbed up and removed the sign from two hooks that held it on the canvas. Then he grabbed the chair and disappeared back inside.

Josh had followed Earl's gaze and said, "Who's that?"

Earl glanced around the restaurant, and satisfied that no one could hear he answered, "That's the man I want you to kill tonight."

7

MATTHEW—TIED IN KNOTS

MATTHEW SAT HIS HORSE ON A ROCKY BLUFF AND STARED up at the foothills of the Blue Mountains in southern Washington State, fifty-five miles from Walla Walla State Penitentiary. He was weary to the bone and disgusted with himself. He had just wasted two precious weeks on a wild goose chase.

No one knew better than him how crucial time was in chasing people and clues down in an active criminal investigation. So, chasing the one lead he had found was decent police work but the clue had led nowhere. He shook his head in frustration.

Going to Seattle, once he had found the St. Patrick's medal in Bandit's teeth seemed the logical choice, especially since the Irish connection had screamed out-loud in his mind. After situating himself properly in his mountain cabin, he had boarded a train in Spokane and followed his tenuous lead into King County.

That was where he came up short. It had been a

long time since he chased the Donnellys across state while searching for his kidnapped niece and honestly, he didn't know the names of half the minions who had once served Patrick Donnelly in his schemes. That was when he decided to pay the crooked politician, Martin LeVesque, a visit.

Face flushing in remembered anger, Matthew gritted his teeth and spat on the ground. Even now, he cringed at how dismissive Lévesque's lackeys had been when he asked for an audience with the city official. They had studied his Marshal's star, and then stared at his dusty clothes in scorn before closing the doors to Lévesque's inner sanctum with a resounding thump.

Matthew had never gotten the "Bum's Rush" before and his blood boiled with anger. After being dismissed, he marched quickly toward the closest hotel, washed and changed his clothes. Then he walked back to the county courthouse and settled in to wait for LeVesque to appear at the grand entrance but hours later, Matthew realized that there must be a back door to the building. Leaving his hiding place from behind a copse of trees, he moved through the twilight to the back of the large building.

Sure enough, a road ran directly behind the court-house where a normal-sized door hid under a small portico. Sometime within the last few hours, LeVesque had skedaddled, leaving Matthew fuming.

The next morning he rode a buggy to the King County jailhouse. He had not made himself popular with the officers who worked there during his investigation into the scandalous prostitution ring, and Matthew expected a cool reception. Nevertheless, he swallowed his pride, stepped up to the counter and asked to speak to the sheriff.

After an inordinate amount of time, Sheriff Adams appeared by the front desk. Matthew studied the man's face and his shoulders slumped. He had inadvertently wreaked havoc in Adam's police department during his search for Amelia and he could tell now that the sheriff was not in a forgiving mood.

Matthew knew that there was a certain amount of graft in every sheriff's office. It was the way of things. Police protection was highly sought and sometimes bought from east coast to west, and gifts given gladly in exchange for a police presence was not only acceptable but, sometimes, expected.

That fact that Sheriff Wilcox had discovered a deep vein of corruption within the King County sheriff's department was merely a by-product of his search for Amelia Winters, one that did not surprise him but had ultimately led to a total shake down of this man's police force. No wonder Adams glared at him now.

"Well," the fat man grumbled. "Look at the bad penny."

Matthew stood up and held out his hand to shake. "Hello, Sheriff Adams. You look well."

Adams stared at Matthew's hand and turned on his heel. "Follow me to my office," he growled. Marshal Wilcox followed the sheriff down a long hallway and noted many veiled glances and grimaces of disgust from the lawmen that milled about the large room adjacent to the hallway. Sighing, he walked behind the fat man into a cluttered office.

There were wanted posters pinned all over the walls and a calendar hung askew behind the desk. As he sat down on a chair in front of the desk, Matthew was amused to see a large campaign poster of Marty LeVesque on the far wall. An elaborate mustache and devil's horns had been drawn over the man's mug and the picture was pierced by barroom darts.

Apparently, Adams was no more impressed by LeVesque than Matthew was, and he turned to the sheriff with a smile...which froze on his face the moment Adams opened his mouth.

Pointing a blunt finger in Matthew's face, Adams hissed, "I know why you're here and I'll give you what I can but, honestly, I can't believe you had the nerve to set foot in this building!"

Matthew studied the toes of his dirty boots. He really hadn't wanted to come. His investigation had torn Adam's division right down the middle and, for a while, Adams himself had come under scrutiny. Matthew had felt bad about that—really—but the King County sheriff's office had needed a shakedown, in his opinion, and in the long- run, Adams had held up under fire.

Still, now that he needed the man's help, he could see why Adams might not feel obliged to render assistance. Staring at the floor, Matthew murmured, "Did you hear about what happened?"

Adams studied the younger man's face and, despite his anger, compassion took over. A *deadman's revenge* (the term "deadman" referred to a heinous outlaw who was scheduled to hang for his crimes and the revenge on that man's part usually directed toward the lawman who brought him down.) What had happened to Matthew Wilcox's wife was every lawman's nightmare... and Adams was not without a heart.

Nodding, he answered, "Yes sir, I did hear about what happened and you have my heartfelt sympathies."

Matthew looked up. "I thank you but it's not sympathy I need right now, its information!"

Adams nodded and patted a dark brown parcel on his desk. "I know, Matthew. That's why I had one of my men put this packet together for you. In here is everyone we know of who was in on that prostitution ring, and a few more, besides. There are wanted posters and prison rosters in here dating from 1892 until present day...from King County to Walla Walla." He sighed and leaned back in his chair.

"This is the best we can do, Marshal Wilcox. Now, if I was you, I would focus my search in yer own neighborhood, instead of causing me and mine any more grief than you already have. After all, the crime was committed right in yer own home!"

Matthew's green eyes grew wide and his face turned red. "I am aware of that, sir. I am equally convinced that there is a connection between this city's Irish population and what happened to my... my—" his voice trailed off.

Adams stood up. Looking down at the misery on the younger man's face, he said, "I am deeply sorry for yer loss, Marshal. Retribution is a terrible fear for all law-enforcement officers. Still, I think you better go back and search your back forty. Whoever did that to your wife is probably running around loose in your own territory while you're wasting time here in my town!"

Hearing the heart-felt sympathy in Adam's voice, Matthew quickly stood up and grabbed the thick folder, before his own emotions unmanned him. He thanked the old sheriff and made his leave. It was almost evening by the time he got back to his hotel room. He had stood for a moment, and stared at the new-fangled telephone in the hotel lobby and thought about calling Iris' father or Dr. and Amelia Winters but he didn't have the heart.

Moving slowly up the staircase, Sheriff Wilcox felt like he was eighty years old, rather than forty. His feet felt like lead weights and his gizzard was tied up in a knot. Once he reached his room, Matthew fell onto his bed and stared up at the ceiling, remembering how he and Iris had made love so many years ago in this same hotel. For the first time since he had found his wife's body, Matthew wept.

Catching the train the next morning, Matthew made his way back to Spokane. Then he rode for the mountain cabin to fetch Trickster. After arranging for the dog to be shipped to Granville, he rode quickly back to Spokane. He found Lincoln munching oats in the city livery and led the horse onto a flat car on the next train to Walla Walla. Cursing himself for a fool, Matthew realized now that the state penitentiary was the first place he should have looked.

Most of the worst criminals tried in Washington State eventually ended up in Walla Walla and, if nothing else, Matthew would be able to access the warden's files and find out who had been released—and when.

Now, as Matthew sat his horse and stared up at the misty foothills, he sighed in frustration. He could ride his horse back to Spokane and ask for the Marshal's aid or he could head on home for a rest and go through the sheriff's wanted posters for a clue. But first, he needed to peruse the release papers he had obtained from the prison warden.

Seven prisoners had been released within the last three months. Two old men who had served at least twenty years, each, for murder were let go last May. Those two couldn't have had anything to do Donnelly, and Matthew signed them off his mental list.

He felt a thrill of dreadful excitement as he studied the next names on the list. Frank and Mary Owens... the murderous preacher and his psychotic wife had been incarcerated in Walla Walla for a while, until Mary was finally sent to a lunatic asylum. Apparently, Frank was released from custody this last June but had been found shot to death three days later, just outside his own property in Wenatchee.

Four down... three to go, Matthew thought and then

tightened his legs around Lincoln's belly as the horse did a skittish little hop and laid his ears back with a snort. The horse's flesh crawled and his tail rose up in the air.

"Whoa, Lincoln... knock it off!" Matthew snapped, irritably. Usually his horse was as sensible as they came but he did not like to be kept waiting, and Matthew was forcing him to stand still.

There were three more names on the list; a Negro woman who had been caught stealing, (Matthew placed that sheet under the others with a disgusted sneer) and one retarded man named Joshua Manning.

Shaking his head, Matthew read up on the kid who was apparently the younger brother of a dead outlaw named Martin Manning. He was a simpleton whose only claim to fame was a friendship he had struck up with a dangerous Irish mobster named Earl Dickson.

Spotting the word *Irish*, Matthew grabbed the next sheet of paper and eagerly perused the man's likeness. Like most WANTED POSTERS, the facial features were blurred and practically indistinguishable from the faces on any other poster. The devil, though, was in the details.

The black and white drawing showed a bony face and a long, pointy nose. The eyes were blue, apparently, and the man's age thought to be forty-five or forty-six. The one *distinguishing feature* (and what lawmen looked for in Wanted Posters) was the notice-able gap of a missing right incisor.

Matthew's heart quickened and a smile etched his

drawn features. He didn't remember all the men he and his men had disabled that fateful night in Potter's Field. It was too dark and foggy to distinguish his enemy's features, and this likeness did not jog his memory. But still... it was a good start.

He was just starting to put the folder back in his saddlebag when Lincoln suddenly screamed and reared up in the air. Matthew clutched the horn and stared about wildly. Before he had a chance to register what was frightening his horse, a freight train of long, tearing claws and the snarling, meaty breath of a mountain lion struck him from behind.

8

MATTHEW AND THE BEASTS

THE COUGAR HIT MATTHEW SO HARD HE FLEW FROM HIS saddle, rolling down slope ten feet away into a bed of rocky shale and sagebrush. He felt a line of fire across the back of his neck and knew that either a fang or a claw had marked the big cat's passing. Luckily, the cougar was more interested in Lincoln than the human being who was lying in the weeds trying to regain the breath knocked out of him during the fall.

Gasping, and trying to ignore the hot, red blood running down his neck, Matthew stared at the showdown taking place on the bluff above him. Most horses would have taken off running at the threat—a horses' normal response to a live predator, but Lincoln was having none of it.

Matthew saw the rage in his gelding's eyes as he faced off against the cougar, which hissed madly and growled deep in its throat. Gathering its hindquarters to pounce, it subsided with a screech as Lincoln advanced with a whinny and kicked out with both front hooves, narrowly missing the cat's head.

Matthew, finally catching his breath, struggled to his feet and climbed up the small embankment to help his horse. At the same moment, the cat, rather than go backwards over the bluff, changed its strategy and cut to its right, running back up onto the ledge from which it came. Just as Matthew got to the horse and yanked his shotgun away from its scabbard, the cat pounced again, this time landing directly on top of Lincoln's back.

Matthew fell back with a cry of rage and Lincoln's squeals of agony echoed throughout the canyon as the cat's back claws dug into his hindquarters. The mountain lion crawled over the saddle, wrapped its front legs around the horse's neck and bit into its crest as Lincoln screamed.

Matthew knelt on the ground, took aim (as much as possible with the flurry of activity taking place in front of him), pulled one trigger on the hammerless double-barrel shotgun and aimed just over the cougar's body. Hoping against hope that the buckshot had not killed Lincoln as well as the predator, Matthew stood up, placed his finger on the second trigger and watched as Lincoln let out a bellow of fear, hobbling away a few feet. The cougar fell straight down to the ground with a snarl.

The gelding stood shaking and blowing hard with shock, as Matthew walked slowly toward the cougar. It was mortally wounded, but did not know it yet. It twisted around and around on the ground like a top, futilely trying to soothe the pain of its bloody wounds. It alternated between screaming out its rage and meowing, pitifully, like a kitten.

Shaking his head, Matthew pulled the shotgun's second trigger and shot the animal in the chest. The cat collapsed into a silent heap as both Matthew and his mount stood still, shuddering and panting into the silent, autumn afternoon.

A few moments passed as Matthew's heart slowed down and then he made his way on rubbery legs to Lincoln's side. The horse nickered softly and turned his long, ugly face toward the sheriff. Matthew assessed the damage and his heart sank. There were a number of bite marks and puncture wounds on his animal's neck and terrible, deep scratches scored Lincoln's rump and neck.

The animal needed medicine and time to heal. He might be made to walk but would, most certainly, come up lame and maybe even die of shock if he wasn't allowed to rest and recover. Even now, Lincoln made to lie down but Matthew pulled his head up by the reins and crooned, "Whoa, there boy. Let me put some medicine on those cuts before you try to sleep it off."

Lincoln snorted and tossed his head but Matthew was able to pull the saddle off his back and grab some supplies out of his medicine kit. Holding the horse steady with one hand, he rubbed medicinal ointment over the bloody scratches and poured a little bit of whiskey into the puncture holes on the animal's crest and withers.

The whole time, Lincoln jinked away from Matthew's ministrations, so that horse and man moved about in a circle on the rocky ground. Finally, Lincoln stopped and placed his long muzzle in the crook of Matthew's neck. The horse's nostrils fluttered noisily as he caught the scent of blood and then he pulled his head back with a snort and trotted away a few feet, huffing nervously.

Matthew let him go and felt at the wound on back of his neck. Now that the excitement was over, the pain from his wound began to register and Matthew winced as he untied the bandana on his neck. Feeling a little faint, the sheriff made his way to the saddle, fished the medicine kit out and sat on a large rock to assess the damage.

Pulling a hand mirror from the kit, Matthew stared sideways at the blurry reflection in the glass. Sure enough, the cat had dug a claw into the back of Matthew's neck in its mad leap. A bloody gash went from one side to the other and the sheriff could see bruises already forming under his skull. The bleeding had mostly stopped, except for the far right end where the animal's claw dug in more deeply.

He sighed. The wound stung like hell but it was not serious. He applied ointment on the wound and used water from his canteen to wipe away most of the blood. Taking a moment to let his still jangled nerves settle, Matthew stared out over the valley. *It's too bad,* he thought, *that I'm so far away from a town. I need to get Lincoln to a vet and let him recuperate, but getting there...*

He grimaced in frustration. Even now, Lincoln stood still, legs splayed and head hanging, despite the tall grass within easy reach. The horse never missed an opportunity to grab a mouthful of anything tasty. The fact that he was not interested in a treat spoke volumes to his master.

Matthew climbed to his feet and walked over to where the ruined cougar lay stretched out on the ground. It was an old female, Matthew saw, slat-ribbed and almost blind with cataracts. No wonder he had not become the cats primary focus... Matthew doubted whether the starving animal even saw him when it decided to attack.

Looking back from where he and Lincoln came, Matthew thought about the farmhouse he had seen about fifteen miles back. He had thought that it might be a pig farm/whore house and had steered clear. Now though, remembering the horses, cows and pigs that wandered about the place and the rather tidy loafing sheds and paddocks, Matthew thought his bet best for assistance might come from there.

It might not be a whorehouse at all and besides, not all brothels were places of ill-repute. Older whores often ended up there or girls that were either too frail or homely were taken in—sometimes in charity, and sometimes as slaves. Knowing he was in no position to be choosy, Matthew walked back to where Lincoln stood swaying slowly on his feet.

Matthew removed Lincoln's bridle and applied a little more salve to the wounds on his neck. Then he pulled all the grass he could find in the area and placed it in a pile as close to the horse as possible. He also took three of his remaining canteens and filled his cook pot with water. He dug a little hole to place the bucket in, in case Lincoln decided to kick at it, which he was wont to do.

Matthew thought about hobbling the gelding and then changed his mind. If something were to happen, Matthew wanted Lincoln to be free to find water and sustenance... or escape, without having to hurt himself trying to break free of restraints.

It was turning cold and the bleak autumn sky dimmed with the gray and lavender colors of dusk. Not caring to hike too long in total darkness, Matthew stowed most of his gear under a shelf of rock, shouldered his saddlebags and took off walking toward the pig farm.

A LITTLE OVER four hours later, Matthew saw faint, dim lights on the horizon. It was almost 8:00 in the evening, and Matthew was cursing his slow progress. A heavy cloud cover filled the sky overhead and twice he had stumbled, once over a rock in the road and once into a shallow ditch. Now, his right ankle throbbed, and the big toe on his left foot had swollen and seemed to be butting heads against the front of his boot.

He stopped and pulled a tiny lantern out of his bag. Holding a scant half-cup of oil, the lantern had three clear glass sides but the back had been tinted red. It was meant to signal an emergency or distress signal to those who spied it in the dark. Matthew had no way of knowing if the occupants of yonder farm knew the lantern's meaning but at least he wouldn't be caught lurking in the shadows.

Just then, he heard the excited yip, yip of the farm's watchdog and he held his lantern up in the air. Walking down the long drive leading to the farm he saw the lights in the windows and the front door open. A large silhouette darkened the doorway and Matthew heard a man shout, "Who's out there?"

"Hello! My name's Matthew Wilcox. I have a stricken horse, up the road about fourteen miles. I was hoping I could get some hay and medicine for him… and maybe some extra water while I tend to his wounds. I've got money!"

Here is the proof of the pudding, Matthew thought. If this place was filled with bad people, they could easily murder him where he stood, take all his belongings and ride ahead to seize his horse while they were at it. He fingered the grip of his pistol, wondering which way the wind was going to blow, and then he heard the hammer cock on a pistol, not ten feet away from where he stood in a sudden gleam of moonlight.

"Drop yer pistol, Mr…" a feminine voice called out from behind a tall tree.

Matthew shoulders drooped, setting off the pain he

had kept at bay for most of the over-land trek. The cat scratch seemed to be festering, probably ripe with infection from whatever that old cougar carried in its mangy, broken claws. He reached down with his right hand and unbuckled his gun belt, letting the equipment drop on the ground behind him.

Then he called out, "As you can see, I have a shotgun as well. Let me put it down, along with my saddlebags, okay? Don't shoot me!" Keeping his right hand up, Matthew shrugged his saddlebags and the shotgun off his left shoulder and then stood straight, with both hands in the air. "There," he shouted. "I'm unarmed. Will you help me out or not?"

A moment or two passed, and Matthew heard whispering coming from behind the tree. Then, a woman and a young girl stepped out and walked slowly toward where he stood waiting. The woman was well past her prime but Matthew could tell by the moonlight that streamed down from the heavens that she must have once been beautiful.

Now, though, she was quite heavy and her large breasts swayed ponderously beneath the nightgown she wore under her coat. Her long gray hair fell in a plait down her back and she wore huge, knee-high leather boots. She also held her pistol with authority.

Her companion was heavy as well, although quite young. She had small and slightly slanted eyes and the heavy brow of a retarded person. She stared at Matthew with moonstruck eyes as though she had never before seen such a spectacle and she said, "Hi!"

"You hush, Hildy and get behind that tree!" the woman snapped.

The girl jumped and scooted backwards out of sight. The woman said, "What did yer say yer name was again?"

Matthew, who stood sweating, slightly, under his duster despite the chill in the air answered, "My name is Matthew Wilcox, Ma'am. I'm not here to cause you and yours any trouble. I just need a little assistance with an injured horse up the road a few miles. I have money to pay for whatever you might have that will help."

The woman dropped her pistol and placed it in her coat pocket. She had studied Matthew's face carefully while he approached and decided, apparently, that he was no threat. Walking forward a few feet, she extended her hand to shake and said, "My name's Patricia Hanson... you can call me Patty. This is my place, but we're closed to business except fer weekends, which, you know is three days off, yet. Still, I have some supplies and a wagon if'n you want to go back and fetch yer horse."

Reluctant to leave Lincoln out all night on his own, Matthew nodded gratefully. "That would be much appreciated Ma'am. I could leave all of my gear here for assurance, and pay you, up front, for any costs incurred..."

Patty shook her head. "Tell you what. My son's will accompany you on yer way—and they will hold yer firearms while you fetch that hoss back here... fair enough?" She raised a quizzical eyebrow.

Although the thought of turning his firearms over made him feel queasy, he nodded and said, "Fair enough."

Turning around, Patty put two fingers in her mouth and whistled. In short order, two young men came running up. They were both big, like their mother, but they had open, cheerful expressions on their faces and they seemed excited to be taking an unplanned outing.

Patty said, "You two get the wagon ready. You'll be escorting this gentleman up the road a ways to his horse. Put the medical kit in back and bring a bale of hay and a bucket of oats along as well. GO!"

At this, the teenagers sprang to life and disappeared into the darkness. Turning back to face Matthew she said, "Bring yer pony back here and we'll nurse him back to health, if possible. If he's real bad off, the traveling doc should be here day after tomorrow. He'll know what to do."

Matthew reached into his pocket and pulled out a couple of bills. Handing them to her he said, "A downpayment, Ma'am, for your kindness."

She took the money and dropped it down the front of her nightgown with a grin. "Won't say no to that, Mr. Wilcox. Here are the boys now."

An old wagon and two draft horses approached from around the back of the house. Matthew saw that a number of people, mainly women, were standing on the front porch watching and he gave them a polite, little wave.

He heard a few girlish titters and Patty yelled, "You girls get back in the house!"

Turning to the old madam, Matthew saw that the little retarded girl was standing by her side again, despite earlier orders. She stared up at him with wide eyes and grinned when he smiled at her. "Hi!" she said, and he replied, "Hi, yourself!"

Beaming, she turned to Patty and exclaimed, "Mamma, he's nice!"

Patty rolled her eyes, but wrapped the girl in one beefy arm. "This is my youngest, Hildy. She ain't no genius, but she's a good girl and a marvel with horseflesh."

Matthew tipped his hat and said, "Pleased to make your acquaintance, Hildy." To which the girl clapped her hand over her mouth and giggled.

"Okay boys, be on yer way, and come back slow if that horse is stove up. Don't want him getting too stove-up on the way back!"

As the wagon headed back down the road from whence he came, Matthew Wilcox had no way of knowing that Patty Hanson would eventually become one of his most cherished friends.

9

THE NEW BOSS

ALLEN O'DONNELL (AKA EARL DICKSON) AND JOSH stepped off the coach three weeks later, in Billings, Montana. Earl had spoken to Spiles, at length, about their final destination and found out that there were two towns situated along the Yellowstone River—the original settlement of Coulson and the newer and apparently booming town of Billings, named for the railroad baron, Frederick Billings.

According to Spiles, the money... and the men who wielded it were in the newer section of town and if it were him starting out fresh with cash in his pocket, he would settle on the north side, in Billings.

Dave jumped off the bench and went to grab the horse's bits, while his passengers stared about in pleasure. *This place certainly is a going affair,* Earl thought. *A man can be anything he wants to be, here, without anyone the wiser!* (Back in Orofino, Idaho, a certain notary by the name of Stapleton, and the only true witness to

Dickson's change in identity, was buried by now, another sad victim of suicide by hanging… at least according to Josh, who had strung the man up, himself.)

Turning to Josh, Earl murmured, "Remember Josh, from now on, I am Mr. O'Donnell, Allen or Sir, okay?"

Josh nodded with a grin and replied, "Yes, sir!"

Earl stared at the side of Josh' face and thought, *I wish the kid didn't act like my name change is some sort of inside joke. I wonder, after all, if it's such a good idea bringing him in on the game.* Knowing, though, that he would need muscle a-plenty in his future schemes, Earl settled for snapping, "Bring those bags down off the back of the coach."

Josh cut his eyes sideways at Earl in hurt surprise but moved quickly enough to carry out Earl's orders. While the driver and Josh were otherwise occupied, Earl stared over at the front façade of an elegant building calling itself, The Grand Hotel. Stately carriages moved in and out of the front entrance and he saw finely dressed men and women milling about by the large double doors. Servants dashed back and forth, lugging carpetbags and trunks and a stern-looking maître d loomed over everything and everyone like an angry, black hawk.

Glancing down at his worn and dirty clothes, Earl knew that even though he had enough money to buy his way into that fine establishment, he would, imme-diately, be pegged as a low-sort of man… and that was the last thing he wanted at this point. Deciding the first order of business was to outfit himself as a wealthy man, he called out to Josh, "Meet me at that milliners store in two hours, Josh, and when you do show up, I expect you to be as clean as a whistle!"

Josh nodded with a grimace of distaste and Earl walked up to Dave Spiles. He asked, "How much is the fare?"

Spiles grinned. "Well... how does thirty bucks grab ya?"

Earl studied the man's face and wondered, for the tenth time, if just killing him would be the better way to go. He hated to, though. Spiles seemed like a game bird, and one whose services might come in handy in his future endeavors. Thinking hard for a moment, he stared into the man's eyes and said, "Dave, how would you like to work for me?"

Spiles frowned in consternation and answered, "Well, I got my coach here and the two nags... and they're paid off! What would I do with them and... well, what would I be doing fer ya and how much would it pay?"

"I want you to be my driver and maybe help run one of the liveries here in town. I will buy this coach from you and the horses too. If you accept my proposition, I'll buy you a few sets of good clothes and some good livery. Then you will go and purchase a fancy coach and four... and I mean high-end. I'll pay you two dollars a day, plus room and board. Interested?"

Spiles had started to grin halfway through Earl's pitch, and said, "Done! And, I know just where to go for a good outfit. It's down the road a ways... Cothron and Todd. They have some real nice coaches and buggies, and a line on the best horseflesh."

Earl nodded. "Okay, but first, I want you to clean up. I am going to be running a first-call outfit, here in town, and first impressions are everything! I want you to take a bath and get a shave and a haircut. Go over to that bathhouse, and I'll send Josh by with some new duds." Earl stuck his hand out to shake and when Spiles reciprocated, he pulled the older man forward, whispering, "Do right by me and I'll make you a wealthy man. Do wrong... well, I think you know what will happen..."

Dave Spiles stared down into Earl's eyes and swore, "Don't worry... sir. I'll do right by ya."

Earl released Spile's hand and walked toward the nicest of the three bathhouses on the busy street. He had brought his best suit along, and emerged an hour later, clean and wearing a respectable outfit. Then, he moseyed toward the milliner's shop he had pointed out to Josh earlier. Sure enough, Josh was standing in front of the business, clean but still wearing his old, stinky clothes.

Earl took one whiff and said, "Stay here—I'll be out in a little while."

He sailed into the clothing store, and was met at the front door by a fussy, little man who claimed to be the owner. Earl stared at a number of male mannequins toward the rear wall that sported, according to the small hand-printed signs on each, the "season's" latest fashions. There were seersucker suits and wool, herringbone and tweed, embroidered vests, chaps, knee-high stockings with tiny garters, velvet collars and silk ties.

Wicker heads showcased the latest in headwear. Top hats, derbies, straw boaters and the latest in cowboy hats... giant, ten-gallon hats, low-brimmed sombreros and even some slouchy-looking horsemen hats from far-off Australia.

Making up his mind, to buy one of every outfit for himself, Earl smiled at the shop-owner and said, "Good afternoon, Sir. I will be making a number of purchases today, but first, I would like two simple wool suits... one extra-large and one large, extra-long for my men. Unfortunately, we had to ford a river on our way here and most of our luggage was lost to water damage."

The little shop-owner smiled and picked out two inexpensive suits, shoes and coats for his new customer. Packaging them separately, he handed the suits to Earl, who took them outside to where Josh waited on the front stoop. "Okay, Josh. I want you to go and find Davey, who is working with us now... he should be over there at the bathhouse. Give him this outfit and the two of you go up the street to that hotel... see it?"

Josh stared down the street to where Earl pointed and nodded. "Yes, Sir."

Earl grinned and handed over some clink. "Okay, you and Dave go and buy a room for the night. Get some rest, and eat dinner in your room. Wear these suits and, for God's sake, stay clean! Tomorrow... say, 8:00, I'll meet you outside the hotel."

Josh couldn't help himself. "What are we doing, Ear..., uh, Sir?"

Earl glared. "Never you mind that for now! Just go, and be ready to meet me at eight o' clock, sharp!"

Josh scurried away with his packages, and Earl saw Dave step out of the bathhouse just as Josh reached the boardwalk. Satisfied, he walked back inside the men's store and commenced to reinventing himself.

THE NEXT MORNING dawned bright and cold. Earl sat outside the Grand Hotel sipping a cup of strong, black coffee and smoking a pipe. He stared at the surrounding horizon and saw a number of mountains —large and small. He would later find out that Billings was situated in a large valley ringed by the Bighorn and Cloud Peak mountains, with vast tracks of land stretching as far as the eye could see that once was home to the Crow and Blackfoot Indians.

He was dressed in a fine, gray wool suit, and he wore a purple silk scarf tied around his neck. He sported a white carnation boutonniere in his coat's lapel, and wore his new Australian hat. He looked like a gentleman, and (testing his theory) he nodded graciously to the men and woman who passed him on the outdoor veranda. Each, and every one of them smiled pleasantly

—even some stuffy-looking gents who passed by his table looking like a well-dressed gaggle of turkeys with their round, glassy monocles and red, wattled necks.

Finished with his breakfast, Earl tipped his waiter and strode down the boardwalk to where his men waited patiently in front of a shabby hotel. Springing to their feet, he saw both of them stare at him in shock. Josh even took his winter cap off in nervous respect. By the looks on their faces, he knew that he had succeeded in changing his appearance.

Josh hardly knew what to think as he gazed at his mentor. Earl had gotten a bath and a shave, but that was only part of it. He had also shaved the rather thin, stringy hair on his head, and he was now as bald as an egg. His beard was gone as well. In its place, thick black mutton-chop sideburns were groomed to perfection and met up with lush, handlebar mustaches on either side of Earl's thin lips.

His nose, although obviously scarred, was almost improved in appearance from his former, pointier proboscis and he had gotten himself a pair of spectacles, which gleamed within shiny gold rims. He did not look anything like the man Josh had come to know... rather, he looked like one of those fancy swells he had learned to avoid.

Earl studied the two men, in turn, and was satisfied by what he saw. Although neither man was dressed in anything fancy, they had washed away their former grime, shaved their chin whiskers, and wore their new clothes well. For once, both Josh and Dave looked... respectable.

Nodding in approval, Earl handed Dave a bundle of cash and said, "You look good—both of you. Now, I want you to head on down to that carriage company you were talking about and buy the best four-seater money can buy. Then, find a matching pair to go with it. Take the wagon, and pick up some hay and oats for the stock. While you're at it, you might as well outfit the horses with the best tack."

Dave answered, "Yes, sir! Er, I hate to say it, but I never really caught yer name..."

Earl grinned. "That's because I never gave it. Now that you're working for me, you will call me, Mr. O'Donnell... Allen O'Donnell."

Dave looked a little intimidated, but answered, "Pleased to make yer acquaintance, Mr. O'Donnell."

Josh asked, "What about you, Sir?"

Earl turned around and stared up the street a ways. "First, I am going to the Yellowstone National Bank, and then I'll head on over to the Montana and Minnesota Land and Improvement Company. I expect to be business owner by the end of the day and own a new home by weeks' end."

He paused for a moment, adding, "Meet up with me about 7:00 this evening for supper. I'll be at The Grand Hotel. Just tell the maître d that you're meeting Mr. O'Donnell... I'll make sure he knows you're coming."

"What kind of business do you plan on starting up?" Dave asked.

Remembering a place he once visited back when he was a younger man in New York City, Earl grinned and answered, "I've been thinking about it all night, and decided I'm going to open a dance hall, across the tracks, in the new part of town. I'll call it, The Little Haymaker Dancehall. There will be high-dollar dancing girls, a can-can show, a good restaurant and the best bar in town. Billings is ripe for the pickin' boys, and I intend to make the most of it!"

When Earl turned around to face Josh and Dave again, both men saw an avaricious gleam in their boss' eyes that promised two things. Earl Dickson (now known, forevermore, as Allen O'Donnell) was going to be the new boss in town—come hell or high water!

10

MATTHEW—AN AWFUL RUCKUS

MATTHEW, AND PATTY HANSON'S SONS, TREVOR AND Lucas, found Lincoln right where Matthew had left him. He was snoozing when they pulled up in the squeaky wagon, but awoke with a snort and whinnied when Matthew walked up with a little blue bottle of mercurochrome in one hand and a bucket of oats, in the other.

"Hold him steady, boys," Matthew said, handing the bucket to Lucas and placing a rope over the horse's ears and nose in a makeshift halter. Lincoln, normally an overly friendly horse, jerked his head and rose up, slightly, on his back hooves in alarm at the strangers who suddenly surrounded him.

"Whoa, son!" the younger boy, Lucas, said with a nervous chuckle. Lincoln stood over seventeen hands tall, after all, and if he wanted to, he could take out all three men where they stood with one quick kick of his front hooves.

Matthew simply stood with his arms around the horse's neck, crooning meaningless endearments into its ear while Trevor emptied most of the medicine into the gashes on Lincoln's rump. There was a little ointment left and while Trevor finished the doctoring with a little sage-paste and Lucas fed the horse plump oats from the bucket, Matthew poured the rest of the mercurochrome into the gouges on his mount's neck and crest.

Finished with their ministrations, Matthew tied Lincoln to the back of the wagon and said, "Let's head on back, boys. We need to go slow, though, okay? I don't want Lincoln blowed any more than necessary."

"Yes, Sir," they answered at once.

Matthew grinned into his whiskers. Placing the rest of his hidden gear in the back of the wagon, he decided to compliment Patty on how well behaved her boys were, and to caution her as well. The first thing Lucas and Trevor had done (once out of their mother's line of sight) was hand Matthew's guns over. He worried that one of these days their trust would be rewarded—and in the worst possible way.

They drove the cart slowly toward the homestead in the darkness as Lincoln, nickering irritably, trailed behind them. The boys chattered like magpies while the sheriff alternately checked his horse's progress and stared into the shadows. He held his shotgun at the ready.

Glancing at his pocket watch, Matthew saw that the time was 11:34 pm and he felt weariness press down on him like a heavy quilt. The same arduous road he had walked before was a mere jaunt now by wagon, and soon he saw lantern light on the whorehouse's porch and above the open barn doors.

An old Negro man met them in front of the barn and walked back to where Lincoln stood behind the wagon, quivering. "Ho, boss man... how you doin?" he whispered, and scratched his fingers under the horse's chin as though he knew, exactly, where Lincoln liked to be petted the most.

Matthew watched as his horse shifted his weight and leaned into the old man's embrace. He felt both pleased and, almost, a little jealous of the man's effect on his animal, but thanked his lucky stars that this isolated whorehouse was a decent place, filled with good people.

"I'll take your horse into the barn and put him in a stall for the night, suh." The old man stared at his feet when he spoke, and the marshal understood that this man would always be frightened of white folk.

Doffing his hat, Matthew replied, "Thank you very much. I appreciate it and so does Lincoln, apparently."

The black man glanced up quickly—a mere flash of white eyes and teeth in the moonlight, and ducked his head again. "This be a good horse, suh. I'll take care of him proper." With those words, Lincoln followed the old man into the barn and out of sight.

When he turned around, Matthew saw the boys leading the draft horses out of their traces and in to a nearby paddock. Then they walked up, grinning. "Let's head on in. Ma told us to let you sleep in the parlor," Trevor said.

This was welcome news to Matthew, who felt like was ready about to melt right into his boots with pain and fatigue. The last hour or so had not improved the long scratch on the back of his neck and he wished he had a little more of the mercurochrome for himself.

He followed the boys up on to the long porch and into the house. Finding himself inside an alcove, he looked through a curtain of beads on his left and saw a number of pretty women sitting here and there in assorted states of undress. One plump girl sat in nothing but a union suit with her feet in a pail of sudsy water, while another lounged on a settee in a see-through, scarlet negligee.

Still another sat in a prim, high-collared, cotton nightgown playing the piano. Perfume and a deeper, earthier odor wafted from the room to where he stood, staring.

"Mister," young Lucas said. "The house is here on the right."

Matthew jumped slightly and turned toward another door, following the teenagers inside to a worn but clean kitchen. The room was empty of people but a coffeepot steamed on the woodstove and a rough, plank table held a loaf of bread, preserves and slices of cold ham under a dishcloth.

He sat at the table with the boys and enjoyed the good meal and the warmth of the cook stove at his back. Finally, when hardly a speck of food remained,

Trevor stood up and said, "Come on in here, sir. Ma has a bed made up for ya."

Matthew followed the boy into the small parlor and saw that a couch was made in to a bed. Trevor smiled and said, "See you in the morning, sir. Sleep tight."

"It's Matthew, Trevor…" Matthew grunted, as he pulled off a boot that seemed welded to his foot.

Trevor just smiled and said, "Yes, Sir. Good night."

Matthew pulled off his other boot with some effort, and winced as he stripped his shirt off. The dried blood on the back of his neck and shoulders tore and he yelped, slightly, in discomfort. Eyeing the pretty, clean quilt on which he was about to lay his head, he pulled his only other clean shirt out of his bag and laid it on the pillow for protection.

Then, finally, he laid his head down, asleep before he hit the pillow.

THE NEXT MORNING, Matthew awoke to sunshine streaming into his eyes and Patty Hanson standing over him with a steaming pan of water in her large hands. "Fer God's sake, Marshal Wilcox… why didn't you let on you was a lawman and… that you was injured?"

Matthew blinked, discombobulated and tongue-tied. He cleared his throat to speak and the woman said, "Turn over on yer belly, Matthew, and let me tend to this scratch on yer neck!"

Helpless to move and pinned to the back of the couch by the woman's ample bottom, Matthew submitted to her ministrations and listened as she talked a mile a minute.

"Oh, the stupidity of men, I swear!" she grumbled. "Look at this, Hildy…"

Matthew cringed. Patty had removed what was left of his shirt and, except for his britches, which had somehow come unbuttoned during the night; he was laid out as naked as a Thanksgiving turkey for all the world to see.

The girl popped up from where she had stood, hidden, behind the couch. Staring into his face with wide, worried eyes, she reached down and patted him on the head with clumsy fingers. "HI!" she cried.

"Hi yourself, Hildy," Matthew sighed.

"Hildy!" her mother admonished. "Quit mooning over the man and hand me some wet rags to clean this wound!"

Patty pulled Matthew's too long hair away from the scratch and placed a warm, wet rag over the injury. The marshal stiffened, hissing in pain, but Patty slapped him on the rump. "Oh, stop yer belly-achin! That's what you get fer ignoring a cat scratch like this! It's a miracle it ain't festered! Men…"

After the first shock of warm water, Matthew relaxed and let the woman tend to his wound. She went on a bit more about the pig-headedness of men and then she asked, "Seriously, why didn't you say you was a law man?"

He shrugged which was a bad move and earned him another swat on the rear. "Stop that, dammit, I'm trying to fix you up!" Patty bellowed.

"Sorry!" he replied. "I didn't think to mention it, that's all. Besides, right now, I'm operating outside of the marshal's service. How did you know, anyway?"

Patty laughed. "Weren't too much of a mystery, Marshal. When you pulled yer shirt out of yer bag, yer coat came with it."

Matthew looked down and saw that, sure enough, the black coat had come out of his bag, sporting his marshal's star on the lapel. *Well,* he thought, *It's not as if I'm trying to hide anything, after all.*

Finished, finally, Patty gave him a parting pat on the backside and stood up. "Come on in to the kitchen when you've gotten dressed. The boys cooked some flapjacks and should be coming in, soon, with a side of bacon for breakfast."

After his hostess and her daughter exited the room, Matthew sat up and pulled clean pants out of his bag. Standing up, he shook out his one clean shirt and buttoned it up. Then, grunting, he shoved his sore feet into his boots and walked into the kitchen.

"Wash yer face, Marshal, and sit down at the table. The boys have already come and gone, but I wanted to have a word with ya before ya leave, if you please."

Matthew grabbed a washrag that sat beside a bucket of warm water on the cook stove, and commenced to washing his face and arms and then using the rag to wash his teeth. Refreshed, he walked over to the table and sat down while Patty bustled around her kitchen.

Finally, she placed a plate of bacon, and pancakes in front of him and sat down with a cup of coffee. She watched as he dug into the feast with gusto and then she said, "Marshal, I think you and your horse could leave in a couple of days if you wanted to. Murray... that's my stable-hand, says that Lincoln is should be healed up enough to travel by then. If you are in a big hurry, my fee for the time and medicine will be five dollars. Does that sound fair?"

Matthew nodded, for the moment unable to speak past the food in his mouth.

Patty frowned. Surprisingly, the slight frown emphasized her former beauty as she stirred an extra spoon of sugar into her stiff, black coffee. "Good... that's fine, Matthew. But, there's something I would rather you did than pay me cash..."

Wiping his mouth with a napkin, Matthew sat up and asked, "What is that, Patty?"

Patty stared in to his face for a moment and said, "You might as well finish yer breakfast... it's a long story."

Matthew nodded and dug in again while Patty spoke about a cattle baron by the name of Miles Atkinson, who was bound and determined to run her off her property.

11

THE HAYMAKER SALOON AND DANCEHALL

TWO MONTHS AFTER ALLEN O'DONNELL (FORMERLY known as Earl Dickson) stepped down from the coach in Billings, Montana, he walked from his lavish office onto the balcony overlooking the bar, stage and dance floor of the Little Haymaker Saloon. His saloon...his pride and joy.

It was 11:00 in the morning, one hour before the doors opened for business. The day-shift bartender, Joey Landraith, was stocking shelves behind the bar with new bottles of hooch. His janitor, a one-armed man named Kyle Burley was pushing a broom around and his madam, Goldie Adams, sat at a table by the front window, sipping coffee and reading the "Weekly Times".

As he watched, the local doctor stepped in the front door. Walking up to where Goldie sat, he spoke to her for a minute and then they both moved to the back of the room where the door to the whore's quarters was located. *Here on pussy patrol,* Allen thought with a smirk. His nostrils quivered with the smell of today's offering from the restaurant's kitchen.

"Hey Joey!" he called. "Bring me up a pot of coffee, and have one of the girls in the kitchen bring me some lunch when it's ready."

"Be right up, Boss," Joey shouted in response.

Calling out to the janitor, Allen said, "Kyle, make sure you wash that wall in the far corner. I think I saw someone pissing on it last night."

"I already got it, boss. Bet yer boots it was that asshole, Little John Barbre. That damn scroat don't think a bar is legit unless he christens it, himself!"

Allen waved in acknowledgement and stepped back inside his office. Sitting down at his desk, he lit a cigar, and spun the chair so it faced toward the room's one large window. Puffing the expensive tobacco with pleasure, he looked down at 28th street and watched carriages and buggies dodging past over-laden wagons and one large herd of cattle. He grinned in satisfaction.

It's all working out as planned! he thought, gleefully. The day he sent Dave and Josh to Cothron and Todd's coach and buggy store, he had marched into the Montana and Michigan Land and Improvement office. He spent most of that day riding around in a fancy coach looking at homes and businesses alike, and had finally settled on the new but abandoned warehouse in which he now resided and ran his dance hall.

Almost a city block long, the warehouse was, originally, built to process and bale wool, but the owners had lost their financial shirts somewhere along the way, and were forced to sell out.

Even as Allen walked around the huge, empty building that day, his mind pictured the stage, the two bars that would run adjacent to one another and the restaurant in front by the street. The upstairs rooms were already built. Intended as office space, they could easily be transformed into living quarters and rooms for the girls he planned to hire.

Turning to the land agent, Allen had done his best to mask his excitement. "How much for this property?" he barked.

The agent, a sweaty, little fat man said, "Well, the previous owners *are* motivated to sell, but one must consider the size of the building, and its newness when setting a… a price…" he stammered, as Allen turned on him with a glare.

"I asked, how much?" the dapper gentleman snarled.

"The asking price is $30,000, but you can make an offer…"

"I'll pay $25,000 and not a penny more!" Allen snapped, hoping he wasn't over-playing his hand. He had watched many a rich man over the years, and seen them act… and talk, exactly like this. They often acted cavalier about money and the power it could buy, but the whole time they were busy calculating how best to turn a piece of silver into a gold dollar.

The little agent smiled and said, "I should have an answer for you by day's end, Mr. O'Donnell. May I inquire as to what business you plan on opening?"

"You may not," O'Donnell snapped.

"Oh... well alright then, Sir. Can I have my driver drop you off somewhere?"

"Yes," O'Donnell answered. "Take me to the Yellowstone National Bank, please. I am staying at the Grand Hotel if you need to send me a message. Please don't dally... I will be happy to find another agent if you can't get this deal done for me in a timely manner."

A few minutes later, O'Donnell stepped out of the carriage, leaving a red-faced land agent behind and walked into the bank. He emerged an hour later with a $35,000 line of credit, and a powerful need for a drink.

The rest was history and Allen thanked his lucky stars. No sooner had he finished a couple of stout whiskeys and returned to the hotel, the desk clerk handed him a note saying his offer had been accepted for 25,000.

The next three weeks were spent hiring an army of carpenters to build the dance hall to Allen's specifications, hiring staff, and outfitting the whole establishment from Yegen Brothers... the magnificent dry goods store down the street.

Taking up two square blocks and three stories tall, the store boasted everything from flour to tractors. One whole floor held suites of furniture and what could not be found within the building itself could be ordered and was guaranteed to arrive within two weeks' time on the new transcontinental railroad.

By the end of the first month, The Little Haymaker was almost ready for business. Cartload after cartload of tables, chairs, beds, desks, stools, bureaus, china, glasses, and silverware arrived daily, sometimes twice a day. Every-day accouterments arrived as well; chamber pots, light-fixtures, spittoons, bar towels, door-hooks, bath towels... anything and everything Allen could think of.

Crowds gathered outside and watched as a beautiful, bright red, grand piano arrived by train from Chicago, and a different sort of crowd gathered as, a couple of weeks later, a gaggle of high-priced whores arrived in three matching carriages just as the sun began its descent behind the mountains. Goldie Adams had arrived, along with ten of her finest and many of the men, who had come to watch, threw their hats in the air and whistled as the women disembarked from the coaches.

As the Little Haymaker took shape in front of his eyes, O'Donnell hired his own, personal army of men. Some would be strong-arms and others, simple messengers, runners and bookkeepers. He did not fool himself; although the Sisters of Mercy had taught Allen to read and do simple mathematics when he was a child, he had no real sense of figures and, more importantly, how to make those figures expand.

There was a knock at the door and Allen was startled out of his reverie. "Come!" he called and Joey stepped into the room with a sterling-silver coffee pot, cream and sugar and pastries on a matching tray.

"Here you go, Boss. Cookie says that he'll send some stew and fresh bread up in about an hour. Is that alright?" Joey placed the tray on Allen's desk and stood up with a sunny smile. Allen liked Joey, although he was not the sort of man he would normally hire.

He was too young, too fresh and as Irish as a shamrock. He had come to the Little Haymaker, hat in hand, and asked Dave if he could speak with the man (Allen O'Donnell himself) directly. At first, Allen was tempted to boot the kid off his front stoop but when he heard the soft lilt of Ireland in the boy's voice, a memory stirred in his heart; of times long gone, when he didn't have to live and die by his wits (and the blade of his knife) in this harsh new country.

He was just starting to interview bartending positions and, after a brief hesitation, he had hired Joey on the spot. So far, the kid was doing well. Picking up a cup of the strong, heavily sweetened coffee, Allen took a sip and said," Thank you, Joey. Tell the cook that will be fine, and when you're done with that, go and fetch Josh up here."

"Will do, sir," Joey said and left. Turning back around and staring at the wall of the opera house across the street, Allen smiled. There was only one fly in the ointment of his carefully, crafted plans. He wanted, more than anything else in the world, to be considered "high salt."

But that had not happened yet. Allen knew, by God, that money could buy anything, including social and political standing but, so far, his attempts at fitting in to this town's elite had failed. *The goddamn mayor is nothing but a trumped up grocery store clerk!* he fumed, referring to Christian Yeger, of Yeger's Dry Goods, who was voted in as mayor in 1899.

He was shunned, though, at every turn! He had tried to join in the Men's Auxiliary Club last month, and was met with regret. He had also dragged Dave and Josh to the closest Catholic Church one Sunday but had felt a distinct chill from the parishioners and the priest, alike.

It wasn't his clothing, he was sure, nor was it his faint Irish accent... in truth; O'Donnell had never heard such a dizzying assortment of accents and dialects before he first took up residence in Billings. It must be the whore-end of his business, he thought ruefully. That was the only explanation he could conjure up for his failure to blend in.

It was a cold comfort though, especially since he knew, as fact, that half the big wigs in town were nothing but crooks. Hell, one of the biggest cattle barons around was a known thief and rustler and the chief banker, President Walker Thompson, at the Yellowstone National Bank, was rumored to be a sodomite. It was that same man, though, that had offered Allen O'Donnell the deepest insult.

Since his first day in town, Allen had looked toward the west side of Billings and coveted the grand homes that sat like handsome, dozing dowagers amongst tree-lines cobbled streets. One, in particular, a redbrick mansion with pale, yellow pillars and black shutters had sat empty since his arrival.

He had walked through the empty, echoing rooms

with the same land agent that sold him the warehouse, and asked the cost. The little agent, obviously bolder now and afflicted with the same lofty attitude toward Allen and his men, as his betters answered, "This is the Landry estate, Mr. O'Donnell. I really shouldn't have let you in here, since it's not on the market."

Stopping, Allen had gazed into the man's face and something in his cold, blue eyes caused the fat man to back up a step. "Why then, is there a FOR SALE sign in the front lawn?" he growled.

"Well" the fat man gulped. "That was a mistake on my part, I'm afraid!"

They had left the house then, but Allen swore he would own it someday, and the devil take the hindmost!

There was another knock on the door, and Josh called out, "Boss, you wanted to see me?"

"Yes, Josh. Come in!" Allen said and watched as the young man entered. Josh was much improved, as of late. He was bathing regularly now, and his hair was cut, and combed. He had also grown a little mustache, which served to hide his weak mouth and rubbery lips.

"Pull up a chair, Josh, and sit down," Allen said and walked over to bolt the door. Returning to his chair behind the desk, Allen said, "Do you remember the bank president, Walker Thompson?"

Josh nodded. He would never forget the murder in Earl...er, Mr. O'Donnell's eyes when his bid for that house on the west side was first rejected by the bank. "Yes, sir!"

O'Donnell smiled. "Well, I got a job for you."

Josh sat still and listened to instructions, as his boss planned the murder of his biggest obstacle in purchasing the home of his dreams and acceptance into the "Upper Crust of Billings' society.

12

THE GREEDY BARON

MATTHEW SAT AND LISTENED WHILE PATTY HANSON talked about her life, her family and the threat that hovered over all of them, since Atkinson had bought land adjacent to hers a year earlier. The longer he listened, the sadder, and angrier, he became.

Patty said, "As yer must have guessed by now, Marshal, I was a whore for most of my life. A high paid one, mind you, but a whore just the same. That all changed when Lanny Hanson showed up one day at the whorehouse I used to work in." She shook her head and her cheeks flushed with pleasure at the memories her words recalled.

Looking into Matthew's eyes she stated, "I wasn't always fat, ya know. Used to be, I was known fer my beauty and the gents came from miles around to spend the night in my bed. Well, one night, the dirtiest man I ever clapped eyes on showed up. Whoeee!" she chortled. "I could smell him clear across the room!"

Sobering, she continued. "He asked my boss, Arnie, if he could spend the night with me and I almost refused, but Arnie said the man had promised to take a bath before he came to my room. Plus, Arnie said that filthy man was willing to pay fifty bucks fer the honor and there was no way Arnie was going to pass that kind of money up. Needless to say, I couldn't say no."

Standing up from her chair, Patty walked over to the cook stove and asked, "Want another cup?"

Matthew said, "Sure, thank you."

Pouring each of them a fresh cup, she sat back down and continued her tale. "Well, I can tell you, that man cleaned up just fine. So fine, in fact, some of the other girls were ready to fight me over him, but he wanted me—and only me. It was the luckiest day of my life."

She sighed, and a tear slipped from the corner of her eye. Smiling through her tears, Patty said, "Lanny was a mule-skinner, Marshal... a good one. He had scrimped and saved, and bought a freight wagon and six good mules. He contracted out, mainly, to the Army and made a pretty penny over the fifteen years he worked that job. He saved every dime he made, too."

Patty grinned. "He told me, that first night, he had visited the brothel a few months earlier and saw me working the room... said, he hadn't ever seen anything prettier in all his days and he told me he was ready to hang up his mule-skinnin' days and settle down if I would agree to be his wife."

She snorted, "Well, I had heard that before, of course, plenty of times. I laughed at him, thinking he was a touch loco, but I still gave him a good ride that night and sent him on his way."

Patty's eyes glowed. "Well, he came back the next night—and the night after that and he kept coming, paying that greedy old bastard, Arnie, fifty bucks each time until he finally talked me into it. If nuthin' else, I admired the man's stubborn streak!"

"We got hitched a couple of days later," she continued. "And I jumped into that wagon of his. Truth to tell, as we headed out over-land, I had to wonder what had gotten into me. For all I knew, he was going to murder me...or sell me to one of the rogue tribes who like to trade women for whiskey. But Lanny, he was true-blue, Marshal. It took about a week to get here, but when I saw this little valley and the house he had already built, I couldn't believe my luck!"

"Anyway, we made a good life fer ourselves here. The boys came along, one after the other, and a couple of years after that, we got our little Hildy." Patty sat up a little in her chair and glared. "That's the real test of a man, in my opinion. It's all well and good when a child comes out of its mother's womb sound, but when a young'un comes out wrong... well, I seen it happen before. A lot of men will skedaddle, or turn hateful toward a baby like that.

Patty smiled again. "Not my Lanny, though. My God, he took one look at my little crooked girl and fell in love all over again. He was a saint, my man and I miss him still, although he's been gone almost eight years, now."

"What happened... if you don't mind my asking?"

Patty shook her head. "It ain't no secret... one of his own mules kicked him in the head. I had the whole team shot, right after." Staring at the table, she added, "Weren't one of my finer moments, I reckon."

"My family and I have made out okay, since Lanny died. There weren't much of the way of spending cash, though, so I called on a few of my old friends to see if they was interested in moving out here and servicing the cattlemen and Buckaroos that live in these parts."

"It's been a successful endeavor, too, by God. We ain't rolling in the clink, by any means, but we have a fine home, with a good Doc who comes by once every couple of weeks. Some of my girls were raised on farms and they take care of the pigs, sheep and cattle just fine."

Matthew sat back in his chair and stared in to Patty's eyes. "Tell me more about this Atkinson guy, why don't you?"

"Oh yeah, I mean to." She responded. "About a year ago, the honcho of this new cattle outfit rode in with a bunch of his paid cowboys. They rode in blazing, too, like they was fixing to light the whole place up!" Patty glared. "Well, I sent the kids inside and met them on my front porch. My heart was pounding to beat the band, I tell ya, but I can be tough when I need to be!"

Matthew grinned. *I just bet!* he thought.

"Atkinson was in the back of the pack, first time he rode in. Once, his boys had me in their sites, he rode through like some sort of king and says, "My name is Col. Miles Atkinson. Are you the owner of this estate?""

"Well I knew, right then, that he already knew who I was. You hardly ever hear of a stranger not asking to speak to the man of the house. I answered yes, and he said that he wanted to give me a hundred dollars to vacate my property. Said, he had a mind to turn my home into a bunkhouse for his men and wanted to run his cattle, unimpeded, through my fifty acres!"

Patty scowled. "Marshal" she said, "I ain't no genius, God knows, but Lanny paid close to two hundred dollars for this land fifteen years ago, and that was without the house, and the barn, the well, and the fence-lines!"

"I tried to be polite about it, but I told him and his boys to go hang! He didn't take kindly to that and, before they left, three of his boys put bullet holes into the front of the house!" She shook her head and said. "They have come in once a month, since that first time. Every time they ride in, they shoot their guns, steal a pig or two, maybe slaughter one of my sheep... last time they was here, one of those boys set fire to the back of the barn!"

She sat very still, and stared into Matthew's eyes. "Marshal, you and the star you wear are an answer to my prayers. You know, Atkinson and his men could ride in here and take what they want... all they would have to do is kill the lot of us. Something is holding them boys back, though. Although the local sheriff hasn't showed up to help, I have the feeling that Atkinson doesn't want to be tangled up with the law. That cattle baron is greedy but he ain't stupid."

"So, what I was hoping is this... come the weekend, I fully expect another visit from the Colonel. I was thinking that if you was here, wearing yer star, he might get scared off enough to look elsewhere for more land." She grinned. "I also know that the doc will be here in a day or two. He is pretty handy with a needle—maybe he could fix up a couple of those scratch marks on yer pony's rump?"

Matthew thought about it for a moment or two. Although he was in a hurry to chase down the dirty, low-down dogs that killed his wife, right now he was clueless on which way to go in his search. His horse was lame and he, himself, was stiff and sore from the bottom of his feet to the top of his head.

He knew that three or four days wouldn't make any difference in his hunt, so he nodded and said, "I'll stay through the weekend, Patty. If the Colonel shows, I'll do my best as a marshal to make him see the error of his ways. If he doesn't show up by, say, Sunday, I'll pay you twenty dollars for your hospitality and be on my way. Deal?"

Patty nodded with a smile and spit in her hand, sticking it out over the table to shake. "Deal, Marshal. Thank you!"

He shook and stood up. "Now, what can I do around here to make myself useful?"

A few minutes later, Matthew strode across the barnyard with a long list of chores in his back pocket.

IT WAS late Saturday morning now and Matthew was beginning to wonder if Patty's Colonel was going to prove a no-show. He wanted to help the kindly lady out, if he could, but time was wasting and he simply couldn't afford to waste much more of it.

It had been a fine and restful interlude, though. He had spent the last three days helping around the house and ranch doing everything from helping bring in firewood, to fixing the barn's roof. Lincoln was doing better as well. Most of the deep scratches and puncture wounds on its rump and neck were healing nicely, and the gelding was growing restive in the corral.

Except on weekends, the whores rolled up their sleeves and worked around the ranch, as well. They tended to the pigs and sheep, washed laundry, tended to the garden, made soap, and tallow candles and generally made everyone in their vicinity smile with their bawdy jokes.

They weren't the prettiest women Matthew had ever seen but they were healthy enough and obviously happy with their decision to move here and keep their old friend, Patty, company.

A few of the whores had approached Matthew and

asked if he would like to partake of the wares, but he politely declined. Although he was a very attractive man, something in his expression kept the women from taking offense. They sensed that his heart belonged to another and with a smile and a wink, they faded away, leaving him alone again to yearn for his lost wife.

One of the women, a redhead named Dixie, did take umbrage, however. Of the three, she was the prettiest and when Matthew declined her free offering her cheeks blazed red in embarrassment. "Too good fer the likes o' me, eh?" she hissed.

Matthew tried to explain, but she picked up her skirts and flounced off. He heard her speaking to the other whores who were sitting on the porch in a loose group, and he also heard a titter of derisive laughter follow her complaints as he made his way across the front yard and into the barn. He shrugged... even if his broken heart allowed him to have his ease; he doubted whether he could perform the deed.

One thing was constant and that was little Hildy. She had shadowed his every boot-print from day- one. Patty thought it was because Matthew reminded Hildy of her daddy. She also worried that her daughter's constant attention would anger the marshal, but Matthew just smiled and said, "Oh... let her be. She's no bother."

Matthew had just finished cleaning his shotgun and both pistols. His hands were covered in gun oil and he wiped them on a soft towel. Then he laid the shotgun on the towel and holstered his 45 Long Colt and his placed his back-up 38 pistol in his shoulder harness. Walking to the well to take a draught of cool water from the bucket, he was staring down the road when Hildy ran up, waving something long and green in the air. "Marsh! Marsh, lookit wha I made ya!" she yelled.

Matthew turned around and saw that she had a woven a dandelion chain. Most of the yellow blossoms were facing inwards and some were nothing but bits of fluff, but his lips twitched in a grin. Remembering Chance, and how he had once commanded his pa to wear the same kind of necklace, he bowed to the girl and said, "Very beautiful necklace, Hildy. Thank you!"

The girl grinned with delight and held the weedy contraption up in the air. Knowing that the chain wouldn't quite fit over his head, he removed his hat and placed the dandelion chain around the brim. Hildy jumped with joy and Matthew knew his simple gesture would stick with Hildy for years to come. Glancing up, he saw Patty standing on the front porch, watching them with a fond smile.

"I'm going to take Lincoln out for a bit and see how his gait is," Matthew called to Patty who nodded in acknowledgement.

He walked into the corral and mounted his horse, bareback. *This will be a good test*, Matthew thought as he gently nudged Lincoln's belly. The horse sprang into action with a nicker and they trotted quickly up the hill behind Patty's house. Easing up on the reins, Matthew gave the beast room to run and they flew up the incline and onto a plateau overlooking the valley. Matthew gauged his animal's progress and smiled in satisfaction. Lincoln was sound now… and it was high time for both of them to be on their way.

He figured he would tell Patty as soon as he returned to the house. Just then, he heard the sound of gunfire. Turning Lincoln around, Matthew stared down at the house and barn. He couldn't see too much from where he sat his horse but he could hear screaming and another round of gunfire echoing off the distant bluffs. "Heeyah!" he shouted and gave Lincoln a light slap with his reins.

They cantered down the hill and around the back of the barn into a scene of blood and chaos. At first glance, it looked like three gunmen had come up the road and shot Patty Hanson where she stood on the front porch. An old man sat on his horse surveying the action with sullen eyes. Matthew heard him shout, "I told you I'd be back…"

Two cowboys were standing on the front steps. One of the men still held a smoking pistol in his hand as he observed the stricken woman. Most of the whores were inside, safe from harm, but Patty's sons and old Murray were kneeling next to her on the front porch.

"Put your guns down, NOW!" Matthew roared.

There was such authority in his voice, the two buckaroos by the steps backed away with their pistols held low in their hands. They were just about to set the guns on the ground when the older man barked, "What in the hell are you two doing? Don't give up your firearms, dammit! Put that man in your sites!"

The men looked torn but their boss' orders carried weight and they tightened their grip on the guns. Now, Matthew was at a disadvantage, and he slid off the far side of his horse. Knowing he had to put a stop to things—quick—Matthew took aim and fired at the man he assumed to be Atkinson. He grinned as the old man tottered in his saddle and gripped his left arm.

"He shot me, boys! Goddammit, he shot me in the arm!" Atkinson howled.

There was a sudden silence as the cowboys tried to figure out what to do, and then Matthew heard a distant scream. Turning to his right, he saw a flurry of activity from the corner of his eye and took off running. The one person he had not seen yet was Hildy, and something about the scream he had just heard tickled his memory. Running around the back of the barn, he saw two more of Atkinson's buckaroos.

One man was crouched by Hildy's head, pinning her arms to the ground and the other man was hunched and heaving between the thirteen-year-old girl's legs. It was obvious to Matthew that the men were raping Hildy and he could hear her thin cries from thirty-feet away. He lifted his pistol and shot the man who held Hildy's arms down. The cowboy fell backwards, and Matthew took off running.

The man who was, actually, in the act of raping Hildy, either didn't see what had happened to his part- ner, or he was too far-gone in his own sexual frenzy to notice the threat that stalked up behind him. He was in mid-heave when Matthew reared back and kicked him as hard as he could in the temple. The man collapsed onto the girl's body, out cold.

Hildy let out a wail of fright and disgust. The marshal pulled the man's limp body off her and holding her tight, he whispered words of comfort in her ears as she sobbed. Then he felt a line of fire scorch his left arm and his lap grow wet. Staring in shock, he saw that Hildy had been shot in the back, the bullet entering her body from behind and exiting into his own arm.

A high-pitched whistle rang in Matthew's ears as he gazed across the girl's dead body at Colonel Miles Atkinson, who was leaning heavily against the back of the barn and grinning at the work he had just done. His other two men were by his side and both of them were pointing their pistols in Matthew's direction. Matthew let the girl slide to the ground and then he pulled the 38 from his shoulder harness.

The only thing Matthew could see in that moment was the hideous face of every, single outlaw who had ever done him, or the people he was sworn to protect, wrong. In one swift movement, the marshal lifted both of his pistols and shot Atkinson and his two men full of holes. Then he turned around and shot the rapist too. Standing over the buckaroo he had wounded earlier, Matthew saw that the boy was gut-shot. Knowing he would die anyway, Matthew shrugged and put a bullet in the back of his head.

A few moments later, as Matthew stood gasping within a cloud of acrid gun smoke with the absurd crown of weeds on the brim of his hat, he understood that life, and his accustomed place in it, had just come to an abrupt and violent end.

13

SUDDENLY, AN OUTLAW

WITHIN A FEW MOMENTS, TREVOR, LUCAS AND MURRAY appeared from the front of the barn. The youngest tripped over the dead body of one of the Buckaroos and almost went sprawling. Trevor and Murray saw the carnage immediately, though, and stepped over the dead bodies in their way, making for the marshal and the dead girl at his feet.

Trevor stared at his little sister and tears filled his eyes. Behind him, Lucas said, "Oh no... Hildy!" The old Negro's lips drooped in sorrow as well and he crouched low to pick her up off the ground. Shooting the marshal a glance, he murmured, "Best come back to the house with us, Suh. The Mrs. will want to hear about what happened, here."

Matthew nodded silently and accompanied the others back to the house. Most of the whores were milling about on the front porch, shock and fear written plainly on their worn faces. "What happened, Marshal?" he heard, and, "Oh my God! Is that Hildy?"

Patty was lying on the settee in her front parlor. Her plain white blouse had been removed and a red-tinged square of white cotton covered a bullet wound just under her collarbone. One of the older whores, a woman named Dee, was cleaning blood away from the wound and Matthew heard her say, "It went in the front and out the back, Patty. Thank God I don't have to dig around in your shoulder for a bullet!"

Patty wasn't listening, however. She saw her boys enter the parlor and then her groom with Hildy in his arms. Letting out a cry, she pushed Dee away and tried to rise but Matthew took two long steps and held her down as she shouted out in grief. There was another couch by the back wall and Murray laid Hildy's body down with great care.

Turning around he swept his hat off his head and said, "She gone, Mrs. Little Hildy's gone."

Patty's face was white with shock and sorrow. Falling back on the settee, she stared up at Matthew. "What happened to my little girl, Marshal?"

Matthew decided not to go into too much detail. The end-result was terrible enough. "She was shot in the back, Patty. I am so sorry—you have my deepest sympathies."

"How did those men get the drop on her like that? I thought you, of all people, could have kept my girl safe!" Tears streamed down her cheeks from angry, brown eyes.

Matthew was wondering the same thing... he was a lawman, an experienced shooter and he had failed in his duties. Then Trevor spoke up, "Ma! Mr. Wilcox killed every single one of those bastards! It ain't his fault they got to Hildy first!"

Patty eyed the marshal. "Did you kill them all, Matthew? My God—you gotta go! The sheriff will see you hang if'n you don't!"

Matthew had already started to feel the long arm of the law squeezing the back of his neck. A man like Atkinson didn't operate on his own. Chances were he had a whole army of men back home just waiting on his return and when that return never came, another army of lawyers and crooked lawmen ready to seek justice.

"Is the sheriff in Atkinson's pocket, Patty? What I did is justifiable. They came on to your property with malicious intent, shot you and your daughter and... worse. I *am* a Washington State marshal and well within my rights to use deadly force..."

Patty, who was staring at the still form of her daughter shifted her gaze to him and murmured, "What do you mean worse, Marshal?"

Matthew, who had not intended to mention the rape he witnessed, cursed his loose tongue. There was enough damage done already, without having to torture Patty's memories with images of her daughter's final moments. He looked at the other people in the room and asked if he could have a private moment with Patty.

Lucas, Trevor, Dee and Murray filed out of the room and Matthew pulled a chair up to the side of the couch. Looking into Patty's sad eyes he said, "Patty, two of those bucks were raping Hildy when I came around the back of the barn. I didn't want to burden you with that knowledge but the rape, on top of everything else, would exonerate me... at least in a court of law."

Fresh tears welled up in the woman's eyes as she absorbed the information. It was true, she thought. Blood had soaked the blanket in which Hildy was wrapped, and Patty realized, had the marshal not told her directly, she would never have investigated her daughter's maidenhead... or lack thereof.

She had become accustomed to being treated like a lesser citizen because she was once a whore and ran a brothel. She knew that Atkinson had all the power in the world, whereas she had none. Her first thought was that Matthew Wilcox would be dealt with in a swift and final act of retribution because she, herself, held no sway with the powers that ruled the land.

She had forgotten, though, that Matthew Wilcox had his own power—the star on his coat proclaimed it, and she allowed a small smile of triumph cross her lips even as more tears leaked from her eyes at what had become of her little girl. She also realized that for the first time in over a year, she, what remained of her family and her business were finally safe from harm.

The shock of the last hour or so, and blood loss made her head spin and she lay back on the pillow with a weary sigh. "What are we going to do now, Marshal?"

"You are going to stay right here and rest, Patty." Matthew replied. "Murray, your boys and I will wrap the bodies up and take them into town. I have some explaining to do, but I don't want you to worry about that, okay?" Leaning forward slightly, Matthew asked, "Do you mind if I have a look at your wound?"

She nodded and he peeled back the cotton bandage. It *was* a simple in and out, and Matthew said, "This looks pretty clean, but I think I'll fetch the doctor back here when I go to town."

There was no response and he realized that Patty had fallen into a swoon. Matthew stepped into the kitchen, where her friend Dee waited, impatiently. Nodding to the woman to go in and see to her friend, Matthew said, "We need to wrap those bodies up and head into town and the sheriff's office."

Murray shuffled his feet. "Suh, I will help you with those fellas but, please don't make me go into town. The Mrs. might need me here, anyway!"

Studying the visible fear on the black man's face, Matthew nodded. "That's fine, Murray. You stay here, but we would appreciate your help getting those men loaded into the wagon."

"Yes, Suh," Murray answered and the four of them trooped outside to face the havoc Matthew's pistols had wrecked on Atkinson and his buckaroos.

MATTHEW and the boys rode into a little town that

made Granville look like a small city. The dirt road running though the town of Victory sent up plumes of dust that covered the whole area in a reddish-gray shroud. There was a grand six buildings—a general store, a post-office, a small church and a bar stood on one side of the road, two houses and the sheriff's office stood opposite.

A number of chairs on the boardwalk in front of the sheriff's office were occupied, and as Matthew and the boys rode up in the wagon, the chair's occupants stood up and stared at the back of the wagon, which was, unfortunately, piled high with bodies. Immediately, one of the men (the sheriff, Matthew assumed) undid the leather strap on his holster and rested his right hand on his gun. "Who are you and what have you got in the back of that wagon?" The man shouted.

Matthew eyed the man's companions who were now holding their firearms and looked prepared to start shooting. "My name is Matthew Wilcox... State Marshal, Matthew Wilcox... don't shoot!"

The sheriff, a tall, skinny man, studied Matthew's star and said, "Put your guns away, men. That star is legit." The deputies did as ordered, but remained standing by the sheriff's side.

Tensions eased, for the moment, and Matthew stepped down off the wagon. He extended his right hand and shook. The sheriff said, "My name is William Purcell... sheriff in these parts... and I ask again, Sir. What are you doing with a pile of dead bodies in the back of your wagon?"

The man seemed friendly enough, but none too pleased with the trouble that had just ridden up to his front door. Matthew sighed and took his hat off, wiping sweat away from his forehead. Things could go very wrong at this point of the game—if the sheriff was in Atkinson's pocket; he was likely to be pissed as hell, but maybe...

"I was lying over at Mrs. Patty Hanson's place, while my gelding recovered from a cougar attack." Gazing up into Purcell's weathered face, Matthew paused. "You know of whom I'm referring to, Sheriff?"

Purcell nodded and his eyes slid sideways to the back of the wagon again.

Matthew's heart rate accelerated, slightly. "Then you probably know, already, that a man named Atkinson has been trying to run Patty off her land?"

"Yessir, I'm aware of that, but Patty never filed an official complaint, so my men and I decided to just wait it out. Surely you know that there are land squabbles every day of the week in these territories?"

Matthew hid his grimace of distaste. "Yes, Sheriff. I know that land boundaries can be a mite... fluid. However, earlier this afternoon, Atkinson and four of his buckaroos rode onto Mrs. Hanson's property. One of those boys shot Patty in the chest, and two others raped her youngest child, a little girl named Hildy."

Matthew heard a stifled gasp come from one of the two boys who still sat on the wagon bench. He really didn't want Hildy's brothers to hear about what had happened in this way, but he also knew he had one chance (and one chance only) to clear his name.

Continuing, he said, "I shot one of the men who held the little girl down and kicked the other man away, but then Atkinson shot Hildy in the back while I held her in my arms. I ended up dispatching the intruders, Sheriff." He studied Purcell's face and thought he saw... relief, maybe.

"They had obviously come onto the property with malicious intent and, as a Washington State Marshal, I was well within my rights, and lawful jurisprudence, to act with deadly force," Matthew finished.

Purcell said nothing but gestured to his two deputies. "Take a look at these stiffs and see if they are who the marshal thinks. If so, you boys can take that wagon around the back of that house, there."

He pointed to a two-story house at the end of the road. "The town doc lives there and runs his practice out of one of the downstairs rooms. There's also a graveyard behind the house, although I'm thinking that Atkinson's people will be heading to town to fetch his body back home."

The deputies snooped around the back of the wagon and one of the men said, "Sure 'nuff, Sheriff. These are Miles and his men."

"Okay..." Turning to Lucas and Trevor, the sheriff said, "Boys, go and drop your load and then head back here and wait while I have a word with the marshal.

Matthew spoke to Sheriff Purcell for an hour or so, while Trevor and Lucas left the dead men off at the doctor's office. Purcell informed Marshal Wilcox that the circuit judge was scheduled to make an appearance by the end of the month... two weeks hence.

Purcell made it clear that although he believed Matthew's tale, and felt that the greedy cattle baron had received his just desserts, Matthew would need to repeat his story to the judge before any charges could be, formally, dropped.

Matthew agreed with the sheriff, knowing that if he were making the call, his decision would be the same. Although Matthew felt that Purcell could have been more pro-active in the whole affair, the fact that Patty Hanson had never pressed charges, ultimately led to a "hands-tied" situation for the sheriff.

However, there was no way he was going to hang around for two, whole weeks until the circuit judge showed. He had his own demons to hunt down and neither the time nor inclination to wait on justice to be served here in Victory, Washington.

He rode home with the boys in the now, empty wagon and talked with Patty about how he supposed things would play out. Then he told her he would not be waiting for the circuit judge to show up... and why. Tears filled Patty's eyes as he told her about what had happened to Iris, and the outlaws he was in a hurry to apprehend.

Although they both knew that Matthew's actions would label him as a fugitive from the law, Patty hugged him with real affection and swore she would stand as a witness if he ended up on trial. The whores bid him a fond farewell, and the boys begged him to come back someday. The old Negro groom, who had filled Matthew's saddlebags to overflowing with food and water, kissed Lincoln's nose and, staring into the horse's large brown eyes, wished its master a safe journey.

One pair of cold, green eyes followed the marshal's diminishing shadow as he rode away with hostility, however. Dixie despised Marshal Wilcox with all her being. Not only had he spurned her advances, he had shot the man she loved (and spied for), dead.

Her lover, Alex, had sworn that once his boss, Miles Atkinson, ran Patty off her property, he would receive a big bonus and once he got the cash, he would come back and marry her. Well, now Alex was dead—shot by the same man who had made her feel like a piece of cow-dung stuck on the bottom of his boot.

Well, she thought, *there are two sides to every story and just wait until the Atkinson family hears what I have to say about Matthew Wilcox!*

14

THE NEW ELITE

ALLEN O'DONNELL RESTED HIS ELBOWS ON THE balustrade and stared down at the seething mass of people in his saloon. He grinned. It was a packed house again, just like the night before and the night before that. *Good thing, too,* he mused. It had cost a pretty penny to hire the can-can girls and dancing band that held his customers captive.

There were fifty, four-top tables, twenty-five tables for two and forty bar stools. All of them were full. There were people plastered along the walls and the dance floor was teeming. Glancing to his left, Allen peered into the gambling section and saw that the Roulette table and the six poker tables were full as well. He could hear the roar of the crowd even over the band and his heart swelled with pride.

Waiters were running back and forth from the restaurant, hauling dishes of food from the kitchen and returning with trays of drinks. A fight seemed to be brewing by the back bar but Allen saw that Josh and one of his new hires, a knuckle-buster named Bob Showers, were putting a stop to the quarrel.

One voice rose above the others. Hearing the strident and all too familiar tones, Allen gritted his teeth in frustration. It was that damn Calamity Jane* again! Stinking drunk, as usual, she had talked a man into letting her ride on his shoulders. Now, the two drunks careened around the customers and tables while she whipped his backside with a short quirt and he neighed like a crazed pony.

From where he stood, he could hear startled yelps and outraged squawks as Jane's quirt found its mark on an unsuspecting bottom or a dislodged hat. Allen was just about to don his derby and head downstairs in order to stop their antics when he saw Josh and Bob muscle their way through the crowd and wrestle the two miscreants to the floor.

Two more of his bouncers joined the fray and Allen stood still, watching, as within moments both Jane and her human pony were hauled outside. The immediate crowd quickly returned to their seats and called for more whiskey, rum and gin. The can-can girls lifted their skirts with a boisterous cry and squealed, "Aieee!" The crowd responded in kind, "Aieee!"

Allen thought, *Aieee indeed,* and made his way to the one, empty table by the back of the room, closest to the bigger and longer of the two bars. Taking a seat, he gestured to Joey, who nodded in acknowledgment.

Within moments, a double whiskey and a wicker

bowl of peanuts were sitting in front of the Little Haymaker Saloon's owner, along with the day's books. He thumbed through the ledger and stifled a grin. He was learning more about arithmetic from his book-keeper and he was not certain but it seemed that he and his business were in the black... way in the black!

Sitting back in his chair, O'Donnell felt the warmth of his success cover him like a cozy blanket on a cold, winter day. A few of his patrons saw a slow, rather ugly smirk cross the man's face as he sat and stared at noth-ing, but they were too inebriated to take much notice.

Three weeks ago, after an insidious smear campaign, the bank president, Walker Thompson, committed suicide. This wasn't a fake suicide, like what had happened to the luckless notary, Howard Staple-ton, back in Orofino, Idaho. (Josh had snuck back to the man's tent that night, throttled him and strung him up in a tree with a suicide note pinned on his coat jacket. Allan was rather proud of that note—he had mentioned the man's wife and daughters by name and wrote how sorry he was for being such a loser and for kicking the bucket in shame.)

This suicide was no fiction. Committed by Thomp-son's own hand, the lofty bank president had stuck a 22 in his mouth and pulled the trigger after everybody in the towns of Billings and Coulson heard he was as queer as a two-headed calf and saw the crude, porno-graphic graffiti that graced every storefront and outside wall within the two towns and beyond.

Thompson's associate, a pleasant but weak young

man, was easily cowed and cognizant of his newness in management. All it took for O'Donnell to, finally, own the home of his dreams was a well-timed (and somewhat forceful) private meeting with the banks new president. Within days, Allen was given two sets of keys to a house he had never, ever dreamed of owning, even during his wildest flights of fancy.

O'Donnell frowned. The first time he had walked through the large, echoing rooms as owner, he felt a keen sense of fear. It was though the house itself held its breath, affronted and disappointed that it must suffer the likes of him in its hallowed halls. Allen quickly fled, but wasted no time in ordering all new furnishings and household staff. He planned to move in, this coming weekend, and hoped that the new furniture and the starchy new staff would drown out the building's subliminal whispers of scorn.

Picking up his glass and seeing it was empty, O'Donnell glanced toward the bar. The bartenders, Joey and another man named Bradley, were knee deep in customers, so he decided to go fetch a bottle of whiskey for himself. Just as he started to stand, a wild-looking man in animal skins walked up to his table. He crowded in so close, Allen felt a thrill of fear and put his hand on his vest pocket where he had hidden a small, 22. Caliber pistol.

Face flushing, O'Donnell peered up at the man and demanded, "Back away, Sir… at once!"

The man gazed down at him for a moment and then took a step back, holding his two gloved hands away from his stinking, hide coat. "Sorry about that," he said. "I spend a lot of time on my own, ya know, and sometimes forget a man needs room to breathe." He held out a fur-covered mitt and said, "The name's John Johnson. Been up wood-hawking for the ferry steamers for a while and was surprised to see this fine new establishment when I got back to town."

O'Donnell studied the man's craggy face and wild, dirty beard. Hard, hazel eyes peered out from a nest of wrinkles and, although his words were friendly enough, the man's lips curled down at the corners in a U-shaped grimace. *Could this really be "Liver-Eating Johnson—the Crow Killer?"* he thought.

Deciding that he had better change his attitude quick, lest Johnson eat *his* liver, O'Donnell stood up and shook the man's hand. "I'm pleased to meet you, Sir! Sorry... you startled me, is all."

Johnson had been studying Allen's face with cool eyes and seemed, suddenly, to reach a conclusion. Somehow, O'Donnell knew that this man found him wanting and he felt a chill. Maybe it was a meeting of two similar minds, or a hint that Johnson was not impressed with his credentials as an upright citizen, but Allen knew, without a doubt, that this man was dangerous and would brook no nonsense.

"I saw your boys hauling a certain woman out of here a little while ago..."

O'Donnell smiled. "Oh, you mean Calamity Jane? Yeah, she was getting a mite lit up, and I run a respectable house here. Can't be having the rabble running customers off, you know."

Johnson pursed his lips, which caused his unkempt beard to bristle like porcupine quills. "Her name is, actually, Martha Jane Canary. She likes to take a drink, for sure, but there ain't any call for your men to kick her like a dog."

"Who was kicking her?"

Johnson turned around and studied the back entrance. "That one there, the big one with the cheap, pocket watch. He hauled off and kicked Martha so hard, it's a wonder half her ribs ain't broke."

"Oh, you mean Josh... he's a simpleton." O'Donnell saw the moron leaning against the far wall, looking pleased with himself. Allen also saw the watch he had given Josh hanging on the front of his vest, although he had told the boy to keep it hidden from view.

"So, you are friends with Miss Canary, Mr. Johnson?" O'Donnell studied the man's face, thinking, *everybody in town knows she ain't nothing but a drunken, whore. Why the concern?*

Johnson screwed up his lips and spat in a cuspidor. Turning back, he stared Allen in the eye. "Not really. I just don't tolerate savages, Mr. O'Donnell, as you might know if you were to study up on me a little."

Gazing over at Josh, who was laughing at something Bob Showers was saying, Johnson added, "Tell your guard dog, I had better not catch him kicking women around on the street, again." He pulled a bowie knife from a hidden coat pocket and used the tip of it to clean one of his fingernails. "Got me?"

O'Donnell felt a deep flush of fury heat his cheeks and it took every ounce of control he possessed to keep from pulling his gun out and putting a cap in the man's hairy head. He struggled against his own anger for a moment, while Johnson observed his reaction with amused eyes and said, "Of course, you're right, Mr. Johnson. I'll have a word or two with my bouncers about the use of excessive force."

"That's good, Mr. O'Donnell. "See you around, I'm sure." Johnson said and wandered away into the crowd, still using his knife to clean his nails. O'Donnell saw that people moved as far away from Johnson as possible as he moved toward the gambling tables. He also realized that he wasn't the only one who felt danger emanating off the man, like stink from a skunk.

"Jesus, what a town!" he muttered to himself as he walked over to the bar, grabbed a bottle of whisky and a fresh glass. Sitting back down in his chair, O'Donnell wondered what would happen in two weeks' time when Buffalo Bill's Wild West Show and rodeo came to town.

With the likes of Annie Oakley, Lillian Smith, Seth Clover and the attending Sioux and Pawnee Indians that made up William Cody's show, O'Donnell thought he had better cozy up to the town's sheriff. Grinning at the irony of enlisting legitimate lawmen, Allen knew he would need all the help he could get if he wanted to keep his grand new saloon in one piece.

He did not notice the pair of cold hazel eyes that studied him from across the room. Liver Eating Johnson was no one's fool. Although some folks had taken to calling *him* an outlaw, lately, he did not think so of himself. He had lived a solitary life and seen more atrocities than he was able to count.

His heart and soul could not take unwonted savagery, never could, and he had made his point abundantly clear over the last few years. That was why the Crow Indians feared and despised him. Seeing the brutality of one of O'Donnell's strong-arm men earlier, made all of his anger toward injustice rise to the surface.

It didn't matter that Martha Jane brought most of her problems down on herself; Johnson wouldn't stand by and watch her get a beat-down for no other reason than being drunk. Half the men and women in this establishment were inebriated.

No, he thought, as he shuffled the poker cards in front of him. *That was sheer meanness and I mean to keep my eye on things, especially O'Donnell* (who he knew—at an instinctual level—was a crook, despite his fancy clothes) *and his boy Josh, with the stupid, tarnished pocket watch.*

Calling the bet, Johnson settled back in his chair with a smile.

Dixie Monroe gave her horse a savage kick and galloped as fast as she could toward the Atkinson ranch —some ten miles away from Patty's place. She didn't have much opportunity to leave on her own but she had used the excuse that the chickens were running low on feed and lied about her need to go into town.

After promising to fetch back some hair ribbons, grain and the new Sears and Roebuck catalogue, she had buckled a packhorse into its traces and headed out. Once she was out of sight, she planned to drop the wagon and go the rest of the way bareback. She did not intend to return, however. Once she got to the Atkinson's (and hopefully gotten a little cash in exchange for information) she planned on heading to Seattle.

She knew that once the other women learned of her involvement with her (now dead) lover, Alexander Guthrie, she would be cast out, anyway… especially once they heard what she had said about Mr. Pretty

Boy, Matthew Wilcox! Kicking the fat, old horse again, she hollered, "Heeyah!" and used the tail end of her reins on the horse's backside.

The draft horse was blowing bloody foam from its nostrils when Dixie entered the high gates of Atkinson's ranch, an hour and a half later. Some of the buckaroos (who liked horses much more than human beings) walked up and took the poor old horse by the reins, clucking in concern as it shook and its knees knocked in strain.

"What in the hell, Dix?" One of the men turned to her with a scowl. "You bein' chased by Injuns... cuz that's the only excuse I can think of for runnin' a hoss to death!"

Dixie couldn't have cared less about her mount—he was a means to an end. She put her pretty, freckled nose in the air and said, "I was in a hurry, that's all. That horse will be all right. Now, I need to speak with Mrs. Atkinson and Mile's brother... come on! Take me to 'em!"

In fact, the draft horse known as Percy was not all right. Even as Dixie demanded to be shown to Widow Atkinson's parlor, the gelding fell to its knees with a shudder. Then it let out a miserable groan and toppled to the ground with a crash.

"Goddamit! You killed that old hoss! I oughtta make you bury it!" the same, old cowboy snarled.

Dixie sniffed. "Okay—I'm sorry! Just, please take me in to talk to Henrietta. I've got important news about the man who shot her husband, and his boys down!"

Tears filled her pretty, green eyes and she batted her lashes as she added, "I'm in a hurry, though, boys! Please?"

"Show her up to the house, Carl," the older man growled and turned to regard the dead horse at his feet. With a sigh, he walked over to a tall post and grabbed a heavy rope. Now, he had to drag the horse to the bone-yard, which was a place he disliked at the best of times.

Dixie composed herself (and her story) as she walked to the front door. Her escort knocked and they stood waiting until a Mexican woman in a servant's outfit opened it. A few minutes later, Dixie was shown to the parlor, where she told a whopper of a story to ears that were only, too, happy to hear that a scoundrel of the first order was responsible for Mile's fate.

Two hours later; and with twenty silver dollars in her purse, Dixie Monroe was headed by coach, to the town of Walla Walla and a train that would take her on in to Seattle.

"I HATE him!" Chance declared, tossing his hat across the office to land in amongst the cups and saucers on a bureau by the cook stove. Tears filled the boy's beautiful, moss green eyes and he wiped them away with an angry swipe of his right arm.

Sheriff Roy Smithers winced, both at the boy's angry words and at the sound of broken crockery. Standing up, he walked over to the bureau and started picking up shards of glazed pottery from the top of the bureau and the floor. He felt a presence by his side, and heard Chance say, "Sorry, Uncle Roy. I didn't mean to break stuff."

They cleaned up for a minute or two, and then Roy said, "Sit down, son. I want to talk to you about your Pa."

Chance, who seemed to have grown a foot in the three months since Matthew left sat down, glaring defiantly. Roy settled into his chair and stared back at him with kindly eyes. "I know you're mad at him for leaving, Chance. But, sometimes a man needs to find his way back from a bad place. Your Pa was in that bad place after your ma was murdered... a place where he couldn't see any other way to ease his mind than to find the man who did this and bring him to justice."

Chance sat up in his chair. "Well, he should have taken me with him. I loved her too, you know!" The boy's cheeks were beet-red with fury and, for a moment, Roy saw Matthew staring out from those emerald orbs.

"Besides, he just upped and left me and my sister behind. He didn't even say good... goodbye!" Chance started to weep again, although he tried to hide it by glaring toward the far corner of the room.

"I know, son. I think he figured you would pester him about coming along for the ride. Even you gotta admit, he can travel faster without you tagging along, slowing him down..."

Chance didn't disagree, although Roy's logic

couldn't ease the hurt for a thirteen-year-old boy who had lost both parents, almost overnight.

There was a light knock on the door. "Come in!" Roy shouted.

Dicky stuck his head around the doorjamb and held a leather dispatch bag in the air. "Mail just came in, Sheriff," he said.

"Thanks, Dicky. Bring it on in here."

The deputy placed a hand on Chance's shoulders as he passed, and Roy saw Chance reach up to touch his friend's hand. "You stop in and see me and Abner before you head back, you hear?"

Chance nodded, but continued to glare at the far wall. Dicky handed the sheriff the mail packet and blinked in sympathy at the expression on Roy's face. They all missed Matthew—deeply—but the boy's grief was unbearable.

They understood the youngster's anger but as grown men, they also understood Matthew's motives. There was a whine at the door and Matthew's dog, Trickster, poked his head in. Sometime within the last few weeks, Matthew had dropped the dog off in Colville, with instructions for its delivery back to Granville.

The half dog-half wolf had escaped though, and followed its nose to Abby's household. It was a lucky thing he hadn't been shot. Although Trickster was only half wolf, he looked more like the predator species than a dog. Both city-folk and ranchers, alike, wouldn't have hesitated to shoot him down, had he been spotted.

Once Abby and Chance fetched him back to Granville, Matthew's pet spent most of his time between Roy's office and the jailhouse.

"Remember, Chance... stop by the jailhouse before you head back to Spokane. I got something for you." Dicky had made a fine, new slingshot for Chance. He didn't know whether the boy still held an interest, but the deputy thought it might serve well to remind Chance that his pa had laid low many a crooked agent with the same type of weapon.

"I will... I promise." Chance murmured.

Dicky left and Chance got up to pour himself a cup of coffee while Roy perused the mail. Sitting back down in his chair, he started to apologize again for his earlier behavior when he saw the sheriff sit up in his chair with a grunt of surprise.

Roy held a large piece of paper in his hand and even from across the room, Chance could tell that Roy was staring at a WANTED POSTER.

"What is it, Roy?" Chance ventured.

"Well, it's a goddam lie, is what!" Roy snarled.

Standing up, Chance crossed the room and stood behind the Granville sheriff. Looking down at the Wanted Poster in Roy's hand, the boy's mouth dropped open in shock... and fear.

WANTED
DEAD OR ALIVE
For Rape and Murder
Washington State Marshal,

Matthew Robert Wilcox
Considered Highly Dangerous
Approach with extreme Prejudice!
$1000.00 Reward

There was also a rather well done rendering of Matthew on the sheet. Roy figured that an enterprising artist had lifted a photo of Sheriff Wilcox from a book about the Granville Stand-off.

"Roy?" Chance's voice trembled. "You don't think…"

Roy stood up. "NO! There's no way your pa would have raped any woman. The killing part…" he hesitated for a moment. "I'll just have to see what's happened, before I can know for sure."

Roy moved to the hat stand and put his fedora on his head. Then he donned his warmest coat and turned to look at Matthew's son. Putting a hand on the boy's shoulder he said, "Chance, I've got to go find your pa, now. Something… or someone is after him and I think he may need my help."

He noticed that the youngster was fixing to complain or plead to come along and he added, "Now, I need you to head back home to Spokane, okay? I want you and Abby to stay buttoned up at home—don't go to school or hang around outdoors, got it?" Chance's eyes were growing shiny with frustrated tears and he shook his head in denial.

Roy shook the boy's shoulder. "Chance! You've got to believe me when I say that not only do outlaws use family members as hostages, lawmen do it too! One of the first things a U.S. Marshal will do to gain leverage in apprehending a fugitive is seize his family and property!"

"If you stay home, like I ask," the sheriff continued, "I can place a district attorney on your doorstep. This will keep you and Abby safe—at least, for a while, and free me up to find your pa before anyone else gets to him, first."

The look in his Godson's eyes broke Roy's heart and he pulled Chance in to his arms. Hugging him close, Roy whispered, "Just give Dicky and me a little time, son. We'll find your Pa and bring him home, safe and sound. I promise!"

Roy could only cross his heart and pray that he wasn't too late.

THE GOOD DOCTOR

MATTHEW AND LINCOLN TRAVELED THE MILES BETWEEN Patty's place and the town of Walla Walla, slowly. Small, hard flakes of snow were sailing out of the low-lying clouds to the North and the marshal shivered. He had decided to make a cold camp earlier, both to rest his gelding and to let his nerves settle after what had happened the day before. He felt chilled now, though, and he wished for a crackling fire to warm his hands and feet. He acknowledged, with a sigh, that it wasn't only the brisk weather of late autumn but a coldness that was growing in his own soul.

He might have killed men before in his life as a lawman, and seen enough death to satisfy a mortician, but he had never grown used to it. He was uncomfortable over killing the four young cowboys that had accompanied Atkinson on the raid. Despite what they had done, they were too young to die and Matthew worried that his own dark demons had put a sudden and irrevocable end to souls that might have been saved... with time and maturity.

It didn't bother Matthew in the slightest, however, that Miles Atkinson had gone on to meet his maker. He fervently hoped that, even now, Atkinson stood waiting on Purgatory's crossroads and he would, eventually, be forced to turn left toward the gates of Hell.

Matthew had often teased Iris about going to church. He simply couldn't imagine some giant, old man sitting on a golden throne up in the clouds, observing—and judging—his many minions here on Earth. Since his wife had been murdered, however, Matthew found himself wishing for such places as Heaven and Hell. Places where a human being's actions on Earth were judged... and either rewarded ... or punished.

He had no doubt that if Heaven was real his beloved Iris was probably cavorting amongst heavenly horses and celestial cows on weekdays and singing with the angel's choir on Sundays. By the same token, he hoped that if there was such a realm as Hell, Atkinson was even now being poked at and prodded by the devil's own pitchfork!

Sighing, Matthew rubbed at his sore arm. So much had happened yesterday, the bullet that killed little Hildy and passed through her body to graze his left arm seemed like nothing more than a mosquito bite. He had woken up this morning, though, realizing that the bullet wound was more than just a graze.

After peeling off the crusty neckerchief he had used

to staunch the flow of blood, he saw that the bullet had plowed a six-inch long furrow in his upper arm. The wound cut into the muscles as well, which was causing his arm to swell and the fingers of his left hand to tingle and burn. Luckily, Murray had put a small, blue bottle of mercurochrome in his saddlebags, along with clean bandages.

The wound would heal, Matthew knew, but right now, it was aching something fierce. Staring down the road, he wondered how he was going to find Iris' killer. The only thing he could think of was to go back to the prison and search for more clues. Maybe, if he could find that Josh kid's whereabouts, he would find the Irish man as well.

Matthew gave Lincoln's belly a light squeeze. They were walking so slowly the gelding was nipping at weeds growing alongside the road. At his rider's prompt, the horse dropped the weeds that hung from the sides of its mouth and started trotting up the road. Matthew figured it was about thirty miles to Walla Walla. If they made good time, they would arrive back at the prison by late afternoon.

They trotted along for a while, until Matthew's arm throbbed so badly he thought he might faint. Clicking his teeth, Matthew said, "Let's run for a minute, Lincoln... Go!"

The horse snorted and dug his back hooves into the packed dirt. Then, man and horse flew up the road in an easy canter. The gelding's ears pointed forward and Matthew could feel Lincoln mouthing the bit.

Knowing the horse wanted to gallop, Mathew said, "Whoa, Son. Let's not get ahead of ourselves! Whoa..."

Lincoln fell back down into a trot. They were approaching a blind corner and Matthew heard a donkey bray. This caused his horse to crow-hop a little, and Matthew pulled the reins taut. They stopped by the side of the road and waited. A minute later, a tall, skinny man with iron-gray hair and a lantern jaw hove into view, pulling a recalcitrant donkey behind him. "Come on, Lewis, goddammit!" he swore.

The donkey saw the man and large gelding standing on the road in front of him and immediately set all four hooves on the road, pulling the reins of his bridle backwards. The man almost went flying face first, but let go of the reins, instead. Cursing, he shook his leather-burned palms and turned around to face Matthew and Lincoln with a rueful smile of greeting.

"Good morning," he called. "Guess this is all the animal I deserve for only five dollars! Still, for the most part, Lewis is a friendly enough fella. He's just scared of his own shadow!" The man walked forward a few paces and held his hand out to shake. "The name's Lawrence Talbot... Doctor, Lawrence Talbot. How do you do?"

Matthew smiled and stepped down off his horse. "Matthew Wilcox... pleased to make your acquaintance." He made no mention of his status as a lawman, or the star that was hidden in his saddlebag.

The men shook hands and eyed each other in a friendly manner. One never did know what or whom they might meet on the road—friend or foe—but both men were at ease as they seized their animal's reins and moved off the road onto a grassy clearing.

"Where are you headed, Doctor?" Matthew asked after they had settled their mounts down. He was starting a small fire to make a pot of coffee and put a little more medicine on his arm.

Talbot was feeding his donkey a handful of oats, but he turned to the marshal with a smile. "I'm heading out to a pig farm about fifteen miles down the road. I take care of the women who reside there. You know what I mean, I suppose."

Matthew *did* know, and he was thankful that Patty had found a physician who was willing to tend to her whores. Those women were prone to all sorts of diseases and unwanted pregnancies. Some folk might think that a doctor who performed abortions was the very devil... he, himself, would rather those girls be looked after by a good doctor than risk the sharp implement of a traveling huckster.

Matthew nodded. "I do, and I appreciate your efforts, doctor."

Talbot looked pleased, and Matthew continued, "I just came from there, in fact. Patty is good people. There has been a sad change of circumstance, however..."

Talbot took a tin cup of coffee from Matthew with a look of concern and said, "What has happened?"

"I stayed there for a few days after my gelding got scratched up by a cougar. Their man, Murray, took care of my horse, while I helped do some chores around the place. More specifically, Patty asked me to run point on a certain problem she has been having with a cattle rancher named Miles Atkinson."

The doctor looked affronted. "Why, that old bastard! He has been systematically running one family after another off their own properties for a few years now! I didn't realize that he was after Patty's holdings, too."

The marshal nodded. "Well, he's not doing it anymore, Doctor. I killed him and the four other men he rolled in with."

Dr. Talbot eyed the man with whom he was sipping coffee with the new eyes and his heart started thudding hard in his chest. This was one of those times he wished he didn't have to risk life and limb on the open road. You just never could tell whether a stranger was good or bad until it was too late to do anything about it!

Matthew could feel the change in the air as the older man tried to decide whether he was an upright citizen or an outlaw. "Don't worry, Sir. I am a Washington State marshal and I was well within my rights to shoot those men down. They not only shot Patty in the shoulder, they raped and killed her daughter Hildy."

A strange expression crossed Talbot's face but then he glared. "Blast their hides! Patty's a good woman and Hildy is… was a doll! Why did they have to shoot them?"

Matthew shrugged. "Sheer meanness, I suspect. At any rate, I'm glad you're heading there now. Yesterday, it looked to me like Patty's shoulder wound would be all right, but I'm no doctor. I would feel better knowing that you were there to help, if she takes a turn for the worse."

Talbot stood up and tossed the dregs of his cup away. "I had better not dawdle then, Marshal, if my services are required."

Mathew stood as well. "I wondered if I could bother you with a little stich work before you go. Shouldn't take long and I would pay you for your time."

Talbot had heard *that* before but he remembered his oath, even if his pocketbook was as skinny as a willow switch.

Staring at the marshal, the doctor said, "Sure. Let me have a look-see."

Matthew peeled off his shirt and the clean cloth on his upper arm. Talbot whistled. "Why, that wound never would have healed up proper without sewing! Sit down, please."

Matthew sat while the doctor pulled a large black case from one of the bags on his donkeys back. Then he knelt down and poured some foul-smelling concoction over the injured flesh. The marshal gritted his teeth against the fire as the liquid soaked into his skin and then the doctor started sewing.

"There you go... I think you only need a few stitches and the rest of the flesh will knit itself closed. Still, it's a good thing I could help, because you were really risking infection with this wound gaping open... what's this?" the good doctor cried out in exasperation.

He had apparently found the second bandage that was still stuck on the back of Matthew's neck.

"Well," Matthew winced as Talbot lifted the crusty cloth and snorted in disgust. "Remember that cougar I mentioned... he took a swipe at me before he decided to chew on my horse, instead."

Talbot lifted the day-old bandage and threw it into the fire. "Well, both of these wounds need tending to, Marshal. Just let me do my work."

It sounded to Matthew as though the doctor thought he would not be compensated for his time and medicine, and Matthew held up his right hand. "Hold on a minute, Doctor."

"What!" Talbot complained, and stood back as Matthew got to his feet and rummaged around for a minute in his money-belt. Handing the doctor two twenty-dollar bills, he smiled and thanked the man for his help.

Talbot eyes gleamed and he grinned in return. "Too many folks these days think that doctors can live on air alone, Marshal. It reminds me of a couple of men who came along about two months ago. One man, a young simpleton, said the other was attacked by a bear... and would I come and help?"

Talbot ran a warm washcloth across the still painful cat scratch on Matthew's neck. "I admit to feeling ashamed by what I did, then, Sir. I took one look at the man's wounds and knew that they weren't bear claws— it was a dog bite... or maybe a wolf that almost tore the man's nose from his face."

Matthew sat up straight and his nerves tingled with excitement. His painful wounds forgotten for the moment, he listened as Talbot continued his story.

The doctor sighed. "Well, thinking the two men were at worst a couple of liars and at best a couple of crooks, I asked them for a lot of money for my services...more than was proper, really. But I've been wanting to get out of town for a while now... maybe even out of this state and open up a nice new practice, in a new place... get a fresh start." The doctor's face was red with shame and self-loathing.

"Did you happen to catch the crook's names?" Matthew asked through numb lips.

"Yeah... kind of. The older man's name was Earl, I'm sure, and the younger fella was named Josh. Those boys sure proved my suspicions correct, though. No sooner did I patch Earl's face up, he knocked me over the head and tied me up in a closet!"

Matthew turned to look the doctor in the eye. "You didn't happen to catch which way they were headed?"

Talbot stared at Matthew for a moment and said, "Do you know these men, Marshal?"

Matthew shook his head. "Not personally, no. But if my suspicions are correct, I think my wolf, Bandit, did the damage to Earl's face... after the man killed my wife, Iris."

The doctor saw the marshal's wide, green eyes and the grief that lingered in them still. "I can't be sure, Sir, but the young one stepped back in the room after I thought they were gone for good. He was muttering to himself about not wanting to go to Billings, Montana."

Matthew's lips peeled back in savage smile. Somehow, through sheer luck or maybe, God's providence, he had found his clue. He didn't know who Earl was or why he had killed Iris, but he aimed to find out... right before he filled his body full of holes.

THE BIG SHOW

Allen stood at the window and gazed at the activity below him on the streets of Billings. It was unbelievable. A huge wagon train was moving like a parade through town. There was everything from small buggies to huge covered wagons, fancy broughams, and run down whiskey wagons. There were rodeo clowns and mimes, actors dressed up as all manner of western characters, and street vendors selling caramel apples and popcorn.

Many of the wagons were gaily painted and some barred, like patty wagons. Wild-looking Indians cavorted inside them brandishing tomahawks and beating authentic-looking war drums. A large, flatbed wagon carried a number of dancing girls, who swept their ruffled skirts up in unison, giving the cheering crowds a glimpse of forbidden pleasures.

It seemed to O'Donnell that half of the town's citizens had come out to cheer and gawk at the strange assembly. The town father's had decided to build a new, covered barn for Buffalo Bill's Wild West show. They figured that not only would this large, new building shelter this season's smash hit, but it would also serve in the future as a meeting hall, and a rodeo grounds.

Train car after train car had arrived daily, disgorging horses, cattle, sheep, dogs and even an exotic zebra, to the fascination of the watching citizens. More than one fistfight had erupted in debate over what manner of creature the zebra was or if it was just a pony, embellished with black and white stripes.

O'Donnell's saloon had been filled to over-flowing for the last two weeks, and he could only smile and rub his hands together in greedy delight. Staring at the crowds that milled below him, though, he was beginning to wonder how he was going to house the growing masses. He had already suffered losses that were beginning to cut into his profit margin. Three nights ago, an angry gambler had picked up a heavy glass pitcher and shattered one of the saloon's largest and finest marbled mirrors.

A week earlier, a frustrated patron had taken offence at one of the whores... an attractive but none too bright blonde, out of Missouri. Before he was through, the cowboy had torn two of the whore's rooms to bits and injured the prostitute... to the point she might never work again. The building repairs and doctor's bills stole that week's income.

He hoped that his idea of opening four beer gardens

inside the new building would ease the burden on his establishment. Maybe, if the citizens got drunk enough outside of the saloon they wouldn't bother coming inside the Little Haymaker to wreck additional havoc. It was his product, after all, so his pockets would still feel the weight of success.

A gaudy, painted wagon approached now and Allen could hear the crowd roar. A tall man with a fancy white suit and long, golden brown hair was standing at the front of the wagon, bowing and throwing candies to the children in the crowd. There were two women with him, standing in back. Glancing down at one of the flyers that had been circulating all over town for the last two weeks, O'Donnell realized that he must be looking at the sharpshooters, Annie Oakley and Lillian Smith.

They were both attractive women, if a little care-worn. The female facing Allen was dressed properly with a high collar and a fashionable, feathered hat. *Annie Oakley*, he thought. The other woman was dressed more provocatively with a red satin, low-cut blouse. As O'Donnell watched, she twirled around and shook her bosom at the men in the crowd... who crowed appreciatively.

The show was scheduled to start tomorrow afternoon, but O'Donnell could already hear a crowd gathering downstairs in the bar. The saloon was open for business and he could only pray that it would still be standing by tomorrow's opening performance. *Oh well,* he mused. *The girls are ready and waiting, and we have enough booze to fill the Missouri River. Bring 'em on!*

He smiled as he sat at his desk but within moments, his smile fell flat. *What's wrong with me?* he wondered. *I should be riding high on my success, not wallowing in the muck!* Nevertheless, life as a respectable business-owner was starting to pall. All the shiny trappings of wealth were just that... trappings, and as time wore on, he felt more and more like a fraud.

He was smart enough to know that a mogul must remain aloof—far above his cronies—or he risked being-taken advantage of. Still, he was lonesome. He missed some of his pals—long dead now—that he had hung around with on the docks in Seattle. It was rough company but it was his... and valid.

This charade was taking a toll, both on his nerves and his feelings of self-worth. There were eighteen men in his employ now, and each one of them either, stuttered in fear when he spoke to them, or gazed at him out of the corners of their cold, calculating eyes. Much the way, he acknowledged, he used to assess his old boss (and new namesake), Patrick Donnelly. At least Patrick had a couple of friends... Freddie Marston and Dan O'Reilly. He, himself, had no one.

The society he had so desperately sought, here in Billings, finally welcomed him in to their circles. But, like nervous deer in the presence of a predator, they kept him at a distance; showing through the disdain of a lifted eyebrow or a chill shoulder that they knew him for what he really was... a wolf in sheep's clothing... a crook and a low-life dressed up in fancy clothes.

He couldn't even enjoy his beautiful new home. Although his staff was impeccable and did everything he asked them to do, they were not capable of making him feel that he belonged there. He would climb into his giant, four-poster bed and lie awake at night with beads of nervous sweat soaking the snowy, white sheets. Anxiety and doubt colored his dreams with a dark brush and he would inevitably flee to the only place that felt like home—The Little Haymaker Saloon.

Glancing over at the bed in the corner of his office, he felt the weariness of sleepless nights press down on his shoulders. He was tired... morose, and there was a long night ahead of him. Loosening the tie around his neck, he walked to the door and stepped out onto the balcony. Staring down at young Joey Landraith, Allen made a special gesture.

Nodding in acknowledgement, Joey finished serving up drinks and made his way upstairs to the whore's quarters. There was one whore, in particular, that O'Donnell fancied. She was tall and willowy with long, black hair and bright blue eyes. She was older than the other girls were but still beautiful and quite athletic.

Knocking on Lilly's door, Joey stepped inside the threshold and gave her the boss' orders. Lilly nodded in weary resignation. She would rather screw every stinking cowboy and drunk in the state than have to suffer O'Donnell's attentions. For one thing, he always had to make a rape out of their love-sessions although she gave freely of herself.

For another, after he finished with her sexually, he would always turn her over on her belly and whip her backside, all while he muttering, "That's what you get, Maggie", or "Serves you right, Mags!"

Lilly didn't mind a little roll playing, but the boss' spankings were harsh and... who in Hell was this Maggie, woman? Sighing, and knowing that she had, long ago, sown what she reaped now, Lilly got up from her bed, dabbed rosewater behind her ears and between her breasts and made her way around the balcony, to Allen's office.

SIX HUNDRED AND fifty miles away, Roy Smithers and Dicky McNulty started tracking their friend, Matthew Wilcox. It was not easy, as Matthew had backtracked many times over the last few months.

First, he headed toward Colville and an old miner's cabin he had inherited. Then, he left there and headed back to Spokane where he had boarded a train and traveled on to Seattle. There was no telling what he had done there but the records indicated that the marshal had left the Seattle area within a couple of days and come back to Spokane.

There was a two-week delay, and then Matthew was on the move again... this time to Walla Walla, State Prison. As far as Roy could tell, that was where

Matthew eventually ended up, although by now he could be anywhere.

Nodding in understanding, the sheriff could see why Matthew had gone to the state pen. The prison was a good place to track down an outlaw. God knew he and Matthew had put at least a hundred crooks in there themselves.

But, where was he now... and what about this ridiculous arrest warrant? Roy pulled the warrant from his coat pocket and stared at the bottom of the page. Sometimes, the origin of an issue was typed on the bottom of the page, but not this time. Glaring in frustration, he jumped a little when Dicky said, "What should we do now, boss?"

Roy stared at the diminutive man by his side. Matthew had picked Dicky up like a stray puppy, seven years ago in the town of Wenatchee. He was just a kid of twenty then, and timid because of a severe stutter, but he had grown into a fine deputy over the years. He could shoot the eye out of a bullfrog, and had an unerring knack of tracking down any lost thing—whether it be friend or foe.

Dicky had grown to love his friend and mentor, Matthew Wilcox, and he adored Matthew's family as well. He had truly suffered when Matthew's wife, Iris, was murdered. When he first saw Marshal Wilcox' arrest warrant, he had turned red as a beet and his brown eyes blazed as hot as coals. "I'll be damned if he di...di...did!"

Roy hadn't heard that stutter in years, which just

went to show how upset and appalled Dicky was. Now, looking down at his deputy, Roy said. "We will go to Walla Walla. I have no way of knowing if Matthew's still there but that's where our trails leads, so we have to follow it."

Two days later, once Roy brought in some replacements and made sure that the town of Granville was safe during his absence, he and Dicky boarded a train to Walla Walla, Washington.

ARRESTED!

MATTHEW COULD SEE THE STOCKYARDS ON THE outskirts of Walla Walla, Washington in the near distance. *Finally, I've made it!* he thought, with a rueful smile. After running into Dr. Talbot and finding the one real clue he needed in his search for Iris' killer, he had decided to backtrack to Patty's place.

Although the doctor seemed stout enough, Matthew couldn't abide the thought of him having to walk the seventeen miles to the pig farm (dragging a spooky donkey), when the two of them could take turns riding Lincoln. Not only did he feel the need to repay the doctor's kindness, Matthew wanted to make sure Patty was still okay and getting the best possible care for her injury.

The two men had made good time and after installing Talbot in Patty's guest room, and hugging her goodbye once more, Matthew left again. It was quite late in the day when he rode into town, more like evening than afternoon. Matthew was weary and in need of a bath and a good night's sleep so he found a hotel and ordered a bath tub brought up to his room.

Matthew inspected himself in the mirror and he didn't like what he saw. His hair was clear down to his shoulders and his gray- speckled beard was wild and over-grown. There were shadows under his eyes and he had apparently, lost weight. He glared at his own gaunt reflection. *I need to take better care of myself,* he thought. *I still have a long way to go, tracking down Iris's murderer and once I do, I need to be strong—not skinny as an old wolf and weak with nerves and lack of sleep.*

He took a long bath, shaved his beard off and donned clean clothes. Then, he went downstairs and, after dropping off his dirty clothes to be laundered, sat down in the hotel's restaurant for dinner.

He finished his meal and made his way slowly upstairs to his bed. Then, he slept over nine hours—a fact that truly amazed him when he awoke the following morning. Always a somewhat restless sleeper, Matthew understood that he must have been weary to the bone. Since he was just a boy, the marshal had slept with one ear listening and one eye open. The devastating events of his youth had forced him into a life-long state of hyper-vigilance.

Last night though, his body had said, "Enough!" Shaking his head, and realizing that he felt better than he had in months, Matthew looked up when there was a light tap at the door.

When he opened it, Matthew saw a brown, paper-wrapped parcel on the floor. *Good...* he thought, *my clean clothes.* Taking the parcel back into his room, Matthew nodded in satisfaction. His tattered, dress shirt was white again and sweet smelling. His wool pants had been mended and his socks were clean as well, and rolled into small bundles.

Getting dressed was a pleasure and he took some care in brushing the dust and dirt off his boots and hat. Finally, because he was going to the prison under the auspices of the state marshal's service, Matthew spit on his star and rubbed it into a shine before pinning it on the lapel of his coat. Finally, he headed downstairs for breakfast.

Looking out the window, he saw that snow was falling and Matthew realized, with a start, that was December 14th. His momentary sense of well-being diminished as he recalled Iris' joy at Christmas-time. She had made a habit of sending him and Chance out every year to find the best Christmas tree, and she spent hours decorating the house and even the barn in boughs of holly and wreaths of evergreens.

She would spend months ordering the best presents she could find for her friends and family and the kitchen was always filled with the warm smell of Yule cakes, venison pie, and mince, warm apple cider and fig pudding. She embraced her husband and children with all the joy in her heart, and made a point of filling her home with any orphans she could find over the holidays.

Iris and the other members of her church choir

would ride a sleigh from farm to farm distributing small gifts and food baskets to the poorer citizens around the Granville area, and singing Christmas carols. He remembered seeing her run up to him in excitement one day, her cheeks pink from the chilly air, her large brown eyes bright with laughter and her lips... as warm and sweet as honey when he bent his head and kissed her...

As Matthew stood, still as a statue and lost in his own memories, he didn't see the two sets of calculating eyes that moved from him to the arrest warrant on the table they shared. One man was the prison warden and the other, a Walla Walla city deputy. This particular deputy met with the warden once every week to go over the latest warrants issued in the state of Washington.

It behooved the warden to know who the latest outlaws were, how much danger they posed to the general population of his prison and when he might expect them to darken his doorway. This latest batch of warrants were nothing out of the ordinary—except for one... a state marshal, named Matthew Wilcox.

They were, frankly, amazed that the man was standing right in front of them where the chill, white light from the window illuminated his handsome face like a beacon. Matthew Wilcox didn't look or act, like a criminal. In fact, he seemed to be completely oblivious to anything but his own, dark thoughts. The proof was right there, though, in black and white on the pile of arrest warrants, and the deputy slowly reached down to unsnap the pistol in his holster.

He was of the mind to take the marshal in, right this minute, but the warden (older and wiser than his companion) put a hand out and shook his head whispering, "No, Smitty... not here! There are too many people!"

Deputy Wynn Smith looked around and couldn't help but agree. The dining room was filled with customers, and the warrant said, in bold letters, that this marshal was considered Highly Dangerous! The last thing he wanted to do was get into a gun-battle, with the hard-looking man... especially in a crowded place like this!

"What should we do?" he asked.

The warden, whose name was Samuel Albright, said, "There is a telephone at the concierge desk. Let me go and make a call. I'll have this place surrounded in no time. We can take him out on the street." He stood up, just as Matthew took a step away from the window and headed into the restaurant.

The deputy watched as the marshal tipped his hat to the warden, and then sat down at a nearby table. *That man has a set of cajones,* he thought and then realized that he must have been staring when Matthew Wilcox caught his eye and smiled. "Good morning, can I help you?"

Smitty started and said, "Excuse me! No sir... you just looked familiar to me for a minute, but I see I was mistaken."

The marshal gazed into his eyes for a moment and then said, "Well, have a nice day, Deputy." Then he turned to the busy waiter who had just come to his table with an order pad in his hand.

Smitty turned away, shaking with delayed nerves. *That is one cool customer!* he thought with resentment. The warrant said that Wilcox was a rapist and a murderer, but he was just sitting there—as big as you please! There was a special burden the lawmen in Walla Walla carried, and that was dealing, off and on, with some of the worst scum in the whole state.

The one thing they all had in common, the deputy mused, was their absolute disrespect of the law and total disregard for the men who enforced it. Just looking into Wilcox' cold, green eyes made his blood turn to jelly and his trigger-finger itch!

The warden returned then and said, "Well, Deputy, shall we go?"

Smitty nodded and stood up from the table. Catching Matthew's eye once more, the deputy tipped his hat, and gave a slight wink of scorn. The marshal blinked in surprise but looked toward the waiter who had just arrived with his breakfast.

Matthew wondered what *that* was about but he was so hungry, he fell to his eggs and ham with gusto and forgot all about the deputy's strange gesture. Watching through the frosty windows as the deputy and the older gentleman spoke to another deputy out on the street, Matthew didn't see the five other lawmen who were taking positions up and down the busy thoroughfare.

It wasn't until later, after he had finished his meal, grabbed his bags and paid his hotel bill that Matthew understood the deputy's sardonic wink. He had just stepped out onto the boardwalk in front of the hotel with his bag in one hand and a few dollars in the other (for the stable man who had housed his horse overnight), when he heard a man shout, "Matthew Wilcox, we have you surrounded! Drop your gun belt and put your hands in the air. You are under arrest!"

18

BEHIND BARS

FOUR DAYS HAD PASSED SINCE MATTHEW WAS ARRESTED. After he dropped his gun-belt and put his hands in the air, the deputies who surrounded him kicked him in the back of his knees, dropping him onto the street's cobblestones. Additional boots stepped on his back then, hard-pinning him to the ground, as rough and inquisitive hands frisked his body for additional weapons.

Finally, after cuffing his hands together behind his back, Matthew was hauled upright. He stood facing a crowd of curious by-standers, some of whom stared into his eyes with the feral demeanor of hungry coyotes as gigantic snowflakes drifted from low clouds like elaborate, lace doilies.

The sheriff, a rotund man of middle years, announced in a loud and somewhat pompous voice that Matthew was wanted for the rape and murder of Hildy Hanson and the cold-blooded killing of Miles

Atkinson and four of his hired hands. Matthew felt like protesting his innocence, but he knew that officers were known, sometimes, to use an outlaw's verbal proclamations as fodder; twisting the crook's words into a rope—until a braid of lies and half-truths was long enough to use as a noose.

Matthew allowed himself to be marched down the middle of the street toward the jailhouse. A crowd of citizens, all of whom seemed to think that this public arrest was an excuse for a party parade, accompanied Marshal Wilcox and his arresting officers. Even as he was pushed and prodded by the over-zealous lawmen, Matthew thought about whom to contact, once the dust settled and he was firmly ensconced behind bars. And he wondered, *am I being set up... and, if so, by whom?*

Should he reach out to Patty, or... had *she* been the one who let her grief turn sour with anger and hatred? Some people could not settle their losses until justice balanced the scales, whether the scales tipped fairly— or not. Still, and Matthew shook his head in a swirl of confusion, he had just talked to her yesterday afternoon. She was weary with pain and sorrow, but she had seemed genuinely happy to see him, again.

She was also badly, wounded. The bullet might have been a clean through and through... but it was still a serious injury, which would take time to heal. This meant that even if she *was* on his side, getting her in to town to testify on his behalf might be out of the question.

Did the laconic sheriff out of Victory, Washington

turn the table on him? If so, Matthew figured he must really be off in his appraisal of people, for he would have sworn on a stack of bibles that the lawman was on the up and up. Or—and this seemed the most likely explanation—someone with a grudge and a lot of power and (more importantly) money, from Atkinson's camp had come forward and sworn false testimony against him.

I could call Roy, he thought, but discounted that notion as well. Roy had better things to do than chase after a missing Marshal. Besides, he really didn't want his old friend to take his eyes off the town of Granville and, more importantly, his son Chance and his daughter, Abby.

Maybe I could call on Marshal Adams... Matthew thought. He knew that his boss was upset with him for leaving his duties without forewarning, but he also felt he could depend on his old boss as a character witness, if nothing else.

The crowd that followed them suddenly turned ugly as Matthew heard the words, "Rapist! That man should hang, right here and right now!"

The town sheriff, Bill McCrady, called out, "You all just hold yer horses! This man will be tried by a jury of his peers!"

"Screw that Sheriff! I heard he's a US Marshal... the way it goes around here is, he'll get let off with a slap on the wrist, and you know it!" A short man with an outlandish handlebar mustache stood closest to the deputies surrounding Matthew. His close-set eyes simmered with anger, and Matthew noticed that he held a small notepad in his hands. Something in this town's past had raised the journalist's ire and the little man was using Matthew's arrest to fuel some sort of personal agenda.

Still, it was unprofessional conduct and served to fan the flames of the unruly mass of people around them. *The unbiased press!* Matthew thought in disgust, and then ducked as some sort of missile sailed past his head and landed with a splat on the hat of one of the deputies who clutched his left arm.

"Gawd-dammit, Howard!" the deputy howled. "Knock it off or we'll set you in a jail cell right along with this big 'un here!"

The journalist faded away into the crowd, but the spectators had only gotten a nibble of forbidden fruit... they were incensed about... something, and wanted blood. Fruit, rocks and sticks pummeled Matthew and his escorts as they made their way down the street until, finally, the jailhouse came into view. "Hurry up, boys, before we end up having to hang a corpse!" Two rocks had hit Matthew within the last few second—one so large that he saw stars and his knees grew weak.

Matthew felt a thrill of fear. Mobs were always a concern and one of the hardest things to contain as a sworn-officer. On one hand, a sheriff and his deputies were honor-bound to protect the citizens in their towns... on the other hand, sometimes those same citizens took the law into their own hands and acted as bad—if not worse—than the outlaws who persecuted them.

This was one of those times, and Matthew heaved a sigh of relief as he and the rest of the Walla Walla's city law officers flew through the front door of the sheriff's office. "That damned reporter is really getting on my nerves!" Sheriff McCrady snarled when the front door closed behind them with a resounding bang.

Turning toward the men who still held Matthew's arms, the sheriff said, "Put him in the back cell. I can't keep the nosy-bodies out of this office, but I don't want some assassin coming in here on the sly and taking a pot shot at our wayward marshal, either."

Matthew was hustled down a long hallway with ten cells per side. Many of the cells were occupied, and some of the prisoners had gotten up from their cots and stood staring as he was marched along. "Who you got there, Jonesey... a marshal? No need for a jail cell. Me and the boys will take care of his ass right quick, won't we boys?"

"Shut up, Brian," one of the deputies hollered, clutching Matthew's right arm even tighter.

A few more steps and they were at the last cell, which the deputy named Jones opened with a large set of keys. Matthew was pushed inside, the door was closed and locked and, besides water, which was circulated four times a day and three light but fairly,tasty meals that were shoved under the bars of each cell, Matthew was alone.

There were a few snarled insults and a couple of

hurled objects over the next few days but Matthew's cell was isolated and eventually, he was left in peace. The only visitor he had was Sheriff McCrady, who seemed to take personal offence at the very sight of his latest prisoner.

The first time the sheriff showed up, Matthew said, "I would like to get word of my incarceration to my boss, Marshal Adams, in Spokane."

The sheriff had replied, "First, you can tell me what possessed you to rape and murder that sweet little girl, Hildy Hanson."

Matthew gritted his teeth. "I did nothing of the sort. She was raped by two of Atkinson's men and shot in the back by Atkinson, himself!"

McCrady smiled, but there was no humor in his expression. "Sure," he sneered. "Although a witness told us otherwise... *Marshal.*

Can I place my phone call?"

McCrady shook his jowls. "No! You have to wait until the circuit judge shows up, which will be a couple more weeks." Then he walked away, while the other prisoners hooted in derision.

A couple of days ago, McCrady visited Matthew's cell again. "Tell me, again, why you raped and murdered Hildy Hanson and shot Miles Atkinson and his hired hands." McCrady's demeanor was quite different this time. His eyes were soft with under-standing and his voice dripped with sympathy. If Matthew hadn't been first, a sheriff and then, a Washington State marshal; McCrady's tactics might have fooled him.

Instead, Matthew shook his head and turned to face the wall. The technique McCrady was attempting was known as softening, which, at least, told the marshal that the Walla Walla sheriff was current on his state exams. McCrady clicked in teeth in frustration, hit the bars of Matthew's cell with his Billy-stick and stalked back down the corridor.

Now, Matthew heard footsteps approaching again. He turned over on his cot and faced the brick wall again. He was tired of the sheriff's hostility, and poorly played police procedures and just wanted time to speed ahead, so he could swear his own testimony to the circuit judge and, hopefully, be on his way.

"Leave me alone!" Matthew said, harshly.

"Never, Mattie," Roy Smithers answered.

Matthew's eyes opened wide and he sat up, facing his two, newest visitors. "What are you doing here, Roy... and uh, Dicky?"

"Saw that warrant and thought we'd find out what in the Hell is going on." Roy said.

Matthew grinned. "Didn't buy it, huh?"

"No, Sir!" Dicky said with enthusiasm.

"Can you get me out of here?" Matthew asked.

The Granville sheriff shook his head, "No, not yet. That sheriff out there seems to have it in for you and is insisting that we need, at least, two witnesses to speak for your innocence, before he'll let you out on bail."

Roy took off his hat and scratched at his balding pate. "What did you do to piss him off, Matthew?"

"It's a long story, Roy, but someone is trying to set me up. I wouldn't be surprised if there was some big money at play here, as well." Matthew sighed.

"Well," Roy said. "I don't suppose you have a witness or two Dicky and I could round up?"

Matthew said, "I think so, although no one, alive still, actually saw what happened. Still, if she's up to it, I think that Patty Hanson will serve as a witness. Also, if he can be found, Dr. Lawrence Talbot might be persuaded, if the price was right."

Roy lifted an eyebrow. "And where might I find these folks?"

The marshal gave directions to the pig farm and then he asked, "Roy, I appreciate what you are doing, but I've got to ask… how are my children? Are they safe with you gone?"

Roy winked. "I sent both Chance and Abby… and her family, to Amelia's house in Marysville with Abner. They are safe and sound, Mattie. I wouldn't have come looking for you, otherwise."

Nodding in relief, Matthew turned to the small deputy by Roy's side. "Dicky, will you do something for me?"

"Anything, Sir." The young man replied.

Matthew smiled. "Good. While Roy goes out to talk to Patty, I would like you to go to the prison and find out everything you can about a man named Earl Dickson. It's my best lead so far and I was heading there when I was... interrupted."

"I'll go there, right away, Matthew. You can count on me," Dicky said, stoutly.

Matthew, feeling the weight of the hangman's noose slowly lifting from around his neck, and the deepest gratitude to his best friends in the wide world, stood up and shook Roy's hand, accompanied by the muffled catcalls of their captive audience.

LATER THAT NIGHT, Matthew heard footsteps approaching his cell again. Knowing it was late... very late, Matthew sat up and stared into the darkness. Usually, when the deputies needed to come to the back cells after dark, they brought lanterns to light the way. Whoever approached him now, though, did so in utter darkness.

Knowing that something was wrong, the marshal stood up and made his way around to the front of his cot, where he had hidden a loose piece of brickwork. It was large enough and sharp enough; Matthew figured it would make a good weapon, if the need arose. Grabbing the shard, he knelt on the floor and waited.

He heard the sheriff whisper, "Go in and grab him, quick!"

The door swung open on well-oiled hinges, and Matthew suddenly realized that there were many men with him in the closed cell. Knowing he couldn't hide, the marshal sprang to his feet with a roar and swung his brick at the closest shadow he could see in the enveloping darkness. The brick sent the man to the floor, but it also disintegrated into powder upon impact with his head.

At once, three more men converged on Matthew, kicking and punching. One of those punches landed on the point of his chin, and the marshal's knees buckled. Then, as he struggled to remain conscious, Matthew heard the sheriff say, "Give him the shot... do it now!"

Matthew felt a sharp sting in the back of his neck and he knew then, that despite Roy's best efforts, he had just lost complete control over his life. He made one final effort to break free, but then his eyes closed and he sank to the floor with a sigh.

19

HENRIETTA

HENRIETTA ATKINSON WATCHED AS THE STATE MARSHAL was hauled, facedown, out of the jailhouse. Four stout ward attendants carried the man by his legs and arms while the psychiatrist, Dr. Avery Thompson, supervised from a safe distance. The doctor, who worked for the Eastern Washington State Hospital for the Insane in Medical Lake, had been warned of his newest patient's violent nature.

Henrietta smirked with satisfaction. Although that fat little toad, Sheriff McCrady had come running to her earlier that day, croaking about how another sheriff named Roy Smithers was in town, and was, apparently, determined to get Miles's murderer out of hock, she had other plans. *No one... and I mean* <u>*No One*</u> *can just walk away from killing my dearest Miley, my king!* She mused, silently.

Henrietta had married the cattle rancher over thirty

years ago, when she was a wealthy but rather homely sixteen-year-old girl. They had had a storybook romance throughout their many years together (or so *she* thought) and the shock of losing her husband had pried apart what little remained of wits, long ago, unraveled by bouts of acute hysteria and schizophrenia.

When she was nineteen and had just lost the first of her many miscarried babies, Henrietta started hearing voices inside her head. She didn't know, however, that the conversations she was party to were only inside her mind. Feeling shunned and left out, as she so often did when she was a young and socially awkward teenager; Mrs. Atkinson lashed out at her husband and the household staff.

Demanding to know who was talking to her and why the gabby perpetrators would not show themselves, Henrietta presented the first manifestations of what would become a life-long illness. Not knowing what the crazed lady would do next, the astounded maids used every excuse they could think of not to enter Henrietta's rooms, for when they did, the lady ranted and raved, throwing dishes and glassware and howling like a banshee.

When no amount of sedatives could calm the frenzy in her mind, Miles was forced to have her committed— at first to a local nunnery and later, at the splendid new lunatic asylum in Medical Lake, Washington. She underwent numerous procedures, including shock and insulin therapy, freezing showers and heavy dosages of calming opiates.

Sometimes these therapies helped, at least, temporarily. She was brought home, pronounced cured and spent most of her time either languishing in her rooms or mooning about the garden.

Relapses were inevitable, however. A month or two might pass in relative peace, then she would become hyper-alert and suspicious. She started at any sudden noise and grew more and more paranoid about the hapless maids who tried to help her. Finally, convinced that one of the younger and prettier maids in her employ was trying to poison her, Henrietta waited behind her closed bedroom door one morning with a long, butcher knife.

When the girl (who was not trying to poison her, but *was* having a passionate affair with her husband, Miles) entered the room with a lunch tray, Henrietta flew out from behind the door and sank the knife into the girl's back.

Miles was fit to be tied. On one hand, he loved his poor, sick wife. Although she had never been a raging beauty, her dowry had enabled him to fulfill his dreams. In addition, (at least, when she was sane) her wits were sharp, and her sexual appetites keen.

It was Henrietta who had urged Miles to take what he wanted—to expand his kingdom, so to speak, no matter what or who stood in the way. (It never occurred to Atkinson that when his wife spoke of expanding his kingdom, her words were not rhetorical.

She actually *did* consider herself a queen and Miles her king—especially when she entered some of her more, manic episodes.)

There were too many witnesses, though, to his lovers' brutal murder. A month later, in the spring of 1887, Henrietta was put in a straitjacket and taken, by train, to the Eastern Washington State Hospital for the Insane. Once there, she was subjected to more electro-shock therapy, water therapy and a new procedure... the removal of all her teeth.

Alienists around the world had become convinced that infections of the teeth and jaw were the culprits of madness and many mentally ill patients were relieved of their ivories. Another procedure that had gained favor over the last few years was the lobotomy. A doctor inserted a devise, known as a leucotome, under the patient's eyelid and wriggled it about in the frontal lobes, essentially short-circuiting the nerve endings in the brain that caused seizures and violent behavior. *

Henrietta, once inside the lovely brick walls of the hospital was heavily sedated, and strictly monitored by a vigilant staff of doctors and nurses. She was also aware enough to understand that a lobotomy loomed in her future, if she didn't behave herself. She vaguely recalled the little maid—and how red the blood flowed from the knife wound her *other* self, had inflicted. She could hardly reconcile the fact that she... Henrietta Atkinson had murdered the poor serf, although she was also sure that there must have been a good reason for her actions. *

Henrietta, although she still heard strange noises and saw large, horrid shapes looming in her peripheral vision, made sure not to let on to the staff. It took all of her willpower, and a considerable fortune on her husband's part to convince the psychiatrists that she was finally, cured.

She returned home in the summer of 1897, still beset with mad visions, but calmer now with thrice-daily injections of bottled heroin—a marvelous new invention of the Bayer Company. Perhaps it was the medication, and maybe the uneven distribution of hormones in her body finally calmed enough after menopause came and went, but Henrietta enjoyed a couple of years of relative sanity.

Mile's death, however, brought all of her old demons roaring back to life. Their voices whispered, "Hang him! Watch that murdering marshal die!" and she had surely tried to make that happen. The intro-duction of another sheriff, though and the possibility of witnesses to what had happened at Patty's farm that day put a stop to her devilish dreams. Therefore, Henrietta did something else—something that had been done to her so many times by now, she had lost count.

She contacted the Bughouse in Medical Lake, via Sheriff Bill McCrady. After paying McCrady five thou-sand dollars, he had done as she wished and told the doctors that a mad man was in his custody... and would they please help, for the man was huge and powerful and had murdered no less than six innocent people in his latest fit of lunacy.

Now, Henrietta Atkinson grinned as she watched the marshal's limp body being stuffed into the back of a closed carriage for transport to the state-car she herself had paid for on the next northbound train.

"There!" she murmured. "I bet that one of those white-coated doctors in the hospital will be more than happy to perform a lobotomy on you... for enough cash. That's what you get for killing the king!"

MATTHEW SWAM UP through syrupy layers of consciousness, slowly...painfully. The back of his head felt caved in and the pain was so sharp, so intense, he felt waves of nausea back up behind his throat. Feeling the need to vomit, he tried to sit up, instinctively putting his hands over his mouth lest he soil himself.

But, his hands wouldn't move. Bewildered, he groaned and tried to rouse his fists to usefulness but the only movement he seemed able to perform was to move his elbows, slightly, like the wings of a chicken.

His heart started pounding with fear, which caused the pain in his skull to intensify—he felt like he was a boy again, listening to the rhythmic pounding of Indian drums, as he fished along the shores of the Kettle River. A tear dripped from the corner of his eye. He was grievously, wounded... more importantly, he was trapped!

He tried to open his eyes but they kept drifting closed again, as if lead weights anchored his lids. Another wave of vertigo swept over him and he gritted his teeth. "Hel... hello?" he croaked. His tongue felt thick and another jolt of fear coursed through his body. It seemed as though he had been sick for a long, long time, and in the process had forgotten how to talk.

Trying again, Matthew said, "Hello. Is anyone there? I can't see and I can't mo... move!"

He heard a scuffle of footsteps and heard a male voice say, "Ah ha! The patient is back among the living!"

"Who is that? Wh... where am I?" Matthew turned his head back and forth on a pillow that was probably soft, but felt like stone under his skull.

"Mr. Wilson, my name is Dr. Avery Thompson. I am a doctor of psychiatry and you are in the Eastern State Hospital for the Insane in, Medical Lake."

Matthew shook his head. "No!"

The doctor smiled. "No what, Sir?"

The patient struggled a bit and then stilled with a sigh. "I meant to say that my name is not, Wilson. My name is Matthew, uh... Wilcox. Marshal Matthew Wilcox."

Thompson smiled. "A marshal, you say? My goodness!"

Matthew tried to sit up. "Why can't I see... what has happened to me? WHY CAN'T I MOVE?"

"Steady on, now." The doctor tightened the straps that held the patient firmly to the gurney. "Nurse!

Bring in another ampule, please... 10 milligrams, this time!"

Looking down at the patient, Thompson tried to be kind rather than disgusted and appalled by what the man had done. Still, it was a struggle. Many of the poor creatures he had sworn to help were their own worst enemies but peaceful for the most part. This one though... he grimaced in distaste.

"Mr. Wilson, you have been brought to us by concerned citizens from the town of Walla Walla, Washington. You have been found guilty of rape and murder and, after thorough investigation, I have diagnosed you as a dangerous and violent lunatic. You have been given a strong opiate and, at this moment, you are in a straitjacket. That's why you're finding movement difficult."

Matthew, whose eyes were covered by a thick, black rubber mask shook his head and bellowed inarticulately.

The doctor hollered, "Nurse, quickly please!"

Matthew shouted out in rage and denial. The fog of the last two days was starting to lift. The abduction from the jail cell, being clocked in back of the head by one of his over-zealous captors, a long train ride... the drugs.

"You can't do this to me!" he shouted.

To which the doctor, being five thousand dollars richer than he was two days earlier replied, "I'm afraid I can, sir. The papers are signed and the staff agrees that a lobotomy will do you a world of good. Just think, one little procedure and your desire to hurt other people will simply vanish! Ah, thank you, nurse. Just hold his arm down... there. Very good...."

Then Matthew felt a tiny pinprick, and knew no more.

TRUE COLORS

ALLEN O'DONNELL AWOKE WITH A CRASHING HANGOVER and a grin. He stared at the ceiling for a moment and heard the sounds of busy commerce going on in the streets outside of his saloon. He licked his teeth and grimaced... his mouth tasted like the inside of a chamber pot. Turning his head, he saw the three girls who had accompanied him to his office late last night, sprawled like dead ducks all over the room. In the cold light of day, they looked old, worn out and used up.

Still, Allen acknowledged, he felt good—really good. He had finally stopped banging his head against the impenetrable walls of Billing's high society. Thinking back on the way he acted when he first arrived in town, Allen shook his head in self-disgust. He had suspected, even then, that his vague dreams were never going to work out. Although he had more money than most of the wealthy citizens in this frontier town, he was still considered nothing more than trash, and was avoided like the plague by the very people whose friendship he had so desperately sought.

Well, he sneered. *Not, anymore!* The change in his attitude had occurred during the Wild West show, which had just recently left for Portland, Oregon. Buffalo Bill and his crew stayed far longer than anticipated because of a series of blizzards that had descended in January, covering the train tracks and making travel next to impossible. Since many of the audience members were just as stranded as the cast, the show had continued, unabated, into late February,

Allen's business thrived during those long, winter months, even as other businesses in Billings suffered from the heavy snows. Night after night, the dance hall was filled to capacity. When his own, dancing girls grew weary, some of the more liberal entertainers in the Wild West show stepped in. There were plays and reenactments, sometimes, and impromptu shooting matches between Lillian Smith (who was a most-accomplished flirt) and local marksmen.

The place overflowed with fur-trappers and soldiers; lean and hungry farmers, merchants, and tame Indians from both the Crow nation and the Blackfoot reservation. Although Allen's finest hooch disappeared rapidly, he had planned ahead and brought in enough rotgut whiskey, wine and kegs of beer to sink a ship, despite his accountant's nervous squawking.

The Little Haymaker took a beating, though. Every night, as the boisterous patrons grew intoxicated every beautiful thing within the building became a target. Mirrors and chandeliers were considered fair game and the polished brass spittoons were used as privy pots. When they overflowed, the walls and hidden corners became the next, best choice, as no one wanted to go outside to freeze in the blowing snow and ice.

At first, ever mindful of his precarious status in town, Allen did what he could to fight the citizen's assault on his fine establishment. By the fourth week however, he gave up in frustration. The doors opened every morning at nine and stayed open until 2:00 am. There simply was not enough time in the day to keep the filth at bay.

Now, the black and red flocked wallpaper sagged like ragged, filthy skirts, the pretty marbled mirrors were nothing more than shattered shards and the whole place stunk like an outhouse. Most of the walls were riddled with bullet-holes and half the windows were boarded up. The restaurant had closed its doors two months earlier due to a lack of fresh food and an over-abundance of rats, and the felt-topped poker tables were scorched with burn marks and sticky with spittle.

The general odor of his saloon was rift with *more* than actual dirt. A certain sharp malcontent had entered the double-doors over the last few months, as well. Every man in his employ was run ragged trying to keep the masses from throttling each other. Even life-long friends grew bored and murderous once the snows set in. Local farmers, who worked together in harmony every spring and summer, grew hot with banked coals of resentment and fury and set about to killing each other that winter.

The whores were acting out as well. Being cooped up together like a querulous brood of chickens caused fistfights and hair-pulling sessions on a daily basis, to the amusement of the bored bar patrons. A firm hand...the *very* firm hand of Allen's head bouncer Josh, in fact, quelled the women's wrath.

The young man seemed to thrive in the head-cracking business and he had no qualms, whatsoever, about using his fists to make a point. He only hit O'Donnell's whores where the marks wouldn't show— like the ribs or the cunny. Still, after he hit Madam Goldie so hard one morning, three of her ribs broke; she stole the rest of her girls out in the middle of the night and disappeared forever.

It was easy enough to replace the prostitutes, but the quality of the goods suffered, greatly. The women who replaced the missing whores were of the pig farm variety, but most of the customers didn't seem to mind, or even notice. For one thing, they were cheaper and for another, they seemed willing to endure all manner of depravity, unlike Madam Goldie's girls who held much higher standards of behavior.

Now, after only five months in business, Allen's' beloved saloon was a seedy, sad affair although he continued to make money—hand over fist. At first, during the establishment speedy decline, Allen attempted to stay above it all. He ensconced himself in his upstairs office, and issued orders from above, like God. He paid whole crews to come in and wash the place down every morning and he paid thousands of dollars on repairs.

He still sought acceptance from the town's elite at that point. But, despite all his efforts, he was rejected at every turn. For the first time in his life, Allen O'Donnell, aka Earl Dickson, knew true despair.

He stopped going to his new home entirely, and put it on the open market. It sold with unrealistic (and unseemly) haste. Allen had no doubt that a consortium of rich men had somehow pooled their resources and bought the outlandishly expensive property with the sole purpose of denying *him* access to that stately and *exclusive* part of town. Allen didn't mind losing the house, but those final snubs sent him into first... a two-week drinking spell, and second... total rejection of Billing's high society.

If that's the way they want it, he remembered thinking, *that's just what they'll get!*

From that moment on, Allen reverted into his old self. He let his hair grow out again, and shaved off the thick, ponderous mutton-chop whiskers he had so carefully groomed. He lost the pretentious monocle and stared out at the world through angry, blood-shot eyes. He stopped smearing pancake make-up on his scarred nose and didn't care when his fine new clothes grew rank and soiled.

He also started hanging out with the downstairs boys again. Once he allowed himself to simply, *be...* he felt their acceptance wash over him like warm, healing waters. He took an active part in running the saloon and was hauled upstairs as drunk as a sailor almost every night. He lost a fortune in the gambling room and used his whores as he liked… savagely and often.

Lately, he had taken to doing something else with his spare time. He still felt the sting of rejection although he affected a self-satisfied smirk in public. Three times, he had asked to walk out with one of the eligible young women in town and all three times, he was rudely put in his place, even though he could have bought their papa's properties four times over without blinking an eye.

Only one out of the three girls even attempted to be courteous when she turned him away and for her kindness she, alone, was spared. The other two girls and their families suffered his wrath. Once Allen had chosen his latest target, he and his boys would don black hoods and exact vengeance upon the hapless victim. So far, he grinned with pride, he and his crew had beaten up on all of the girl's fathers, and one of the girl's mother, as well.

There was always enough time between the attacks to confuse the city police, and even under their hoods, the men's faces were disguised. Sometimes they stole the victim's valuables but just as often, their purses and wallets were left intact. In addition, Allen had instructed his men to never, ever utter a sound. That way, not only did the victim suffer fear and pain but the additional anxiety of not knowing whom or why they were being targeted.

Despite the officer's best efforts to solve the chilling crimes, the attacks continued through the last few months of winter. More than one drunk had been hauled in for questioning but no one, yet, knew whom the perpetrators were.

Now, as Allen stood at his window looking down at a herd of longhorns wading through the muddy streets, he smiled in satisfaction. The devil was getting his due. Last night, as one of those rude, snobbish girls walked home alone from a jaunt through the city park, Allen and his men had surrounded her and forced her into an alley. Once there, they de-flowered her and then disfigured her pretty face so she would always be looked upon with scorn and horror.

They left her alive, barely, and now Allen couldn't wait to hear news of the latest attack. He would make all the appropriate sounds of sympathy but, inside, he would be laughing with glee. So far, he and his boys had escaped detection, but he figured they should lay low for a while. Although he paid his cohorts handsomely, a couple of them couldn't hold their liquor and had big mouths. He wondered if it might be better if he arranged for their early demise, as well.

Striding to the door, he stepped out onto the balcony. "Joey, send up some coffee, will ya?"

The young man, who didn't seem nearly as glad to be working behind the bar as he once did, nodded and shouted, "It'll be right up, sir!"

Allen stepped back inside his office. "Hey, bitches! Wake up, and get out of here... NOW!"

The three whores stirred and yawned, blearily. One of the girls turned over and burrowed into her pillow as if she thought to catch a few more winks. O'Donnell took four long strides and planted his bare foot into her ribcage.

"Aieee!" she yelped and scrambled to her feet, tears of pain leaking from her eyes.

The two other girls stopped and stared, and Allen screamed, "I said, get outta here before I put all three of ya in an early grave!"

The girls scampered out of the room and Allen sat down at his desk. Turning around to face the baleful morning light streaming in the window, he thought, *Yeah, the boys and I will wait a little while and let the dust settle. But, I have plans for a bunch more of those snoots in town. There's no way they get to disrespect Earl Dickson... I mean, Allen O'Donnell—not without consequences, anyway.*

21

A CLOSE CALL

Roy met Dicky on a crossroad about a mile away from the city limits of Walla Walla. Two days had passed since Roy rented a coach and traveled to Patty's house. As expected, the sheriff had returned with Matthew's witnesses—Patty Hanson and her two sons, Trevor and Lucas were behind him in the coach.

Dicky was pleased with his progress at the state prison. He had found out just who Earl Dickson was and, he knew now, that Earl was one of Patrick Donnelly's henchmen from Seattle. He wanted to show Roy the sketch he had obtained... maybe the sheriff remembered him from that night in the graveyard so long ago.

Lincoln nickered when he saw Roy Smithers. Dicky had gotten Matthew's horse out of hock yesterday, and the gelding had seemed genuinely happy to see him. When Dicky saddled the horse and drew the bridle up over his muzzle, Lincoln made a game of it by lipping the brim of his hat and tossing it, repeatedly, in the corner of the stall.

Roy smiled and said, "Dicky, I want you to meet Patty Hanson and her sons, Trevor and Lucas."

Dicky tipped his slightly chewed hat, "Pleasure to meet you ma'am...boys."

Patty smiled back. "Hello, Deputy. I am sorry about happened to Matthew. He is in no way guilty of murder. If anything, he saved me and my boys." Tears sprang, unbidden, to her eyes. "He tried to save my little girl too but that scoundrel, Atkinson, took her away from me."

Dicky dipped his head in sympathy. "I am very sorry for your loss, Ma'am. I also want to thank you for coming to our aid, despite your injury."

The plump lady dashed a tear away and announced, "Oh, I'm fine. A little sore and I tire easily but I wasn't about to sit at home and let Matthew stew in jail. I would bet my boots that Henrietta Atkinson is behind this whole thing. She's as crazy as a bedbug, ya know."

Roy smiled. "The good news is; Mrs. Hanson and her boys are happy to swear witness to Matthew's innocence, and the sheriff from Victory, William Purcell, is coming in as well—later this afternoon. He will weigh in on what he thinks really happened, and is also willing to speak to Henrietta's mental state."

The sheriff winked. "And there's more good news... Patty's friend, Lawrence Talbot, is a travelling doctor. He apparently ran into Matthew and said that he cared for a man who almost had his face ripped off. The patient told the doctor a bear had attacked him, but Talbot thought it was either a dog… or a wolf bite."

Dicky's brown eyes blazed with fury. Handing his sketch over he said, "Do recognize this man, boss?"

Roy peered at the rendering and recalled the man who had stabbed him in the back with a knife, long ago in Potter's Field in Seattle. Nodding, he answered, "Oh yeah, I do. This was one of Patrick Donnelly's men." Staring down at the name scrawled under the picture he added, "Guess, old Dickson carried a grudge."

The sheriff pursed his lips, "The doctor also told me that this crittur might look a tad different now. Guess when the wolf…" he paused for a moment, remembering Bandit with grief.

He continued, "Guess when it attacked, he almost tore the man's nose clean off…"

"Good for him," Dicky breathed.

Roy nodded in agreement. "Yes, but the doctor patched him up. Said, there wasn't much left of the cartilage, so his face might look very different from what we remember." Grinning, he added, "He also said that Dickson and a young, simpleton named Josh were heading into Billings, Montana."

"Now, Matthew has a good place to look for Iris' murderer, and we have our witnesses to get him out of jail. Let's head into town and visit with him for a while. I hope that we can get him out of lock-up by evening. I am sure he'll be anxious to be on his way."

They headed in to town and arrived at the jailhouse about an hour later. Patty was quite weary but she insisted on talking to the Walla Walla sheriff. She was offended and terribly frightened for the marshal. Her sons helped her down out of the coach and she said, "Who knows. Maybe we won't even need Purcell to testify." She muttered as she made her way slowly into the sheriff's office/jailhouse.

McCrady wasn't at his desk when they stepped inside. The only man there, besides an oldster who was feeding the prisoners in the back bell block, was Wynn Smith. Looking up, the deputy frowned and said, "What are *you* doing here?"

The words weren't spoken rudely, but in genuine confusion. Roy felt a thrill of alarm and said, "We're here with three witnesses to Marshal Wilcox' innocence, just as promised."

Smith scratched his head. "Why, he's gone, sheriff… transferred out of here, last night."

"What do you mean—transferred?" Sheriff Smithers barked.

Smith shuffled through some papers on his desk and said, "Says here that Matthew Wilcox was admitted to the Western Washington State Hospital for the Insane. He was committed by Henrietta Atkinson and the transfer papers were signed by my boss, Sheriff Bill McCrady."

Patty Hanson sniffed and said, "What did I tell ya, Sheriff? That Henrietta is as crazy as they come. This is revenge, pure and simple!"

"The hell you s…s…say!" Dicky's stutter showed itself as the news registered. No lawman was unfamiliar with his territories Bughouses. Asylums were often a far worse place for a criminal to land in than any jail. "Mr. Wilcox isn't crazy!"

Wynn Smith carefully placed his hands on top of his desk. Not only had these two Spokane County officers provided witnesses to Mr. Wilcox' innocence, they looked more than willing and perfectly capable of taking their displeasure out on him—right this instant.

In truth, although Marshal Wilcox had scared the tar out of him last week in the restaurant, he had proven a cooperative and courteous prisoner over the last few days. Once Sheriff Smithers and his deputy showed up, Wynn was more than ready to concede the fact that he and his boss were wrong in arresting a man who had, quite possibly, been set-up.

He had heard rumors about that crazy Atkinson woman. Wynn's own sister had done some service work out at the Atkinson ranch about three years ago, and told him that old Henrietta was as loony as a woodpecker bird. Still, when his boss Bill McCrady, said that Wilcox was being committed, he had shrugged and taken the information at face value.

Now though, staring into Sheriff Smithers angry blue eyes, Wynn was having second thoughts. He hadn't really put Henrietta and Marshal Wilcox' fate together in his mind until now, and these two fierce-looking lawmen looked so shocked and horrified, he felt ashamed of himself for going along with McCrady's plans.

"I'm sorry, but I just got here myself. I didn't know

about what happened to your friend until this morning and I couldn't have done anything about it, anyway! That was Sheriff McCrady's call."

"Well, where is he?" Roy snarled.

Wynn Smith felt another thrill of alarm. A couple of days ago, McCrady had taken him aside and said he was taking the wife and kids on a vacation to Portland... or maybe Seattle. (Even then, that had seemed like a strange thing to say. He had teased McCrady about it, although his boss did not seem amused...only in a big hurry and, oddly, nervous.) His own boss, Wynn realized now, had acted like a criminal and he wondered, suddenly, just how much money McCrady had been paid to have a Washington State Marshal falsely committed.

Sitting upright, Deputy Smith said, "I am sorry for what has happened. The sheriff is out of reach but I can let you use our telephone to call the admitting office in Medical Lake. At least the staff will be aware that the Marshal is being falsely committed. If you like, you can also call the marshal's office in Spokane."

Roy glared for a moment longer, and then he sagged with relief. Walking around the desk and sitting in the chair the deputy just vacated, Roy set about trying to stop what was about to happen to his oldest and dearest friend, Matthew Wilcox.

MATTHEW OPENED his eyes and realized that the thick,

rubber mask was, finally, being removed from his upper face, although now his mouth was being taped shut. He jerked his head back and forth, grunting with anxiety, but the hands that held him bore down on his head with terrible force.

A familiar voice murmured, "You are only making things harder on yourself, Mr. Wilson. Just lie still… it will all be over soon."

Matthew's mind was awhirl with confused thoughts and images. He felt the heroin in his body moving like a slow but powerful freight train in his blood stream. One part of him wanted another shot. The heavy opiate obliterated all of his anger, remorse and sorrow and, for the first time since Iris died, he felt… at peace.

Still, a tiny part of his mind screamed out in alarm. *Matthew, wake up! Fight this!* It howled, but the drug silenced that whiney, tiresome voice, as well as the bitter knowledge that the love of his life was truly gone.

He felt the familiar pinprick in his upper arm again and settled back to wait for the bliss to carry him off. Then, he felt a strap tighten across the top of his forehead. His eyes opened, briefly, but the heroin closed his lids. He sailed away, lost on an opiate sea, with only vague and indiscriminate memories to keep him company.

Suddenly, he heard a cacophony of voices. "Stop what you're doing right this instant!" a voice bellowed. Matthew shook his head, fitfully. Something was in his right eye and he blinked, frantically, against the pain.

He heard the rude voices again. Someone was yelling and a woman was weeping in terror. Then, one voice registered in his mind. "Get that thing out of his eye, goddammit!" *Is that Marshal Adams?* Matthew blinked in bewilderment.

There was a brief, tugging sensation and Matthew's right eye bled salty tears. He tried to speak, but he had forgotten about the tape holding his lips shut. Shaking his head in frustration, he moaned. Then he felt the tape peel away from his lips. Two hands cupped his face and he heard his boss say, "Matthew... Matthew, wake up!"

Marshal Wilcox tried to awaken, but the drugs stilled his tongue. Still, the last dose must be wearing off because that infernal pounding pain in the back of his skull was setting up a tortuous tattoo, again. He managed to open his eyes and blink up at his old boss in recognition. He also saw a skinny little doctor and a nurse being hand cuffed and led out of the operating theater.

Matthew's boss stared down at his wayward marshal's face and shook his head. "It was a close call, Matthew. Roy managed to call it in a couple of hours ago, and we moved as quickly as possible, but that little squirt of a doctor was going ahead with his idea of a cure despite the "Lunatic Panic" restrictions, and the necessary majority vote from his superiors.

Adams wiped a trickle of blood from the corner of Matthew's right eye. "I guess someone wanted you out of the picture for good, but you're safe now. Roy and

Dicky are on their way. Do you want me to call your children?"

The younger marshal still wasn't quite sure what was happening, but he knew he didn't want either Chance or Abby to see him like this. Shaking his head, he sighed and said, "No, but can I have another shot?"

22

THE DEN

ALLEN LAY BACK ON THE SILK CUSHIONS WITH A HEAVY sigh. His consciousness floated through the room like a steady stream of smoke; over and around the many couches, cots, pillows and silken alcoves. He hovered above human bodies and watched as the oriental prostitutes coached the other customers into climax... or into sleep. He felt like he was home—and it was eight years earlier, as he frolicked in the poppy dens scattered along the Seattle dockyards.

He remembered that time with fondness, knowing now, that he was in his prime then. He knew who he was and how he fit into the world around him. He was Earl Dickson—Patrick Donnelly's right hand man in the Seattle area and he was good at what he did. The rest of Donnelly's crew looked up to him and Patrick, himself, smiled upon him as an equal and a friend.

Thinking about Patrick made Allen remember

someone else and his euphoric mood dissipated. Margaret Donnelly. Patrick's sister was long gone, but now that he was high, his heart wrenched with grief. Sure, he had used her poorly, but that was under orders from her brother. He'd had every intention of seeking her company again, once Patrick got out from under the threat posed by that Spokane Sheriff, Matthew Wilcox.

Instead, Patrick had gone crazy and killed Margaret and then died himself, at Wilcox' hands. After that, the whole house of cards toppled and fell. The last seven years seemed like one, long confusing dream to Allen as he finally gave in to the poppy and allowed himself a moment to relax and be who he really was.

It *had* been fun, he ruminated... finding Donnelly's booty, getting the ultimate revenge on Wilcox, making himself over into a man of means... but Allen was weary now and heart sore. He had once felt like... maybe not a king, but a prince of the underworld. He had stolen, and killed with the best of them and received a certain measure of respect for his efforts.

Moving to Billings, though, under the guise of a California oil magnate had eroded his confidence. Although, by now, he had gotten his revenge (at least on most of the people who had made public their disdain of him), he could do no more... not without casting the law's sharp, suspicious eyes upon him and his men. He had disfigured three young society girls and cast their families into financial ruin. He had also driven one man to suicide and brought four other men to their knees in fear and shame.

More than once, however, over the last month, the Little Haymaker Saloon played host to the local constabulary and the Pinkerton boys. As far as Allen could tell, the law had nothing on him yet, but their attention was so keen, he knew that his acts of revenge must cease.

Unfortunately, revenge was the only dish he found sufficiently sweet. The rest of life seemed trivial... not even real. Of course, he acknowledged with a sigh, his life wasn't real. He was not Allen O'Donnell from California; he was Earl Dickson from New York City. He was a crook and a drug dealer— not some fancy businessman.

Even his saloon was a façade—a front for more lucrative business dealings like drug trafficking and road agency. At first, Allen was able to pretend. The bright and glittering dancehall was a marvel, and his disguise was impeccable. But, the veneer had rubbed off by now, and his mask had fallen away.

Last month, a new restaurant/tavern had opened up catty-corner from him, across the street from the opera house. It was unpretentious from the outside. A stamped wrought-iron storefront was bolted to the front of a simple wooden structure and a small, gold-gilt, oval sign on the front door read, MacAvey's Diner.

The inside was a different story. The owner, some sort of famous chef from New York City, had spent a fortune on the highly polished oak floors, and adorned the walls with gorgeous murals that mimicked Parisian art, and Italian frescos. There were thirty tables in the restaurant, covered in snowy-white cloth and fresh flowers.

The chef served Angus beef, French snails and fresh salmon. The waiters were immaculate and the service meticulous. The private bar in back sported dark, polished wood paneling and scenes of English lords and highbred hounds hung from every shadowed nook and cranny. Brandy was served in deep, fat-bottomed glasses and ladies sipped the best French champagne from long-stemmed crystal flutes.

From the minute MacAvey's Diner opened its doors, the Little Haymaker suffered the consequences. The town's upper crust fled like rats from a sinking ship, leaving only the riff-raff behind. Allen really didn't mind... gilding the lily every night had become bothersome. What he didn't like was the fact that most of the money in town left along with those who bore it.

Now, the only customers that graced his bat-wing doors were roughnecks, shepherds, cowboys and mountain men and Injuns. There was never a more noisome group and from dawn to well past midnight, the stink of their dirty clothes and rotten breath filled his saloon with eye-watering intensity.

More and more often, lately, Allen found excuses to leave his own establishment. Although many of the higher roads into and out of Billings were still icy or bogged down with early spring run-off, he and a few of his men left most mornings to see what mischief they could find.

Allen shifted on his cot, staring up at the small kerosene lantern that flickered on the ceiling. An oriental girl leaned over him, offering another puff of the long-stemmed pipe smoldered enticingly in her hands. Allen reached into his pocket and found a silver dollar. Nodding in satisfaction, the girl pocketed the coin and placed the stem of the pipe on Allen's lips.

Within seconds, the lantern's golden flicker grew shiny… vibrating with rainbow colors. He fell back on his pillow with a sigh of satisfaction and thought about what he, Josh and another new hire, named Bill Guthry had done about two weeks ago. The memory of it stirred his senses and brought a smile to his lips.

They had ridden out of town at dawn to hunt deer. Allen's storerooms were badly depleted from the long months of winter and some of the hired help had resorted to dining at Allen's competitors. It pissed him off but then, he could hardly complain, when it was either that, or starve for his small army of men.

It had been a fine morning, Allen recalled. Pale blue skies shimmered overhead and random rays of sunlight shone down from the heavens above, high-lighting the distant mountaintops with golden halos. He was feeling fine and listening to Josh and Bill conversing quietly and exchanging bawdy jokes when he saw two young men, leading two heavy-laden donkeys down a distant slope.

"Hold up a minute and shut your yappin'," he said.

Allen and his men came to a stop and watched as the two men reached level ground.

"They're prospectors," Josh whispered and Allen agreed. No other profession, besides pig- skinning, made as much of a mess of the doers than tunneling underground for gold and/or silver. Many miners made camp by a stream, especially those in the lower elevations, but they higher up miners dug, the scarcer the rivers and creeks... and water with which to bathe.

Sometimes—especially if a miner found "color"—he would go weeks on end without a bath. Allen had found this out the hard way, in his very own establishment. Looking at the wide, happy grins on the men's faces, Allen's heart starting picking up speed.

The men were quite young... and brothers, judging the similarity in their hair color and build. They had also struck it rich, from the look in their eyes. The older and larger of the two teenagers slowed and pulled his donkey to a stop. He said something to his little brother who also stopped and watched as Allen and his men approached.

"Allo!" the larger man said, in heavily accented English.

Allen thought, *a swede maybe, or a German.* He called out, "Hello! You speak English?"

The older youth shrugged and waggled his hand. "Little bit. How you do?"

Allen grinned. "We do just fine. We'll do even finer, though, if you give us what you got on those donkeys!"

The young men's faces drew down in alarm. "Nay...

you can't have!" the older boy shouted. The younger of
the two stepped back and it was clear to Allen he was
going for the rifle riding in a saddle scabbard on his
donkey's back.

"Take 'em, fellas!" he howled with glee.

Immediately, Josh pulled his shotgun up and sighted
in on the youngest. He didn't hit the boy but he did kill
the crap out of the donkey. Shot in the face, the animal
squealed in pain and reared up, briefly, before falling
over sideways and pinning the boy to the ground. Josh
aimed again and shot the struggling youth.

"Hans!" the other young man screamed and
fumbled at his hip. Sure enough, under the mud-
encrusted leather coat the boy wore, there was a pistol.
It was strapped down though, and nowhere near ready
to shoot. Allen fired his rifle and the older boy was
dying on the ground before he even had a chance to
draw his gun out of its holster.

Allen and Josh trotted over to where the boys lay
dead, staring up into the robin's egg sky with blind
eyes. Josh got down from his horse and started rooting
through the saddlebags. He muttered, excitedly, and
finally came up with two leather bags filled with gold
dust and nuggets. It was a pretty good haul but nothing
to write home about.

Allen was still breathing rapidly, feeling happier
and more alive than he had in months. It wasn't the
gold, but the feeling of power that made Allen, briefly,
feel like his old self, again. "Stow those bags, Josh and
then we need to hide the bodies. Turning to Guthrie,

he was going to say, "Bill, did you bring a rope?" when he saw that the man was trotting rapidly, away.

"Why you sonofabitch," he growled and lifted his rifle. Sighting down the long barrel, he imagined Guthrie's back as the side of a barn and pulled the trigger. Bill toppled from the saddle even before the blast stopped echoing through the valley.

Although he hadn't counted on killing one of his own men during this adventure, Allen knew that the perfect cover had just presented itself. Now that Bill was done and gone, all Allen needed to do was tell the sheriff that two ruffians had started picking them off, whilst they were hunting. "Lookit what they done!" he would cry, pointing at poor old Bill. "It was self-defense, pure and simple!" God knows, he had heard more outlandish tales, plenty of times, and this bucket of lies would hold water just as good as anything.

It had worked out just as he planned, too. He and Josh rode back into town, two-thousand dollars richer, hauling three dead men behind them on the spare horse and one, surviving donkey. Allen told the sheriff that he and his men were bushwhacked and that old Bill was a casualty of the skirmish.

The sheriff took the tale in stride and the county coroner took possession of the three dead bodies. What Allen didn't know, though, was that his former coach driver, Dave Spiles was watching from behind a post beam in the livery stables.

Spiles had spent most of his life as poor as dirt, and he was seduced, months ago, by O'Donnell's promise of wealth and plenty. There wasn't hardly a day, though, he didn't regret signing on with Allen O'Donnell. The man was a skunk of the first order, and Spiles was too old to put up with his guff.

He had seen too much, over the last few months, of O'Donnell's mad rages and random acts of cruelty. Allen seemed to be especially hateful towards women, and that bothered Dave something fierce. Just before Spiles had spotted his boss and Josh talking to the sheriff out on the street, his friend, Martha Jane Cannary had stopped by for a quick nip.

Although he found Jane to be a bit of a pest some-times—especially when she dropped in and drained his whiskey stores dry without ever bothering to re-pay the liquor, Dave felt sorry for her. If she didn't drink her fool head off every single day and make a spectacle of herself sometimes, in public, Calamity Jane would make some man a fine wife.

Still, she was as sober as a deacon when she had flown in the back door of the livery barn and asked to speak with him in private. That was when she told him about what had *really* happened out on the lonely prairie that morning, while she hunted rabbits. Jane didn't care much for people in general, but she did have a soft spot for youngsters and she had cried when she told Dave about how young and green those two boys were, before Allen and Josh dropped them in their tracks.

She had crept away out the back door again as soon as she spotted Allen and Josh, but Davey stood hidden, thinking about how valuable a nugget of truth was against an enemy—almost as valuable as a nugget of gold, and far less hazardous.

STRONG MEDICINE

MATTHEW AWOKE FROM A NIGHTMARE THAT HIS HOUSE was on fire. Sweat rolled down his naked body as waves of heat enveloped him. His dog, Trickster, was barking hysterically and burning up in the flames. He struggled awake with a shout and tried to open gummy eyelids but beads of perspiration stung his vision. He got a glimpse at his surroundings, though, and thought, *How did I get here?*

He was back home in his cabin. A large sheet of metal lay in the middle of the one-room shack and fiery hot coals glowed like malevolent eyes. Matthew reached up with both hands and wiped sweat away from his sopping face. Peering about, he saw a shadowy figure dancing slowly on the other side of the room and another larger figure pouring a bucket of water onto the coals.

Plumes of steam rose from the floor and Matthew closed his eyes again. Listening, he heard his dog barking outside and a low, chanting from within the room, itself. The voice sounded familiar and he concentrated... trying to place the singsong, foreign words. Suddenly, he knew who was with him in the cabin.

Ann Ferguson stood in the shadows wearing a long, leather dress elaborately decorated with beads, porcupine quills, metal Conchos and bits of feather. She was dancing slowly around the room shaking rattle gourds and singing under her breath. She, too, was dripping with sweat and her hair (normally coiled in a matronly bun) fell in wet shanks down her back.

Her husband, Joseph, stood by the front door with an empty bucket in his hands. He was watching his wife carefully and seemed anxious for her welfare. Matthew looked down and saw that, except for his long johns, he was sitting naked on his own cot. All of the blankets had been removed, and the sheet he sat on was completely soaked with moisture.

"Joseph... Ann, what are you doing?" he croaked.

Ann's voice cut off abruptly. She moved around the bed of hot rocks and leaned over the cot. Peering into his face, she put her hand on his forehead and grinned. "You have come back to us, Mr. Wilcox, and I am glad."

Matthew felt bewildered. "Come back?" His throat was scratchy and he felt weary to the bone, as though he had run a long, grueling footrace.

Joseph moved into Matthew's line of sight. "Hello, Matthew. You've been ill. We found you like this yesterday, and have been trying to help you get better.

Sorry—my wife has a different way than most doctors."
Matthew's neighbor gestured toward the hot rocks and
shrugged. "She said you needed to sweat the bad spirits
out before you could truly heal. I hope you don't
mind…"

Matthew had nothing but the deepest respect for
most Indian cures and potions. Their way seemed a
mite more humane than what white docs were prone
to do for sick folk. Staring up into Joseph and Ann's
faces, he nodded and said, "Thank you for helping me. I
didn't realize how sick I was…"

He shook his head as images of the last couple of
weeks ran through his mind. He didn't remember too
much, but he recalled Roy trying to take him back to
the Imes ranch in Granville, and how he had screamed,
"No! Anywhere, but there!"

He vaguely remembered the long and dreadful trip
to the cabin. He was lying in the back of a wagon, while
Dicky tried to give him a sip of medicine. Matthew
thought that, at one point, he had taken the young
deputy by the collar, shook him violently and
demanded another shot of heroin.

He felt ashamed as he remembered his own,
wretched behavior. Matthew realized now that not
only had he sustained a serious injury—possibly a
cracked skull—when the doctor and his orderlies
seized him from the jailhouse, he had also become
addicted to the medicine they had used to keep him
sedated.

He knew about heroin, morphine and cocaine; and

those opiates' addictive properties, but only as a lawman being trained to recognize the symptoms. Never, in his wildest dreams, did Marshal Wilcox think *he* would become one of those addled souls who would do anything and everything, including theft and murder, to get his hands on more drugs.

Feeling a wave of nausea as the memories coursed through his mind, and realizing he was still as weak as a newborn kitten, he said, "I am so hot... could I have a drink of water?"

Ann turned to Joseph. "Husband, please bring Mr. Wilcox some fresh water, and ask the children to help you take the rocks away. We no longer need them."

Joseph nodded and opened the front door. Immediately, Trickster nosed his way through Joseph's legs and ran over to where Matthew sat on the cot. The large wolf-like dog jumped on the cot and stared into his master's eyes. Letting out a whine, his jaws hung open in a happy grin as Matthew slowly reached up and scratched between his ears.

Joseph approached with a mug of water and Matthew took a number of small sips to slake his thirst, knowing he would founder if he drank too much, too soon. Feeling better, he watched as Joseph and his kids pulled the large piece of tin and the hot rocks out through the front door. The room cleared of smoke and steam, and the pungent smell of the herbs Ann had been holding in her hands, dissipated.

Even as Matthew shivered in the sudden chill, Ann held a blanket up in the air. Looking past it at him, she said, "Please stand up and remove your underwear, Mr. Wilcox. You have sweated out most of the poisons in your body, but it will not do to develop a chill now that you're finally getting better." Her head disappeared behind the blanket again, giving the marshal privacy.

Matthew's neighbor held a pair of his clean long johns in her hand. Matthew grabbed them and turned around to face the wall. As he peeled the seat-soaked under garments off, he thought, *Ann turned my cabin into a sweat lodge...Clever!*

He had to hop around on his right foot to insert his left into the underwear and he felt one of Ann's strong hands hold him steady as he huffed and puffed, his meager efforts bringing stars to his eyes. Once he was decent, Matthew sat down on the bed again with a weary sigh. He felt so tired...

As if she had heard his thoughts spoken aloud, Ann said, "Mr. Wilcox, you must understand. You have been gravely ill. You took a terrible blow to the head. Plus, your body was filled with toxins... I don't know what you have been taking, but it was very hard on you."

As Ann spoke, she bustled about the room, piling blankets around him on the clean cot, building a fire in the woodstove and putting a pot of water on the stove to heat. Her daughter, Susan, was pulling food from a basket and placing a loaf of bread, a jug of milk and a small hunk of cheese on the rickety table in the corner.

Ann continued talking, even as Trickster followed her here and there around the room. "In addition, I believe you had the flux, which was eventually burned out of you by fever. That, alone, might have turned into pneumonia and carried you off, but, luckily, you have a strong constitution."

She stopped moving and stared down at him. "Still," she said, "Now is the time for you to rest, to reflect, and to grant your spirit time to heal."

Somehow, when he wasn't looking, the woman had managed to comb her hair and wind it into a tidy knot behind her neck. She had also put her medicine robes away and looked like a prim and proper lady again, complete with a heavy gingham skirt and high, white collar.

Matthew marveled—she had saved his life using the tools of her heritage and yet, because she was an Indian, Ann knew, instinctively, that her very nature posed a threat to the safety and happiness of her family.

"You are very lucky, Mr. Wilcox," she continued. "Not only because my children found you in time, but that you have such good friends. Sheriff Smithers is on his way back here with your children—*who love you, and miss you!*" She added, severely.

Ann sat down on the edge of the cot and took his hand in hers. "Mr. Wilcox, I didn't mean to pry into your personal affairs, but I needed to understand what was making you so sick—what demon I was fighting against. Mr. Smithers told me about what happened to your wife…"

Matthew cursed himself, but suddenly his eyes

filled with tears. Blinking, he said, "It wasn't Roy's place to say anything…"

Ann squeezed his hand. "Shhh, please, Sir. Let me finish."

Struggling against his own weakness, Matthew shuddered and stared at the far wall in silence.

"My people believe that when a loved one passes on, their spirit lingers—at least for a while—to make sure those they left behind will be all right. It is imperative that the living allow those who have passed to enter the spirit world as quickly as possible, lest they become lost." Ann watched as her words sunk into Matthew's heart like a knife.

Seeing the stricken look in Matthew's large green eyes, she patted his hand again. "Your sorrow and hatred is not only making you sick, Mr. Wilcox, but it might be keeping your wife from entering the spirit-world. You must let go of your anger and grief, so she can find peace."

She smiled. "That being said, my people also believe in bringing justice to their enemies—both to please the spirits and to balance the scales of right and wrong in this human realm." She stood up and gestured to her little girl. "Susan, please bring Mr. Wilcox some bread soaked in milk."

Turning back to him, Ann said. "Take time to rest, sir. Sleep… eat well, and heal… both your body and your soul. Then, once you have a clear head… and a clean heart, go and vanquish your enemies."

After Ann left the cabin, Matthew ate a little soft

bread and slept. He slept like he hadn't slept in years. Occasionally, he would rise to consciousness long enough to smell meat cooking, or coffee brewing on the stove top, but then his eyes would close and he slept some more.

Once, he awoke long enough to see his next-door neighbors sitting down at his dinner table, saying their prayers and once, he felt Trickster snuggle up next to him in the darkness.

Later, he saw Iris running through a field of wildflowers. Catching his breath with joy, Matthew called out to her and watched as she turned around and waved at him with a mischievous smile. He begged her to stop and wait for him and he saw her pause, pensively, as though reluctant to stop her headlong dash.

She did stop, though, and face him again. Although he yearned to take his wife in his arms and run with her through the wildflowers, Matthew remembered what the Indian woman had said. Reluctantly, he smiled and waved her on, although his heart ached so fiercely he thought it might crack in two.

His beautiful wife stared into his eyes for a moment, and it looked as though she might weep, but then she grinned with joy. Waving at him one last time, she blew him a kiss and took off running toward the horizon... a horizon that was so beautiful, so unearthly; he understood that he was catching a glimpse of something not meant for mortal eyes.

Iris ran until she disappeared into the radiant

purple, red and gold of a distant lands setting sun, and... finally, Matthew said, goodbye.

———————

THE NEXT MORNING, he awoke to the smell of bacon, and the joyous shouts of children's laughter in the front yard. Sitting up, he realized that for the first time in weeks, he felt like his old self. The back of his head still ached a bit and there was a lingering heaviness in his lungs, but the heroin had worked its way out of his blood, and the sorrow that was killing him had left, leaving his heart and soul free to heal.

Ann Ferguson glanced his way. "Good morning, Mr. Wilcox. Are you feeling well enough to eat with us this morning?"

Matthew nodded. "Yes ma'am... thank you." There was a fresh set of clothes at the end of the cot and a bowl of warm water for washing. It took more time than normal but, after a few minutes, he was washed up, and dressed in clean clothes.

He stepped out on the front stoop and saw little Toby and Susan playing, *Catch the stick* with Trickster. He also saw Joseph sitting on the back of his wagon, mending tack and chewing on a long piece of grass.

Then his eyes landed on his son Chance, who stood looking at him from the shade of a Tamarac tree. The boys' wide green eyes, so like his own, were glued to his face in anxiety and hope.

Abby was there too, along with Roy, and Dicky.

They were all staring at him as if he might dry up and blow away. (*Indeed*, Matthew thought, *in a way that was just what had happened, as far as his children were concerned.*)

Although it shamed him to know that his children were seeing their pa at his weakest, he smiled and held his arms open wide in greeting and felt the warmth of their love as they flew to side in joy.

24

DR. TALBOT—STILL MAD AS HECK

IT WAS A WARM AND BRILLIANT MAY MORNING. THE SKY was like a giant, blue bowl overhead and the sun's warmth had finally dried the mud in the streets. The Granville jailhouse was free of prisoners and Sheriff Smithers had decided it was high time to do some heavy, spring-cleaning and repair work on the jail and the sheriff's office next door.

Abner was crawling around on the roof taking down old, broken shingles and replacing them with new. Bean Tolson was inside, oiling the iron cell doors, the locking mechanisms and even the wood stove door, which screeched like a banshee every time it opened or shut.

Dicky was sweeping clots of mud and piles of dust off the boardwalk. It was hard work—especially since the sheriff's department had been asked not to sweep the leavings out onto the street. Apparently, Granville's main street was about to be paved in cobblestones...

after an electrical line was placed on tall poles, overhead.

The deputy shook his head in amazement and sneezed. Wiping his runny nose, Dicky thought... *This is sure becoming a modern place! I wonder what Mr. Wilcox will think once he comes back home?*

Dicky smiled. About three weeks after they had fetched Matthew's children up to the cabin in the high hills above Colville, the marshal had driven a wagon back to Granville. His horse Lincoln was tied on back and his dog Trickster sat next to him on the front bench.

For the first time since they had found Iris and her farmhand murdered, Mr. Wilcox looked healthy, and... if not happy, at least, accepting of what life had thrown his way. He stayed in town for a while that afternoon, catching up with the latest news and sitting with Roy and his deputies out on the boardwalk.

Matthew had smiled and waved at passers-by and made a show of eating the fresh cookies brought over by the ladies auxiliary club. It was almost like old times and Dicky felt certain that his idol was finally on the road to recovery.

Marshal Wilcox left later that afternoon and met up with his kids at the Imes ranch. Dicky had no idea how that meeting went, but Chance had dropped by the next morning and seemed content. He was also happy to report that Samuel Imes had come back home for the meeting.

Everyone knew that Sam blamed his stepfather for

what had happened to Iris. At first, Dicky felt angry with the kid and wanted to give him a piece of his mind. But, Roy had intervened, saying that each heart grieved in a different way. He had reminded his deputy that Sam was a good boy who just needed time to get past his sorrow. Now, Dicky was happy that he had kept his big, fat nose out of a private, family affair.

According to Chance, Sam planned on spending most of the summer at the Imes ranch, getting things in order and continuing on where his ma had left off. For a while there, he had threatened to make a career of soldering, but it seemed that Matthew had asked his son to reconsider, and Sam had accepted. The young man had one more year left of service to the Army, but Matthew had promised to pick up the slack until Sam's return.

All's well that ends well... Dicky thought and sneezed again. *Now, if Mr. Wilcox would just finish his business, and get back home!*

Sheriff Smithers stuck his head out the door of his office and said, "You boys take a break and come inside for lunch."

Dicky heard Abner scrambling down off the roof, and he placed his broom against the front of the building. Slapping at his clothes to rid himself of dust and dirt, Dicky didn't hear the sound of footsteps approaching. He was surprised then, to turn around and see a tall, thin scarecrow of a man standing behind him on the boardwalk.

The man took off a derby-style hat and smiled.

"Hello!" he said. "My name is Talbot... Dr. Lawrence Talbot. I came to see Marshal Matthew Wilcox."

Dicky was about to reply, when Sheriff Smithers asked, "What do need the marshal for?"

The doctor turned around in surprise. "Oh! You must be Matthew's friend, Roy!" He turned back to the deputy with a grin, adding, "And you must be Dicky McNulty... also Marshal Wilcox' good friend." He stuck out a hand in greeting.

Dicky shook the man's hand, looking past him to his boss for further instruction. Roy was not a big man, or tall, but there was something about him that gave a person pause... he was tough as an old boot, for sure, and quick to take offense but there was also a streak of protectiveness in the sheriff that was showing itself now as he appraised the doctor with critical eyes.

"I asked, why are you looking for Marshal Wilcox?" Roy growled.

The doctor blushed. "I can see that you're being careful for your friend, Sheriff Smithers and I can appreciate that. But, although you don't know me, I wish you would consider me a friend, as well. Let's sit a spell and I'll tell you how I met Marshal Wilcox and what happened after that, all right?"

Roy studied the older man for a moment and then he sighed. "Dicky, why don't you grab the doctor and I, a cup of coffee and a couple of sandwiches?"

The deputy nodded and walked into the sheriff's office. The other deputies followed him in and he grabbed Roy and his guest some lunch. Then, Abner,

Bean and Dicky joined the two older men out on the boardwalk and listened as Talbot spoke.

"I met the marshal out on the prairie between Patty Hanson's place and the town of Walla Walla." Lawrence explained. "He was pretty beat up, you know. He had been attacked by a wild cat… and shot in the left, upper arm. I helped to patch him up and he told me about what happened to Patty and her little girl, Hildy."

"Yeah," Roy grumbled, sarcastically. "I *thought* you were supposed to come back and help exonerate the marshal, but I didn't see hide or hair of you."

Talbot cringed. "And I am sorry about that, Sir. I had one more stop to make before I headed back into town. An old hermit lives another twenty miles, or so, from Patty and I was heading out to his place with a bottle of ointment for his rheumatism. That's when my donkey stumbled over a pile of rocks and fell over an embankment. Never underestimate the stupidity of some of God's creatures, Sheriff…." he sighed.

"Anyway, I had to put the poor critter out of its misery, and then hike the rest of the way to Fitzgerald's place on foot with all of my supplies. I made it, eventually, but then a big snowstorm moved in. I was stranded for about a week, and by the time I walked back to Patty's house, she had already gone in and sworn testimony to the marshal's innocence."

He stared into Roy's eyes and said, "Sir, had I been able, I would have been only too happy to see justice served on Matthew's behalf."

Dicky saw Roy relax as he listened to the doctor

talk, and he felt relieved. Sheriff Smithers pissed-off, was a force to be reckoned with, and it was too fine a day to ruin with a dust-up.

"What are you doing here today, Dr. Talbot, and why are you searching for Matthew?" Roy asked mildly.

"Well," the doctor grinned. "About two weeks ago, a parcel came to Patty Hanson's house. It was from Marshal Wilcox and it contained cash—both for Patty and for me!" Looking pensive, he added, "There was no call for it, you understand… at least as far as I was concerned. Matthew already paid me for my services. Still, I appreciated the gesture and I just wanted to come by and say, thanks."

"Well, the marshal has come and gone, Sir." Roy said. "He headed out a couple of weeks ago to Billings, Montana, on account of the information you gave him." Roy stared into Talbot's eyes. "I hope that info was not an exaggeration?"

Talbot looked offended. "No sir, it was not!" he exclaimed. "I *did* work on a man's ripped up face and heard their names dropped a time or two. I feel that those are the men your marshal seeks, and I won't deny that I'm still as pissed as heck at those two skunks!"

He glared. "You know, I worked hard on that fella with the torn-off nose and used up a lot of my medicinals… it just ain't right to knock your own doctor over the head and skedaddle after he just saved your danged life!"

The doctor sat back in his chair with a sigh. "I had

planned on talking to Mr. Wilcox first... just to thank him, you know. But, after that, I planned to head over to Billings myself, now that I have some ready cash. Thought I might open a new practice in that city and if I find those two men in town, I planned to put a bug or two in the local sheriff's ear about them."

Roy said, "Well, it's a free country, Doctor. Now that the snows have melted off, I think you could travel by train to Billings... probably get there in less than a week."

Talbot grinned. "Yes, I reckon so. Maybe I will catch up to the marshal and the two of us will get the drop on those two rascals, together!"

Dicky doubted that Matthew needed the doctor's help, but maybe Talbot could point Dickson out to the sheriff. There were so many men in the graveyard the night Iris was almost buried alive, and it was so long ago, neither Matthew nor Roy could remember each, and every one of those men's faces. Unfortunately, the sketch that came with Earl Dickson's biography was so vague it could have been... anyone.

Roy nodded, now, in agreement. "Well, if you *do* catch up with Matthew, be sure to give him our regards and tell him for me, if he needs help don't hesitate to either call or send a telegraph."

The doctor stood up, put on his derby hat and shook their hands in farewell. Then, he walked down the boardwalk toward the train station.

ALLEN O'DONNELL ROLLED off his bed with a muffled screech. He was grasping at his face and could feel blood and sweat dripping through his fingers. "Oh no!" he gasped. It was that goddamned nightmare again, the same horrible dream he had experienced time and time again since the Wild West show had come to Billings.

About two months ago, right before the show left town, Allen had gone with Josh to see what all the fuss was about. It was boring for the most part... although he had to admit the shooting was spectacular. He had never been a great shot, and had to give the devil his due when he saw William Cody, Annie Oakley and the other sharpshooters the tarnation out of whatever was put in front of them.

He was just standing up to leave when a wolf flew right at him out of the shadows. He let out a startled yelp, and drew his pistol to shoot the beast, when Josh grabbed his arm and whispered in his ear, "It's just a costume, Mr. O'Donnell... just a kid in a costume!"

Shaking like a leaf, O'Donnell put his pistol back in his holster and saw that a number of wild-looking creatures were cavorting around the arena. Wolves, horses, bears... even kids dressed up as turkeys and eagles skipped here and there and threw hard candies into the crowd. The tame Injuns were setting up a tepee in the middle of the arena, as well, getting ready to perform their part of the act. Allen could hear Buffalo Bill's voice announcing a short intermission over his loud speaker.

His evening was ruined, though, and O'Donnell

walked to the saloon, leaving Josh behind to enjoy the rest of the show. Later, after he made his way to his office and went to bed, he had the first of the many nightmares that would plague him the rest of his days.

It was always the same dream—that damned wolf he had filled with holes coming after him again, and again...all long white teeth, and raging golden eyes. The first time the dream came upon him, Allen had actually pissed in his bed—he was so scared. Lately, though, the dream had changed.

As always, the wolf tore into his face and, as always, Allen knew that the animal had eaten all of him—his eyes, his mouth, his nose and ears...all gone. Now though, as if that wasn't bad enough, once the animal had eaten its fill, it stared down into his missing eyes and grinned. Then it grew tall and wide, looming over his prone and bleeding body.

Allen lay under the horrible beast and howled with fear as the wolf turned into a man. What was worse, the man seemed familiar. It was that goddamn marshal, Matthew Wilcox, who stared down at him with triumphant eyes and a small smile on his handsome face.

25

GETTING BETTER

MATTHEW STOOD ON A FLATCAR, ALONG WITH A NUMBER of other passengers and watched as the train made its way slowly into Billings, Montana. It was beautiful country and a beautiful day to view it. Vast mountain ranges surrounded the Clark's Fork Bottom—the Bighorns, Black Tooth and Cloud Peak summits still boasted snowy white caps, even now toward the last days of May.

Green valleys, filled with wildflowers, oats and prairie grass stretched as far as the eye could see on either side of the tracks. Matthew saw large herds of cattle mingling with smaller herds of buffalo. The Buffs stood two-hands taller than their domestic cousins, and shied away from the approaching train.

Matthew held onto Trickster's leash and murmured, "Steady there, son" as the big dog quivered with excitement, sniffing eagerly at a herd of mountain goats, which skittered back and forth in front of the train. The sun's golden rays shone off the lead rams curling horns and Matthew felt a sense of awe at the beauty of the land in which he found himself.

Patting his dog on the head, Matthew observed his fellow passengers, as well. Most of them didn't like his pet one bit. He had elected to bring Trickster along this time, as the dog had taken to running off in search of him when he left. Knowing that the animal was safe by his side gave him comfort but traveling with such a large, wolf-like creature was not without its challenges.

When he first boarded the train, Matthew thought to tie Trickster up close to the other animals, but the horses and mules would not tolerate the dog's presence, no more than the cattle or sheep on the adjacent car. So, he put Trickster on a leash and watched as the people on board reacted with barely concealed fear to the wolf-like animal. Never mind that Trickster regarded everyone with friendly eyes, those same golden orbs inspired fear in most folk, rather than affection.

The good news... although he was getting better, both physically and mentally, Matthew was in no mood for company. One thing about a long train ride... people liked to huddle together and visit. They were bored and, sometimes, afraid of where they were heading, so they herded up like sheep.

But, Matthew was on a mission. If he had his druthers, he would have stayed home and sewn together the tattered threads of his family, but he had to find the outlaws who had ruined his life. He was in no mood for being overly friendly with a bunch of strangers and Trickster guaranteed his privacy (even though the dog would have loved to play with some of the children who ran up and down the aisles of the train).

When the big animal rose to his full height and woofed at the mountain goats, the passengers on the flatcar gasped with alarm and moved as far away from him as possible. Some of them muttered angrily about wild men who traveled with wild wolves and Matthew grinned, patting the dog on the head. Looking to his right, he saw the actual town of Billings/Coulson in the distance.

Even from here, he could see how big of a town Billings was. Spokane was about the same size, Matthew thought, but not quite so spread out... or populated. If nothing else, animals were plentiful. One stockyard after another filled to over-flowing with cattle and sheep, squatted on the outskirts of town. The high reek of ammonia and manure almost brought tears to his eyes.

Trickster wasn't helping matters any... the train passed so close to the pens, a man could reach out and pat a beef on the rump if he wished. Not wishing to cause a stampede, Matthew took his dog into the passenger car and sat down to wait while the train slowed and finally stopped at the station. As the passengers gathered their belongings and filed out the door, Matthew stared through the dusty window, and wondered where the elusive Earl Dickson might be in this sprawling city.

He saw that a number of structures were being built... mostly taverns, businesses and hotels. He saw a few that looked to be open for business; The Head-quarters Hotel, The International and the Park Hotel, for starters. There was, apparently, another very nice hotel further up the road called The Grand, but Matthew didn't like to spend money needlessly. Besides, he doubted a fancy place like that would approve of a dog inhabiting its hallowed halls.

Once the passengers had all left, Matthew picked up his traveling case and walked back to the freight cars. He paid the attendant for the hay and water that Lincoln had used up on the long trip over from Spokane, Washington. Then, greeting his horse with affection, Matthew saddled it up and slowly rode the length of 26th street, Trickster walking alongside.

It was a spectacle of commerce. All manner of busi-nesses were on display; from prospecting offices, to solicitors, to milliner shops, to dancing schools. There was a whole city block, sporting only one business... Yegen Brothers Mercantile. Matthew marveled at the new, red brick and the real, glass windows.

Further down the street, the more upscale, conserv-ative businesses gave way to different commerce... taverns and social clubs, bawdy halls and assorted restaurants rubbed shoulders and faced-off against each other across the street. Even as Matthew walked his horse down the middle of the road, the bat-winged doors on two of the taverns swung open and unruly customers were heaved, unceremoniously, outside onto the hard-packed dirt... almost under Lincoln's hooves.

Matthew continued down 26th street and saw on his right, a large structure with the words, *OPERA HOUSE* painted on the side. On his left, there was a giant, warehouse-sized building. At first, he thought it *was* a warehouse, until he got to the corner and saw a bullet-hole stippled sign that read, *The Little Haymaker Saloon and Restaurant.* The word *Restaurant* had been crudely painted over, leaving no doubt that dining was no longer a part of the business.

Matthew paused for a moment and realized that he was tired. To his consternation, his protracted illness had left him in a weakened condition. Although he was getting better, day by day, Matthew acknowledged it was time to stable his horse and find a hotel that would accept Trickster as a guest. Turning Lincoln around, he started back the way he came but then a large group of men burst through the double doors of the saloon.

They carried a squalling, leather-clad figure by its arms and legs and proceeded to throw the body out into the middle of the road, narrowly missing the wheels of a swiftly moving buggy. Then, as Matthew watched, one of the men ran up to the unfortunate person and started kicking him as hard as he could in the ribs and head.

Matthew knew he had no jurisdiction in this town as a marshal, but he didn't like what he was seeing. He got down off his horse and as he walked up to the scene, he heard a decidedly, feminine voice screeching, "Gawd damn you! Stop kickin' me... OW!!!"

It's a woman! Matthew realized with a shock. Galvanized, and all weariness forgotten, Matthew ran the last few steps and pulled his revolver to shoot a warning bullet in the air. Just before he could discharge his weapon, though, another set of hands seized ahold of the young man who was kicking the woman like a mule.

"Goddamn yer hide! I told you once, already, I don't truck with woman-kickin!" A wild-looking middle-aged man had seized the younger fellow by the throat and was commencing to squeeze the life out of him right on the street.

Although Matthew couldn't help but sympathize with the attacker, he couldn't very well allow a murder to take place right in front of his own eyes, either. Sighing in exasperation, Matthew shouted, "STOP, in the name of the law!"

"Johnson!" Matthew heard some of the men say as he aimed at the attacker's back. "Come on, Johnson—that Marshal is fixin' to shoot you!"

Matthew had actually planned on wading into the fray and knocking the man named Johnson over the noggin with his pistol, rather than shooting him, outright. Still, the men's muttered words seemed to knock some of the mad out of him. Letting loose of the young kicker, Johnson turned around and said, "Marshal... which one? There ain't one lawman in this town that's worth my spit!"

His eyes landed on Matthew and he grinned. "Well, hot-damn! We got us a new marshal, it seems." He stepped forward and held out his hand to shake. "The name's Johnson... some folks around these parts call me Liver-Eating Johnson on account of the fact that I once took a bite out of an uppity Injun's liver." He paused and studied the look on Matthew's face.

"'Twas only a nibble though, and it served to keep me alive from the Crow and Blackfoot Indians who were seeking to kill me. My reputation as a thoroughly uncivilized man is highly exaggerated."

Matthew grinned, and introduced himself. He liked this rough-looking man, despite the fact that he had no doubt Johnson would have finished the younger man off, had he not intervened. They shook hands and watched as the young tough and his buddies scampered back into the saloon. Hearing a groan of pain, he looked down and saw a most disreputable-looking woman wallowing in the dirt.

Her long, dark hair hung in greasy shanks around a thin face. She wore a filthy flop-hat and frightfully dirty buckskins. She reeked of whiskey and urine and she was spitting blood from a split lip. She, in turn, was staring up at him through dazed, rapidly swelling eyes.

"Tha's okay, Jim. I had those cock-suckers!" she mumbled.

"Yeah, Martha, I know you did," Johnson replied, gently.

Matthew bent down and helped the woman to her feet. She stood, swaying woozily and whispered, "Bill, is that... is that you?"

Matthew cut his eyes toward Johnson in confusion, and the man clucked his tongue. "Now Martha Jane, you know that Wild Bill is long dead and buried. This here is Marshal Matthew Wilcox out of Washington State."

Martha Jane Cannary stared up into Matthew's face and tears, suddenly, sprang from her eyes. She still missed Wild Bill something fierce, although he had been dead and buried going on a decade now. Still, in her muddled state, the man standing in front of her now, with his upright bearing and his gentle voice reminded her of the man she had once adored above all others.

He was also so strong and handsome, the womanly part of her felt horribly ashamed. She had been on a weeklong bender, and she knew she looked a fright and probably stunk to high-heaven. Pulling together the only thing she had left, her dignity, Calamity Jane wiped the blood and snot from her face, bowed slightly and uttered, "Well, now that the two of you spoiled my fun, I'll be on my way."

She hiccupped, adding, "Bye now, boys... don't let the door slam you in the ass on the way out!"

Then she staggered down the street and turned left into an alley, as the two men watched.

ALLEN O'DONNELL TOOK a quick step behind the window curtains with a stifled gasp as the man below him on the street mounted his horse and rode away. He had been watching the ruckus from his office window and was enjoying the spectacle immensely, when he spied an all, too familiar face. At first, he couldn't believe his eyes.

It had been years, after all, almost nine years, since he first clapped eyes on Matthew Wilcox who, at that time, was giving his testimony in the Seattle courtroom. The man hadn't changed one whit. He was still tall and slender. His hair was still thick and long... Allen snorted. A regular Goldilocks was the erstwhile marshal!

Thing is, Allen thought, *what in the hell is he doing here!* He swallowed in panic. *There is no way that the marshal could have followed me here... is there?*

Thinking back on his uneasy travels from Walla Walla to Wenatchee, to Granville, back to Yakima and on into Montana, Allen was sure he had gotten rid of all of his witnesses! Still... Gritting his teeth in frustrated rage, his neck prickled with alarm. Whether the marshal was after him or not, Wilcox was here—now, in Allen's home town!

Making a quick decision, O'Donnell strode to the

office door. Calling down to Joey Landraith, he
ordered hot water brought up for a bath and a fresh set
of razors. He had let himself go, and now it was time to
rejuvenate his image and get back on the straight and
narrow. He could no longer afford to be his old self...
Earl Dickson. It was time for Allen O'Donnell, with his
mutton-chop whiskers, shaved head and high, white
collars to make an appearance.

It was also time to sober up and gather his
resources. He still had enough men to gather a rather
formidable army against Wilcox if necessary and if
not... if the marshal was only passing through town on
his way to somewhere else, Allen thought it might be
high time to move on anyway.

California had a nice ring to it. He actually had
enough dough now to hire a crew to pan for gold and
silver, while he acted the part of a gentleman
prospector in San Francisco.

Meanwhile, he would need to set spies on Wilcox. If
the man was searching for *him*... well, he was in for a
rude awakening! O'Donnell pulled his employee ledger
forward and started checking to see who he could part
with to keep an eye out on the marshal, and who were
his best gun hands. Realizing that his two best guns
were out on the trail, his eyes blurred.

He suddenly recalled the horrible nightmare he'd
had the other night and couldn't help but wonder if he
had his mother's "sight". She had gone on and on for
years about how she could dream the future, and Allen

had always thought she was a loony-bird. Now, though, he was beginning to wonder...

As two men brought the bathtub into his office and filled it full of water, Allen bustled about barking orders. He didn't realize that his face was as pale as a sheet, he was quaking like an Aspen leaf and his voice was almost hysterical with panic. It did, however, give the men something to talk about later that afternoon.

26

SNIFFING OUT A RAT

MATTHEW REALLY DIDN'T KNOW HOW EXHAUSTED HE WAS until he finally found a hotel that would accept his dog as a guest, stabled his horse and walked slowly up the wide staircase to his room. Once inside, he put his valise in the corner of the room next to a highboy chest, unbuckled his holster, set his shotgun upright against the wall and fell onto the bed. Within seconds, he was sound asleep and didn't wake until a light but persistent knocking finally roused him from his dreams.

Trickster was growling where he lay on the small rag-rug by the side of the bed, and Matthew, despite his eyes being practically glued-shut with fatigue, arose quickly and found his pistol on top of the chest of drawers. Then he crept to the door and listened to two people... a man and a woman, engaged in a whispered argument.

"You're a damned fool, Jim!" the woman hissed.

"Well, you're no better, Jane. You say you just want to help, but I'm thinking you just want to flirt!" the man retorted.

Matthew frowned. Could this be Martha Jane and Liver Eating Johnson at his door in the middle of the night? Rolling his eyes in exasperation, he said, "Hold up your knocking, you two. I'm awake."

"Now you done it..." Jim said, just as Matthew opened the door. Sure enough, Calamity Jane and Jim Johnson stood outside in the hallway. Both of them looked worse for wear and a pungent cloud of whiskey fumes wafted into the room.

"Come in," Matthew said and stepped aside to let them enter.

Although both of his guests seemed inebriated, they were also deferent and timid now that they were in his hotel room. Johnson and Martha Jane sat down, he on a chair and she on the foot of Matthew's bed. Trickster crept to Martha's side and allowed her to stroke his ears.

Matthew rubbed his hands over his face in an attempt to wake up and said, "How can I help you?"

Martha and Jim both opened their mouths to speak, and Johnson glared. "Let me talk first, Jane, if you please!"

Calamity Jane glared right back and then she shrugged. "Go ahead, then."

The man turned to Matthew. "Marshal, we came to you to report some crimes. I saw your badge and if I'm correct, you are a United States Marshal, which means you have jurisdiction most anywhere... am I right?"

Matthew sighed. He really didn't want to get involved in Billings, Montana affairs. For one thing, that was a good way to get in trouble with the local authorities. For another, often, criminals sometimes counted on a fresh set of ears when it came time to plead their own cases. Knowing that a local sheriff or deputy had inside (and sometimes, fatal) knowledge, crooks and ne'er-do-wells often sought outside legal aid and council to help their case.

Still, he was awake now, and something about his two visitor's expressions gave him pause. Thinking it wouldn't hurt to hear their story, if nothing else, he leaned against the highboy and crossed his arms. "That's right, Mr. Johnson... although, I usually don't go poking my nose into other lawmen's business, unless I am being paid to do so."

"Well, me and Jim got a couple of stories to tell about that asshole who runs the Little Haymaker Saloon!" Martha blurted and then blushed. "Sorry about my French, Marshal."

Matthew smiled. "That's okay, Miss Canary. What has he done?"

Johnson took over. "There have been a number of incidents this winter and spring, but mainly, I've been hearing talk about how O'Donnell has been knocking off his rivals... and their families... since he first got here. Lots of folks are so afraid, they won't talk about their suspicions on a bet, but the stories I *have* heard are all the same...which has the ring of truth to it—to me, anyhow."

Although the marshal kept his face still, he agreed. Usually, if a story stayed the same, despite an embellishment here and there, the truth of the matter was plain to see. Nodding at Martha Jane who was bouncing up and down on the mattress with her hand in the air, he said, "Miss Canary, what have you heard?"

"Oh, I heard plenty, Marshal, but I seed more!" she exclaimed.

Matthew frowned. An eye witness to a crime... if Martha has actually seen O'Donnell perpetrating a crime, why hadn't she reported it to the authorities? "What did you see, ma'am?"

Calamity Jane sat up straight, seeming much more sober than just moments before. "Marshal, I get myself in trouble, sometimes. I don't ever mean it to happen, but once in a while, usually after I've had too much hooch, I'll get into a fix." She sighed, and then stared up at him again.

"Well, that's just what happened about two months ago. I mixed it up with a couple of cowboys down at Sweeny's Poker Palace. I know they was cheatin' me and I said so, too, but I got booted outta there, anyway. It was pretty late at night, and I didn't have no money and no place to sleep my load off so I headed out of town to a little hidey hole I use every now and again."

She sat still for a moment, lost in thought, until Johnson murmured, "Go on and tell the marshal what you saw, Martha."

She looked up again and said, "First thing I saw was two youngsters coming down off Pig Ridge. I knew them boys, too; Hans and Frederick Diener… they was William Diener's oldest sons… and they was trying their hand at prospecting. I was just about to call out to them when I heard some riders approaching. That's when I hunkered down behind the rocks. You never can tell who you might meet out on the prairie, Sir, so I've learned to be cautious."

Martha Jane Canary, who seemed to be as tough as rawhide, looked forlorn as she continued, "That's when I spied O'Donnell and a couple of his boys ride up. Marshal, I could not hardly believe my eyes but I swear to you now, O'Donnell shot those two kids down in cold blood and took the boy's gold nuggets right out of their saddlebags as I watched!"

"O'Donnell was laughing his ass off," she continued, "and he told one of his men—the same man he first rode into town with, to grab the kid's gold. He done it, but the other man, a man I knew to be down on his luck, but decent enough, got scairt and started high-tailin' it out of there. That's when I saw O'Donnell take a bead on him and shoot poor old, Billy Guthrie right in the back.

A tear rolled down Martha Jane's weathered cheeks. "I know I ain't no proper lady, Marshal, but Billie always treated me with respect—even when I was at my worst." Wiping the errant tear away, she added, "I knowed Billie from way back when, and it wasn't fair at all the way O'Donnell done him in!"

Matthew frowned. "Did you report what you witnessed to the authorities, ma'am?"

Martha glared, "No Sir, I did not. They hate me around here, because of... well, like I said, I got a history of civil disobedience around these parts. Still, even if I did, I suspect the law around here is just as scairt of O'Donnell as I am. I think they are just hoping that the man and his saloon will blow on outta here."

Being under the misconception that O'Donnell was an established element in Billings, Matthew raised an eyebrow. "How long, exactly, has O'Donnell been in Billings?"

Johnson took over talking as Martha pulled a flask out of her vest pocket and wasted no time in refreshing her state of intoxication. "I have been out wood-hawking for the ferry-haulers the last year or so, but I heard that O'Donnell and his side-kick showed up in town about six months ago.

Matthew stood up in agitation. His heart had started pounding in his chest as O'Donnell's timeline suddenly clicked into place in his mind. "Tell me, what is the name of O'Donnell's right-hand man?"

Johnson rolled his eyes. "I don't rightly know the kid's sir name, Marshal, but his given name is Josh. Why... he is the same young scoundrel who was stovin' Martha's ribs, in this very afternoon!"

Matthew felt like slapping his own face in frustrated anger. *Of course*, he thought. Something about the kid had struck Matthew as familiar, although he didn't place it at the time. He had seen that face before

— on a prison release sheet. There was a lot of dust and action going on out in the street earlier, and Matthew hadn't had the time to put two and two together in his mind. Now, though, he smiled. Hadn't Talbot said that Earl Dickson was traveling with a simpleton by the name of Josh?

Turning back to Johnson, Matthew asked, "Tell me, do you know Mr. O'Donnell's full name?"

Johnson shook his head, but Martha answered, "I do! I looked it up, once I saw what he done to those German boys and Billy Guthrie. His full name, if I 'member correctly is, Allen Patrick O'Donnell.

Matthew felt an electric tingle move up and down his spine. *Allen PATRICK O'Donnell...* he marveled, *a very close match, indeed, to his old enemies name... Patrick Donnelly.*

Could it be, Matthew wondered, that somehow, Earl Dickson had gotten his mitts on Patrick's money and fled here to Montana after killing Iris? He knew that a convicted felon sometimes sought revenge on the lawman who had brought him down, but they were not, usually, wealthy men.

Still, if he remembered correctly, Earl *was* one of Donnelly's right-hand men. It stood to reason, that if Patrick fell, Dickson might have a good idea where his boss had stashed his dough.

Wide-awake now, Matthew stood up from where he had been leaning against the tall chest of drawers. "Listen, I have one more question. Is there anything... unusual about Mr. O'Donnell's face?"

Jane shook her head. "I ain't never seed him up close, Marshal, but you have, Jim, haven't you?"

Johnson nodded, smiling. "Sounds like you might know a thing or two about our local hoodlum, Mr. Wilcox. Grant you, it was pretty dark and smoky in the saloon the one time I talked to him face to face, but I did notice O'Donnell has a number of scars all around his mouth and nose. In fact, for all that he's a bit of a dandy, Allen O'Donnell looks like he went five rounds with a grizzly bear... and lost!"

Matthew grinned and said, "I want to thank you, both of you, for bringing me this intelligence. I will do what I can to see that O'Donnell answers for his crimes."

His two visitors stood as well, but Johnson said, "Marshal, there was another reason we came to your room and interrupted your rest tonight." He and Calamity Jane exchanged a look and the woman nodded. "Tell him, Jim," she said.

"Earlier this evening, when I was having a bite to eat at a place I like down the street from the Little Haymaker, I heard a couple of O'Donnell's new hires talking." Liver Eating Johnson stared up into Matthew's eyes.

"That's when I heard them saying that the whole crew has been put on the look-out for a Washington State Marshal by the name of Matthew Wilcox. Seems that O'Donnell knows you're in town and has put up a thousand dollar reward for the first man who can drop you in yer tracks!"

. . .

To the reader;

I want to stress that although I am making free use of two very real historical figures in this fictional story, there is nothing I have found that indicates Calamity Jane and Liver Eating Johnson ever knew each other, much less hung out together as friends.

That being said... although by 1899, Billings boasted over 10,000 citizens, it still seems a secular place to me where people like Johnson and Canary might cross paths and might even have tipped a brew or two in friendship.

At any rate, please pardon my licentiousness... it's an occupational hazard of being an historical fiction writer!

THE BUM'S RUSH

ALLEN O'DONNELL AROSE QUITE EARLY. IN TRUTH, HE had hardly slept a wink. His mind raced as he tried to trace his steps from the Walla Walla State penitentiary, to where he lived now. But none of his memories warned him of where or when he might have tripped up and left a witness to his crimes. (Of course, there *was* a rather alarming lapse of memory right after the wolf attack.)

He remembered the doctor (vaguely), but for the life of him, he didn't recall the man's name or even where the sawbones had patched him up. He thought he remembered telling Josh to kill the man... then again, maybe he had just... *"Bah!"* he cried aloud, in frustration.

Pacing back and forth across his office floor, he wanted to pull his hair out by the roots. Of course, he couldn't because his head was shaved clean again. He stood at his window and gazed down on the street below. There were a few people up and about... shop-keepers opening their doors, a group of Indians huddled around a small burn barrel, one old drunk passed out on the boardwalk and a couple of whores walking arm in arm across the street.

Allen wondered again, is the US Marshal just passing through, or is he here in search of me? Suddenly, he had a thought. There were five reputable hotels in the downtown area and two stables. *Why not go and find out for myself?*

He would dress in his finest, he decided, and take the morning air. What was to stop him from inquiring after a new marshal in town? He would also visit the stables. The horse Wilcox was riding was memorable, after all. It was huge, for one thing but also spectacularly ugly; with its strawberry roan body, and red and white- freckled head, bulbous eyes and broom-tail. It would be easy enough to spot a horse like that.

Once he found out where the marshal was at, Allen could set assassins on him, quick as a wink. If nothing else, he might be able to find out for himself if the marshal was just passing through. Galvanized into action, Allen washed his face and shaved, put some perfumed paste under his armpits and dressed in his best clothes.

Downstairs, he startled Kyle Burley, the janitor, by asking for a cup of coffee. Kyle blushed and said, "Why, I ain't made a pot yet, boss! You want me to?"

Allen frowned and shrugged. "Nah, I'll stop in and

have a cup somewhere else. Mind you—it should be a part of your duties!"

Kyle blushed and mumbled, "Yes, Sir! I'll make a pot right away and do it every day from now on."

"Allen nodded. "See that you do, Kyle. If anyone asks, you tell 'em I'll be back in a couple of hours, alright?"

"You bet I will, Sir!"

Allen stepped out on the boardwalk at just past 7am. It was a cool, overcast morning, the early summer temporarily derailed by rain showers that were a blessing to the local farmers but the very devil for the streets of Billings. He minced down the boards trying, in vain, to avoid the dirt clots and occasional piles of human waste and offal littered here and there in his path.

Coming to the end of the block, he saw that a little café across the street was open for business. He started to step down onto the muddy road when he spied two young bankers headed his way. They also saw him, and he was aghast to see them almost trip over each other in their haste to keep from encountering him on the walkway.

Frowning, he realized that his feelings were hurt—again. It was the same thing over, and over, again in this town. Everyone...young and old, rich and poor seemed to loathe him with inordinate fervor. Allen decided, in that moment, that it was high time to be on his way. His business was still flourishing... he would put it in young Freddie's hands to manage until it sold.

Cheerful at the thought of starting anew in a different place, Allen decided to turn the corner rather than face the two young bankers (and their scorn). There was a little restaurant about halfway up the block and as he made his way there a large, shambling figure lurched out from an alley, almost bowling him over. Allen realized that this was the same drunkard he had spied, earlier, from his office window.

Allen fought against the stumbling oaf, and tried not to gag at the smell of the man who seemed determined to trip him up. The smell of old sweat, piss, and vomit engulfed Allen's senses, and he cried out, "Get away from me, you fool!"

"Sorry... hey, sorry!" the bum gasped and finally got his feet under him enough to stagger on down the boardwalk.

Allen stared after him, and brushed at his fancy clothes in disgust. *I'm probably covered in fleas, already!* he thought. Then, he went on his way and stepped into the cafe for a quick cup of coffee before traveling to the hotels and stables to see if a certain marshal was still in his town.

MATTHEW SANK down on a bench directly across the street from the Little Haymaker saloon. To a casual passerby, he would appear to be passed out on the boards after a long night of inebriation. Which was fine by him as it gave him the opportunity (at least until the local constables showed up with their curt orders and long Billy sticks) to observe his enemy's lair.

Looking up and down the street, Matthew saw that he was, for the moment, alone. He studied the wallet he had lifted from Earl Dickson's coat pocket and riffled through it as quickly as he could. He was searching for proof of identity. In truth, he hardly recognized the man at all. He had observed his quarry carefully, too, before springing out of hiding and picking his pocket. But Dickson was a canny customer who had done wonders on changing his appearance.

There were so many men who had come and gone, like players on a stage, during the ponderous prostitution and human trafficking trial eight years ago in Seattle, Matthew hardly remembered Dickson's face, but the pompous gentleman of a few minutes ago seemed so far different from the Seattle criminals it was like night compared to day.

Still, anything would do... a paper, a forgotten note, a picture... *Ah ha!* Matthew grinned in triumph. The expensive, leather wallet folded in two. One section held a large number of banknotes, and the other side sectioned into small pockets. Seeing the pinked edge of a photograph peeking out from one of the tiny enclosures, Matthew pulled it out and spied an old portrait. A grey, bleak-looking woman of about thirty years stared out at him and he turned it over to read the inscription on back.

Your Loving Mother—Phoebe Mahoney Dickson

Matthew grinned and tucked the picture into his

pocket. Exulting, he thought... Finally, I have proof! He couldn't be sure if this same man had actually killed his Iris, but he did see the pinkish scars gracing the man's countenance. Then, feeling the sharp nip of a flea as it found purchase on his neck, he grimaced and dropped the hoboes borrowed coat, scarf and hat in another alley just a few feet away.

He had traded his fine wool coat and leather hat for the old man's stinking rags so Matthew didn't think the hobo would mind the loss too much. Hesitating for a moment, Matthew knowingly committed his first act of theft, as well. A simple robbery would produce Dickson's ire but not his suspicions, Matthew thought, as he tossed the empty wallet on the dour rags and ran two blocks away to where Lincoln was tied up outside of a sheep pen.

Lincoln lifted his head and nickered as Matthew approached. His ears stood at attention as if he sensed Matthew's excitement, and no sooner had his rider landed on his back, the gelding gave a little kick and headed out of town to where Calamity Jane and Trickster were holed up, hiding.

BY THE TIME Allen returned to his saloon he was smiling widely, despite the fact that he had been robbed. There wasn't too much cash in the wallet, but he had finally found the hotel the marshal had stayed in and the proprietor said that the marshal checked out in the wee hours, saying that he was on his way to Tombstone on official business.

Not sure whether he should believe his good luck, Allen then visited the two main liveries in town. There were actually more than two but he could see no reason why a traveling marshal would board his horse in one of the more out-of-way stables. Again, Allen lucked out... at the first and biggest of the two of the two liveries, the stable master said the big, strawberry roan had ridden out about 5:00 that morning.

He had thought about stopping in at the livery that Spiles ran and checking on his own horse-flesh but he was tired from his restless night and ready to take a nice long nap. Allen decided to have a stiff drink in celebration, and then head upstairs for a much needed rest. He still planned on pulling up stakes, but at least it wouldn't need to be at a dead run!

He drank a couple of whiskeys and... feeling his oats for the first time in weeks, he called out to one of the new whores and told her to head up to his office. A few moments later, he walked up himself, smiling with relief and anticipation of tasting this newest flower's sweet nectar.

Young Freddie was still aglow at what Mr. O'Donnell had just suggested. He had thought long and hard about quitting work as the Little Haymaker's bartender. The atmosphere here was something he had not counted on when he first started. He had thought it was the prettiest and nicest place in all of Montana but now he knew it was nothing but a den of inequity and

O'Donnell was a horrible beast of a man. The pay was good, though and day by day, it became harder to give up the steady salary on moral grounds.

Now though, he thought, *maybe as the saloons new manager, I can wrestle it back into respectability!* He smiled as he dreamed of making something out of the place and becoming the successful businessman he had always wanted to be!

Just as soon as he saw Mr. O'Donnell and Josh' backsides for the last time!

MAKING PLANS

MATTHEW KNELT BY A SMALL STREAM THAT RAN IN front of the ramshackle cabin Martha Jane occasionally called home. He ran a washcloth over his dirty face, neck and hands while Martha dabbed at his numerous flea-bites with witch hazel.

"I got an old duster you can use, Marshal, if you want."

Matthew nodded. "That would be fine, Martha. I don't feel like being assassinated tonight."

After he finished washing up, the marshal stood and put on his best shirt, his vest, his badge and a necktie. He figured there was no way he would be taken seriously by the local authorities if he didn't present himself as a proper lawman. Then, he sat down at a board that Martha had placed between two old barrels for a quick bite to eat.

Feeding Trickster a piece of rabbit meat, he said, "So, we'll go into town looking like a couple of drunks.

On foot and staggering around we should avoid any confrontations from Dickson's men... agreed?"

Martha smirked. "Yeah, I agree. I have first-hand knowledge that the drunker I am, the more folks avoid me."

Grinning, Matthew asked, "Do you really think that the stable master will give us a hand?" he asked. "All my plans, at this point, depend on Spiles' cooperation."

Martha stared into space for a moment and then she replied. "Marshal, you never can tell what a man is made of until he's tested but I believe, deep in my soul, that Dave Spiles would do just about anything to bring his boss down..." she paused and gazed into his face. "I hope that we can keep him from being hurt."

The marshal said, "I see no reason why he would be hurt in any way, Martha. I might need to call him in as a witness but by then, any threat Dickson poses should be neutralized."

"Okay, Marshal," she replied. "It's just that Dave Spiles ain't no crook. He *is* getting on in years, though. His only crime was deciding to take what the new boss offered so's he could feather his nest a little before he got too old to support hisself."

She shook her head. "But, he has told me that some-times the horses brought into the stable... O'Donnell's horses, are covered mane to hock in blood and half the time, some of O'Donnell rough-riders don't even bother to hide what they stole off of folks they robbed, including ladies jewelry, and little girl's poppets!"

She stared into Matthew's eyes. "I'd bet my life that

Spiles will agree to help. Please, just promise me that he don't go down with the rest of those outlaws!"

"I'll make sure of it, Martha." Staring out the door, he said, "Why don't we catch a little nap and head in at dusk?"

Nodding, she answered, "I don't have a proper bed but you're welcome to my pallet. I ain't tired, but I'll keep an eye out while you catch a few winks."

Smiling, Matthew stood up. Groaning a little at the fatigue that was still sapping his strength, he held out a hand. "Martha, I want to thank you, again, for helping me."

Calamity Jane shook the marshal's hand and blushed. Never in a hundred years would she have thought she would be helping a lawman out, but after hearing why the marshal was hunting O'Donnell (or Earl Dickson, according to Matthew) she was itching to lend a hand.

"Right... I'll wake you up about 3:00, all right?"

She watched as the man sat down on her rumpled blankets and pulled his hat down over his eyes. He was so handsome... but he also looked as if he had been ill. His pretty, green eyes were sunk in shadows and there was a frailty about him, Martha worried about. Hopefully; the marshal knew what he was doing or she, and all of her friends, would find themselves dead by tomorrow afternoon.

Dr. Lawrence Talbot stepped down off the train, stretched his arms over his head and started walking to the first livery he could see. He had spent many a year (way too long, actually) being a traveling doctor and he had learned that a town's stables contained some of the best intelligence in town... along with the busiest restaurants.

Stable hands were often overlooked as real people with actual ears... as were waitresses, and many a customer, whether boarding their horses or filling their bellies talked openly about where they were going and whom they were going to see, unmindful of the eager ears that were soaking up their words.

It was a sunny day, although mud-puddles reflected the blue skies all up and down the street. Talbot hopped here and there, avoiding the potholes as much as possible and then he stepped inside the livery office. No one was inside, so he stepped through the back door leading into the barn and called out, "Hello... is anybody here?"

An old man came through one of the open stalls and walked toward him from the back of the building. "What can I do fer ya?" he asked.

The doctor took his hat off and smiled. "Hello, my name is Talbot... Doctor Lawrence Talbot. I just arrived in your fair city and I wondered if you knew of a man named Earl Dickson? He may have been traveling with a young man named Josh."

Dave's eyes grew sharp. He had never heard of an Earl Dickson, but the name Josh was sure familiar... of course, there were probably a hundred Joshes in town. "Well, I don't know about Earl Dickson but I do know a Josh... what does he look like?"

Talbot scratched at his balding head of gray hair. "I remember him as being tall... and stout, too. Scruffy, black hair... he was a bit simple."

Spiles ears perked up. Feeling a tingle of excitement, he looked around to make sure no one was lurking in one of the stalls. Then he said, "Follow me into my office, Doctor. We'll have us a chat."

———

TALBOT AND SPILES traded stories and drank strong, black coffee until late in the afternoon. Once Spiles realized that Josh might recognize the doctor, he kept a weather eye on the street—looking for the young man to come this way. It was unlikely though... Josh and the tough boys he hung around with rarely darkened the stable doors.

The doctor told Dave that the man *he* knew as Allen O'Donnell was more than likely, Earl Dickson out of the Walla Walla State pen. Talbot also told Spiles what he knew about the murder of Matthew Wilcox' wife, Iris. He asked Spiles if his passenger, seven months earlier, had wounds on his face when he had bought the stage ride into Montana.

Dave nodded vehemently. "That is for sure," he said. "He hardly came out of the coach, at all, until we come into Orofino, Idaho and then, I saw that his face was all tore up. Once we got to Billings, he allowed that his name was Allen O'Donnell and did I want a job working for him?" He shook his grizzled head in self-disgust. "What I would give to have said no to that sorry, sonofabitch!"

The evening's shadows were growing long and Talbot stood up to leave. "Listen, Dave," he said. "I made a vow to let the authorities in this town know about Dickson and what I heard he did to that marshal's wife... and, just as soon as I get situated, I will... mark my words. Thank you for your... Say!" he exclaimed. "I almost forgot! You didn't happen to see that marshal and his big red roan?"

Spiles shook his head. "Nah, I never seen him or his hoss. A friend of mine, Martha Jane, has though. If he shows up, do you want me to let him know you're here?"

Right at that moment, two drunken figures lurched down the boardwalk and into the big barn's double-doors. Spiles heard Martha Jane cackle with laughter as she fell out of the equally inebriated arms of her fellow drunk. Falling on the floor, she hollered, "Davey, why is you still open fer business, eh? Close yer friggin' doors and we'll tip a cup or two!"

Glancing down at his pocket watch, Dave saw that it was, indeed, far past closing time. He pulled the doors shut, secretly mourning the fact that not only did he have one drunk on his hands who was more than willing to nozzle up all of his booze, she had brought a friend along to help. Sighing, he put the bar across the doors and turned around to face his guests.

He was shocked, therefore, to see that Martha Jane was standing upright now and staring in perfect sobriety at her companion who had shed his long, dirty duster and was shaking the doctor's hand in welcome.

"Marshal Wilcox! I am so pleased to have found you! I have news, sir, about that rascal Earl Dickson!" Talbot was grinning from ear to ear and Spiles stared at them in confusion.

Matthew smiled warmly and looked at the stable master. Walking over, he held out his hand and said, "How do you do, Mr. Spiles. My name is Matthew Wilcox. Martha tells me you have some information that might help me put Mr. Allen O'Donnell away for good!"

THE NEXT MORNING dawned bright and clear. It was about 10:00… early enough to find most of O'Donnell's crew milling about the saloon but no so early as to invoke Allen's wrath. Spiles wanted to be cheerful, respectful and on top of his game. He had pondered long and hard about how to separate Josh from his master and thought he had come up with a good plan, as long as he played his cards right.

He stepped inside the saloon and saw Josh standing by the bar with a bunch of his cronies. He smiled and called out to the bartender, "Is he up yet?"

Joey Landraith nodded and said, "Yeah, I already brought him up a pot of coffee."

"Well, I need to have a private word with him. Can I head up on my own, or should I ask Josh to go with me?"

Spiles knew that Allen had gotten pretty, paranoid lately and didn't welcome guests upstairs to his office unless accompanied by one of his guards.

Joey looked at Josh and frowned in distaste. Spiles knew at that moment that the young bartender didn't care for Josh one bit. Dave thought that Joshua was malleable like soft dough. If good and proper people had raised him up, he might have become a decent soul. Instead, he had turned just as rotten as the man he had attached himself to.

Joey said, "Nah... I don't think that's necessary, Davey. Just go on up."

Spiles nodded and walked upstairs. Knocking on the door, he heard O'Donnell say, "Come!"

Dave Spiles plastered a big grin on his face as he prepared to ask his boss if he could spare Josh for a little while. He needed an inside man, he said, to help clean the blood and guts off some beautiful, but certainly stolen, tack down at the stables.

O'Donnell smiled in appreciation. Spiles had turned out to be a great addition to his staff. Quiet, hard-working and most of all, discreet, the old man kept the mobile part of his operation running as smooth as silk.

Sitting back in his chair, he said, "I have some work

for him later on this afternoon, but I can spare him for a few hours."

Spiles nodded agreeably. "Sure thing, boss... it shouldn't take more than a couple of hours to get that tack in top-shape."

Allen looked down at his ledger book and mumbled, "Tell Josh I want to see him here in my office at noon, sharp."

"Okay, Allen, I'll tell him. Thanks!" Spiles backed out the door with his heart in his mouth. He knew that by evening, all hell would be breaking loose in Billings but he didn't care. He had done a few shady things in his life but he, by God, had never signed up for the kind of evil shit O'Donnell demanded of him.

He hoped and he prayed that by the time Marshal Wilcox had gotten the info he needed out of young Josh, he himself would be long gone. Wilcox had written him a pardon for inadvertently being an accomplice to O'Donnell's crimes, and he had even given Spiles about fifty dollars in cash (O'Donnell's own pocket change, according to the marshal) in which to make his escape!

My hope, he thought, as he tapped Josh on the shoulder and told the young man to come along with him to the livery, is *that Marshal Wilcox won't be murdered by Allen and his men while trying to seek justice for his poor, dead wife.*

29

THE ROUND-UP

THE MINUTE JOSH STEPPED INSIDE THE LIVERY, DAVE Spiles disappeared and a number of rough hands seized his arms and shoulders. *Bushwhacked!* he thought, hysterically, but before he could call out for help, he was hauled into a stall and thrown, face first, against the far wall.

A sharp, heavy knee landed in the small of his back and he moaned against a gag thrust between his teeth. "What's going on!" he cried, but his words were nothing more than grunts in the oppressive silence.

Scrambling around on the straw and hay covered floorboards, Josh managed to turn his body right side up and face his captors. He saw a tall, well-dressed man sitting on a stool at the front of the stall. The man was staring down at him with cold, green eyes... eyes that both pierced Josh' soul and made him squirm with fear.

"Who are you? What do you want!" his voice bleated against the cloth that stopped his tongue.

"My name is Matthew Wilcox," the serious man said, softly.

It took a few moments but, suddenly, Josh knew who this hard-looking man was. He bucked against his restraints in terror and squealed inarticulately like a trussed pig. Then, he saw an all too familiar figure step into the enclosure.

Calamity Jane stood in front of him. She looked clean and sober... almost pretty in the gloom. She glared at him as she held a bullwhip in her left hand and made a show of studying the toes of her boots. "Well, I don't wear those pointy-toed boots like our young friend here has on but I guess these'll do the trick. What do you think, Marshal?"

"I think you're probably right, Martha," the man said. "Please commence."

Grinning, Martha reared back and landed a swift kick in Josh's ribs. He howled with pain and rolled away from her to the back wall. She approached again and kicked him on the thigh as hard as she could.

"Ow! Stop kicking me you bitch!" Josh screamed, but even he knew that his screams were meaningless.

Martha spat. "You and your boys have been kickin' the shit out of me for months now!" She reared back and lashed out, this time with her whip. She missed, mostly, but the tip of the whip caressed his neck with a fiery kiss.

Josh stared up at his tormentor with tears leaking from his eyes. "I'm sorry... ma'am. So sorry!" he mumbled. Although the gag in his mouth made it almost impossible to talk, the woman seemed to understand his words.

Martha rolled her eyes. "Yeah, I guess you are... now!" She lifted her whip again.

Matthew said, "Let's hold off for a minute, Martha...please?"

She turned around and stared at the marshal for a moment. "You know, that ain't even a fraction of what him and his boys done to me!"

Matthew nodded. "I know, but remember, we need this young man to talk. In addition, giving this young man a few licks might make you feel good, but he, and his cohorts, will be suffering far worse before too long!"

It looked, for a moment, like Martha Jane would argue, but she sighed and murmured, "Sorry Marshal. You're right, of course." Stepping back out of the stall she added, "He's all yours!"

Matthew stared down at Josh and said, "Dr. Talbot, would you come in here and see to this man's injuries?"

Another familiar face suddenly loomed above Josh and he quaked in his boots. It seemed to him that every single ghost of his recent past had come for a visit and he didn't know what to make of it. "Hey! I didn't hurt you! Leave me alone!" Again, he should have saved his breath because his words were unintelligible.

Talbot knelt down by his side with a bottle of unguent in his hand. Dabbing a little cream on Josh's neck, he smiled and said, "Yes indeed, Marshal. This is the man who knocked me over the head and stuck me in a closet after I fixed up his partner's broken nose."

Talbot stood up and stared down at Josh. "Tell me, Josh, did you and Earl Dickson hurt the marshal's wife? Tell the truth, now!"

Josh glanced over at where the marshal sat, studying him with those chilly green eyes. He hadn't wanted to hurt the pretty lady but after what Earl had done and once she grabbed that gun... he didn't have a choice! Surely, the marshal could see that... right?

Matthew was studying Josh's face and saw the guilt running through his eyes like fish in a transparent stream. Then the marshal pulled his pistol out of its holster and pointed it at Josh's face, watching as his eyes got as big and round as silver dollars. "N...N... N!!!" he grunted while trying to back away.

"Josh, listen to me, now," he said softly. "Dr. Talbot is going to remove your gag. If you scream, I'll shoot you in the face. If you try to run, I'll shoot you in the face. Got it?"

The mouth of the marshal's pistol looked like the black, open maw of Hell and Josh nodded, fearfully. The doctor bent over and removed the gag, even as Marshal Wilcox cocked his pistol. Staring into Josh's eyes, Matthew said, "I want you to tell me, right now, what happened to my wife."

Tears spilled from the terrified man's eyes. "I didn't mean fer it to happen! I didn't want to at all, but after Earl done to her what he did and that goddamn wolf attacked, the lady grabbed at the rifle... I didn't have no choice! I shot her twice and she died. I'm sorry!" Then, Josh started bawling like a baby as Matthew sat still in triumph... and defeat.

Then, Josh forgot all about the marshal as the Billing's Sheriff and three of his deputies swarmed into the stall. "You may go now, gentlemen. We'll take it from here." Sheriff Bob Parker said.

The sheriff, who had about had it with Allen O'Donnell and his crew smiled with relief. Now, thanks to this US Marshal, he had solid proof to rid his town of the Little Haymaker Saloon and its owner for good!

Earlier this morning a new doctor in town had come to his jailhouse and told him an interesting tale about Allen O'Donnell and his partner. The man's name was apparently Earl Dickson, and he was wanted for the murder of Marshal Wilcox' wife, Iris.

The doctor had pleaded with Parker to come to Spile's Livery because there was a hit out on the marshal (Dickson's orders) and Wilcox was afraid to set foot outside for fear of an assassin's bullet. Once he and his deputies arrived, they had visited with the marshal for a while, and then hunkered down in a nearby stall and listened as the crook's partner, confessed to the crimes.

The whole thing was as neat as a pin and the sheriff grinned in triumph. Now, all he and his deputies needed to do was go to the saloon and haul Dickson (and most of his men) out in irons. A good ending, for sure, and maybe now the uppity-ups in town would stop pestering him with vague rumors and accusations they couldn't prove!

"Take him to the jailhouse, boys!" the sheriff said. Then he turned to Matthew. "Listen, if you want, I could let you in on the arrest. It's unusual, grant you, but I guess you got a good reason for being there."

Matthew smiled. "That's okay, Sheriff. I'll just stay outside and let you and your men sort out the criminals, alright?"

Relieved, Parker nodded. "That's fine. Don't go leaving town, though, for a while, okay? The man will surely hang, but it would be best if his principal accuser was around, in case the judge who tries the case has any question."

The marshal, who understood the many rules and regulations involved in an arrest of this magnitude, smiled and murmured, "Don't worry—I'm not going anywhere. What time do you think you'll be heading over to the Little Haymaker to arrest Dickson?"

The sheriff stepped aside to let the deputies, with their prisoner in tow, walk past. Josh stared at Matthew and his eyes were truly sad as he whispered, "Your pretty wife was real nice to me, Marshal... I'm sorry, really I am!"

Matthew's throat closed on his grief and for a moment, he couldn't breathe. Feeling tears of sorrow fill his eyes he looked away lest he unman himself.

Martha saw the expression on his face, though. Her heart filled with rage... both at the grief in Matthew's eyes, and at the constant abuse, she had received from most men, her whole livelong life. Growling, she ran up behind Josh and sunk the toe of her boot into the prisoner's butt so hard, he grunted in agony and sank in a dead faint between the two deputies who held his arms.

"Gawd-dammit, Jane!" Parker howled. "Get the hell outta here!"

Martha picked up her hat, tipped her bottle and winked at Matthew before heading out the double doors of the livery.

Turning back to Matthew, the sheriff said, "I reckon we'll be heading over to the saloon about 1:00. I should have enough men gathered up by then.

The marshal smiled and tipped his hat. "I'll see you then, sir."

Pausing, Parker added, "I understand how you must be feeling, Marshal. Just remember, I don't want no vigilantes in on this deal. If you think you can keep your hands off your gun, you are welcome in on the arrest. But, if Dickson is assassinated today, I'll be tossing you into jail along with the rest of the crooks, understand?"

Matthew answered, "Completely, Sheriff."

Then Parker walked out the door. Matthew walked into the livery office and pulled the window shade closed. Dr. Talbot was nursing a whiskey and he asked the marshal if he wanted one too. Matthew nodded and said, "Just a finger is all… there's still a lot of work to do in the next couple of hours."

Talbot brought Matthew his drink and sat down on one of the chairs. "You gonna shoot him, Marshal?"

Matthew felt as if all the blood in his body had drained away while he wasn't looking. His muscles felt weak and rubbery and his heart ached in his chest. He had thought that getting to the bottom, of his wife's murder would set him free but it only served to weigh him down more.

He knew that filling Dickson's body full of holes would probably help, a little, to heal his pain, but he also didn't want to waste any more time away from his family than he absolutely had to... which would happen if he landed himself in jail—again. The fact that the sheriff had just served a warning to him about undue interference, Matthew also understood that the lawman's threats were not idle.

He shook his head. "No. I don't mean to, Doctor. But I don't intend to let him sneak away, either. Are you still on board with my plan?"

Talbot grinned. "Oh yeah, Marshal. We all are!"

30

TOUCH AND GO

AT 1:34 PM ON A LOVELY SUNDAY AFTERNOON, SHERIFF Parker and ten sworn deputies walked down the boardwalk and filed into The Little Haymaker saloon. The streets were unusually quiet, a fact that the sheriff appreciated. Many of the more solid citizens in town lingered at church socials and potlucks and the fine weather had lured other folks out of town into the verdant fields and new green forests for picnics or games of darts and baseball.

At any rate, Parker thought, *we couldn't have picked a better time than right now to roust the saloon.*

The deputies swarmed in the front door and fanned out along the back walls. They held rifles, shotguns and pistols and all of them shouted, "Put your hands in the air, and get down on your knees!"

Sheriff Parker, meanwhile, had gone straight for the weapons locker. The saloon was fairly quiet—he counted twenty men sitting at the bar and the tables closest to it. All of the men, and four whores fell to their knees, holding their hands in the air. "Search 'em!" he hollered.

Five of the deputies set to searching the men and women and, besides a small knife hidden in one of the prostitute's corsets, the new prisoners were unarmed. "Cuff 'em and take 'em to the jailhouse!"

The men and women set to wailing and shouting out about their innocence and the sheriff knew that, indeed, some of the men in the group were just drunks and gamblers. *Oh well*, he shrugged, *we'll sort the wheat from the chaff down at the jail.*

Joey Landriath stood behind the bar and quivered with anxiety. *Damn it*, he thought in disgust. *And here I thought I might be finally be catching a break!*

The sheriff approached. "Go easy on this one, boys. He's my cousin's boy." Most of the deputies closest to Sheriff Parker knew that, and they also knew that Joey wouldn't hurt a fly. He just had more ambition than common sense, sometimes, and had always loathed the idea of taking over his daddy's sheep farm. Now, some of them smirked, unless he wanted to spend time in jail, he had better high tail it back home!

Earl Dickson heard the ruckus downstairs and scowled. *Goddammit!* he snarled under his breath, wondering which one of his hired men had brought the law down on his doorstep. It never occurred to him that he was the main fish on the line... not until one of the whores tapped on his door and stuck her head inside.

He automatically started to berate the tart for entering his office without asking for permission first, but the woman said, "Shut up, Allen! That is, if you want to escape the sheriff and his men!"

Earl closed his mouth with a snap. His blood ran cold... what had happened? Then, Josh' tardiness began to make sense. He had no idea what might have stirred the sheriff's suspicions, but if they had seized his right hand man, and Josh spilled his guts... Why, he could hang!

"Get out of here, Janie, unless you want to spend the rest of the day in the slammer!"

The whore nodded and pulled the door shut. Instantly, Earl took his valise (that already had two changes of clothing in it) out of the wardrobe and put a handful of money in, along with his shaving kit. He stood for a moment, gazing longingly at all of his fine clothes and hats but he could already hear the heavy tread of many boots marching up the stairs.

Earl ran to the window and opened the sash. Then he threw the bag out on the little balcony. He had often judged the height from the balcony to the street below and knew he could make the eight-foot jump. There came a pounding at the door and the words, "Earl Dickson open this door and come out with your hands up!" rang in his ears.

My, God! They know who I am! Earl thought, and he understood that the only way the sheriff could have gotten the drop on him was if that danged Marshal had whispered in his ear! Cursing Matthew, and Josh, and every other person who had ever crossed his path, Earl grabbed his valise by the handles and leapt over the railing to the street.

A few people were standing on the opposite side of the street and he saw them point, and holler, "Hey Sheriff! O'Donnell's getting away! Sheriff Parker!"

Earl turned and dashed around the corner and down the street. The road ran the distance of the building with two, separate offshoots to the next street. He jinked left into one of the alleys and ran as fast as he could. He was starting to grin in triumph when he saw a buckskin-clad woman and a tall, skinny gray-haired man move to the front of the alley, blocking his way. Both of them lifted their firearms and sighted down their barrels at him.

Stopping, he stared. *Who in the hell... is that Calamity Jane and that doctor... what's his name?* he wondered, and then he ran backwards a few feet and cut right down an adjacent alley.

He had only run about thirty yards when another figure darkened the foot of the narrow, rubbish-strewn street. This shadowy form was very tall and slender, and as he approached, Earl saw that the man wore a low-brimmed hat pulled at a slant over his eyes. Marshal Wilcox had not left town after all, and Earl sprang a sweat.

Turning around, he saw Martha Jane Canary and the doctor walking up behind him, even as the marshal drew closer with every step. There was one more side road, just about six feet to his right. He started to turn into it, wishing that the sheriff would show up and call a halt to this god-awful chase.

"Stop right there, Dickson!" Marshal Wilcox shouted and started running in Earl's direction. Earl took one more step, and then gave up. Wilcox was practically on top of him now and Earl could hear Jane and the doctor practically breathing down his neck.

The marshal stopped three feet in front of Dickson. His face was as white as a sheet, and he held a trembling hand over his chest. He studied his quarry's face —saw the blunt bit of nose tissue left over from Bandit's attack and the small and dirty hands that had murdered his beautiful wife.

A rage filled his heart then… a bitter anger so large and profound he could hardly catch his breath. Gasping, he said, "Doctor… Martha, I've got this. You'd better make yourselves scarce."

The doctor wasted no time in disappearing, now that the marshal had Dickson well in hand. Jane hesitated a moment longer, though. "I wouldn't blame you, Marshal, for dropping this dirty dog where he stands, but the sheriff isn't going to take kindly to it."

"I know, Martha. Don't worry about it."

"Okay, then. Bye!" She started to walk away, but then turned around and spat on Dickson's back. Then she laughed out-loud and disappeared down the street.

Matthew held his pistol on Dickson, and tried to relieve the pressure on his chest but he felt like a horse had kicked him. Lifting the pistol and putting it between Earl's eyes, he murmured, "Why? Why did you kill my wife?"

Dickson grinned. "Cuz I felt like it, that's why. Men like you with your pretty wives and pretty houses—you're all the same. You have had everything... EVERY-THING handed to you on a silver platter. Well, I am sick of it! Thought it was high time someone took away from you!"

Even as he talked, Earl saw that something was wrong with the marshal. His face was pale, and he seemed to be swaying on his feet and gasping for air. "Well... you gonna shoot me with that gun of yours or are you just feelin' me up?" he smirked.

Matthew gulped and thought, *Of all worst times to get sick...* "You need to turn around and put your hands in the air. I'm taking you to the sheriff."

Earl grinned and turned slightly to his right. Then he fingered a button on his wrist and felt his little 22.caliber pistol hideaway slide into his right palm. Turning around, he realized that Marshal Wilcox had fallen to one knee and was staring at the ground with his eyes half closed.

The marshal held both hands on his chest and horrid choking noises were issuing from his mouth as he tried, in vain, to draw air into his lungs. Earl grinned, even as he heard the sound of many men running down the street. Knowing it was this man's words against his, Earl lifted his little shooter and started to squeeze the trigger.

That's when he heard a hideous growl. He turned to

see what was behind him, and then he felt himself hit so hard from behind, he was thrown off balance and landed five feet away on his back, with a grunt. Then, to his absolute horror, he saw the beast of his nightmares crawl on top of him and stare, snarling into his face.

Earl tried to lift his pistol but he realized that the 22 had flown out of his hand when he fell. Then, as if his recurring nightmare had become reality, the marshal rose slowly to his feet, stared past the animal's shoulder into Earl's eyes and smiled.

Matthew was still as gray as a ghost, but his right hand was steady as he lifted his big gun and pointed it at Earl's murdering head. Earl struggled and groaned in fear, knowing that his life was just about to end, when he heard the marshal say, "Trickster, get down off the man now… that's a good dog."

Then, as Dickson lay wallowing in the mud and the refuse of the alleyway two streets away from the Little Haymaker saloon, Sheriff Parker and the rest of his deputies came running up the street, guns lifted and voices raised.

"Marshal Wilcox, do not shoot that weapon!" Parker yelled and watched in amazement as Matthew fell over backwards and landed on the ground in a dead faint.

There was a certain amount of confusion then, especially since that horrible big dog wouldn't let anyone near his master except for one of the worst miscreants in town, Calamity Jane. Once she checked the US marshal out and said, "He's alive!" the deputies marched Earl Dickson down the road and into a jail cell.

Matthew, on the other hand, landed in the local hospital. He was diagnosed with pneumonia, and spent almost a week lost between the dead and the living. No matter how hard he tried, or how many potions Dr. Talbot forced down his throat, Matthew burned with fever and his lungs didn't work.

It wasn't until a couple of weeks had passed and his high fever started to cool that a familiar and beloved face swam into view. Chance was sitting on the edge of his bed. The boy held one of his hands and was whispering things like, "... and we had a good foaling season, too, Pa. Ma would be proud! We sure could use a hand, though."

The boy took a breath and continued, "Sam wants you to come back home before he hires any extra hands, though... you know, he wants it to be your decision. But, I sure hope you choose Abner. He's tired of being a lawman and I think he would make a fine ranch hand, don't you?"

Matthew squeezed his son's hand, and murmured, "Sure, I would like that."

Chance's eyes got big. "Roy! Dicky, come here... Pa's awake!" Matthew's son turned back to face him. "Pa! Oh my goodness, I thought you were going to die!" Then, he threw himself on Matthew's chest and wept with relief.

EPILOGUE

Two months later, Matthew was mucking out stalls in the barn, when the postmaster pulled up in his wagon. "Hallo, the house!" he called.

Matthew put his pitchfork against the far wall and stepped outside. "Hello, Bernie. How are you today?"

Bernie Hammond grinned and said, "Well, if the weather could just stay like this all the time, I would be a happy man!"

Matthew smiled and nodded in agreement. The weather was fine, all right. Warm days and balmy nights had brought in a bumper crop of wheat and corn. The sky was as blue as a robin's egg and plump, billowy clouds sailed across the sky like matrons on parade.

His health had improved and he grew stronger every day. The hurt and sorrow of the last year still snuck up on him sometimes, and he knew he would miss his Iris forever, but his sons and his good friends kept him company. Finally, the sharp edge of his grief was growing less keen.

Last week, Bernie had brought a letter from Sheriff Parker in Billings saying that Earl Dickson had been hanged, along with a number of his hired men—for theft, rape, kidnapping and murder. Dickson's sidekick, Josh had been sent back to Walla Walla State prison.

Matthew was glad about that. Although he knew that the younger man had actually pulled the trigger on Iris, he also understood that it was only because Earl had poisoned his mind. At this point, the retired US Marshal didn't want the death of a young retarded man to weigh on his conscience along with everything else.

Bernie stepped down off his wagon and approached with a letter in his hand. "This is addressed to you, Matthew."

Matthew accepted the formal missive, and his hands grew a little clammy with nerves. *This is it!* he thought. *Either I stay home, and learn to love farming or...*

He torn the end off of the envelope and read,

Dear Mr. Wilcox,

We are pleased to inform you that you have been accepted as a student at Washington State University in Pullman, Washington.

The first of term will start on Sep. 21...

There were a few more words and instructions, but Matthew's eyes blurred with tears. Iris had always wanted him to finish law school and so did his uncle Jonathon. Now that they were both gone, he was finally going to fight outlaws from behind a desk rather than a gun.

Oh, how he wished thing could have been different! His heart sunk for a moment and then he saw his son Chance hop on board one of their stallions. The big stud was a fairly, friendly character but still, Chance knew better!

Matthew Wilcox stuck the letter in his back pocket and walked toward the far corral to have a few stern words with his son.

The End

A LOOK AT LUCKY CHANCE (THE DEADMAN BOOK IV)

It has been eight years since Matthew's wife, Iris, was murdered and he went out in search of her killers; risking life, limb and sanity in his search for justice.

Now, he's a simple, country lawyer. It's certainly safer than being a lawman but he is bored, until an old friend's plea for justice sends Matthew in a whole new direction...

Frederick Holland's youngest son, Johnny, was killed in a "fixed" boxing match, and Fred wants Matthew to search for proof that the boxer's gloves were loaded with Plaster of Paris. Problem is, Matthew no longer carries a badge. What can he do to help his old friend?

Become a private investigator, of course. And so begins the Wilcox and Son Investigation Agency.

Matthew's son, Chance, was a boxing champion in the Army and he is the perfect man to prove Snake-Eyes Svenson's guilt but, can he survive the encounter?

Find out in LUCKY CHANCE... the first of the Wilcox and Son case files!

AVAILABLE NOW ON AMAZON

ABOUT THE AUTHOR

Linell Jeppsen is a writer of science fiction and fantasy. Her vampire novel, *Detour to Dusk*, has received over 44- four and five star reviews. Her novel *Story Time*, with over 130 4-and 5-star reviews, is a science fiction post-apocalyptic novel, and has been touted by the Paranormal Romance Guild, Sandy's Blog Spot, Coffee time Romance, Bitten by Books and 64 top reviewers as a five-star read, filled with terror, love, loss, and the indomitable beauty and strength of the human spirit. *Story Time* was also nominated as the best new read of 2011 by the PRG. Her dark fantasy novel, *Onio* (a story about a half-human Sasquatch who falls in love with a human girl), was released in December 2012 and won 3rd place as the best fantasy romance of 2012 by the PRG reviewers guild. Her novel, *The War of Odds*, won the IBD award for fantasy fiction and boasts 18 5-star reviews since its release in February of 2013. It also placed 2^{nd,} as the best YA paranormal book of 2013 by the PRG.